WINGO

THE REMARKABLE LIFE OF AN UNREMARKABLE MAN

MIKE VANCE

Wingo: The Remarkable Life of an Unremarkable Man

Copyright © 2024 by Mike Vance

Library of Congress Cataloging-in-Publication Data

Names: Vance, Mike 1959 – author

Title: Wingo: The Remarkable Life of an Unremarkable Man

Identifiers: LCCN TXu 2-410-906

ISBN (paperback) 979-8-9879432-3-6

ISBN (hardback) 979-8-9879432-4-3

ISBN (e-book) 979-8-9879432-5-0

Dos Dogs Press

Printed in the United States of America

INTRODUCTION

Interviewer's note: My intention is to provide the reader with a verbatim transcription of interviews with Mr. Rube Wingo, done when he was 116 years old. I recorded him over the course of four weeks. With a breathy, drawling delivery, Mr. Wingo proved to be a consummate storyteller whether sharing a memory bawdy or sweet, and I hope that the reader will be as beguiled as I. The words and the unique voice are his alone, and once the rhythm is acquired, they proved to be mesmerizing to me. Hopefully the reader will concur. Though his recollection of some events may appear to be a bit fanciful and far afield, his recall for baseball dates and statistics was astonishing.

Hand me that prune juice. It's nasty stuff, you know. I prefer grapefruit, really, but it jacks with my duodenum. Still, a body's got to have its juice. I swear by my Vitamin C, and I'm older than God's baby teeth. Yep. The soft juice, the hard juice and lots of naps.

Which reminds me, thanks for not waking me up. I'm not a morning person. Never have been. So, I appreciate you not being early.

In my original working days, most all baseball folk were night owls. We'd stay up half near till dawn to wring every last drop of fun out of the previous day. I reckon I just never broke the habit. Even when we played nothing but day games, the fellows didn't get to the ballpark till lunchtime at best. Hell, some guys like

Dizzy Dean would waltz in at 2:30 for a 3:00 o'clock game that he was pitching. It sure ain't like that now.

So, you want to hear about my life? Well, I have spent an awful lot of time in the game, more than anybody living, most likely, and I learned a few lessons along the way. In my youth, of course, I wanted to be a great ballplayer. Instead, in my own tiny way, I helped men with more talent achieve my dreams.

CHAPTER ONE

LEE COUNTY, ARKANSAS

We might as well take it from the start. They tell me I was born in a snowstorm, though I don't recall it myself, of course. Story goes that snow was pouring down like nothing that northeast Arkansas had ever seen. Big, wet snow that piled deep on the ground and drove everybody back inside even though there was nothing to do in there except sit in the dark and warm by the fire if you was lucky enough to have kindling.

My mama told me the story of my birth many times, though I was never sure how much of the retelling was designed to guilt me into doing my chores with a tad more diligence. It was snowing so bad that the mud tracks we called roads were completely impassable. Drifts so deep that fence posts disappeared. Cows in the field was standing on each other's shoulders so their milk didn't freeze, birds and cats huddled together, and Mrs. Adaline Siler, the midwife who delivered nigh all the childhood playmates I ever knew, couldn't make it through to our farm. Hell, I'm sure nobody got word to her in the first durn place.

So, it was left to my daddy, who was not the most worldly of men, to assist with my arrival into this world. I was an only child, so this was a new experience, and I come along somewhat later in life. They was both over 30 which was plenty old enough to be a grandparent in Arkansas. Lucky for me, Daddy had once foaled a mule. Not personal mind you, but he'd helped.

The snow had been falling for better than 24 hours, and they knew there was no traveling to be had, so when my mama said that her water had broke, and the baby was coming, the first thing daddy done was take her out to the barn. He laid her in fresh hay and lit an extra lantern. Labor took six or eight or ten hours. I reckon it varied depending on what mama was trying to get me to do.

By the time my head appeared, daddy had already enjoyed several nips off the shine. Always a team player, he done it to dull my mama's cries, he said. Nevertheless, he helped guide me out, at least at first. I was a big baby, they told me. North of ten pounds. Once my shoulders cleared, mama give a big contraction, and I shot clean through my daddy's hands, skipped a couple of times, and slid into the edge of the snow before the cord bungeed me back to my poor mama's arms.

Daddy was a little embarrassed by the whole experience, and I always reckoned my delivery into the world could be scored an E-2. There was a very brief discussion about how the mare had licked the little mule clean before a pair of fresh towels and some pruning shears were produced.

For my part, I never was partial to cold weather even a lick, which will tear skin off your tongue under those circumstances. I wonder if it's on account of me arriving during the snow?

That all took place on the first of January 1901, first day of the twentieth century, as any fool who can count will tell you. Now, New Year's Day is one lousy birthday. I never did have a decent party. Everybody was always too hungover to bake me a damn cake.

Funny. As I say that, it occurs to me that when I was a youngster, it's likely I didn't even know what a birthday cake was. Back home, cakes was something you fried up in a cast iron skillet. I think one of my earliest memories must be the sweet taste of a perfect hoecake.

I'll bet you don't even know what that is, do you, son? Well, it's just about the most useful item of food ever invented. See a hoecake is a thick round of cornbread that comes from the pan with a crispy outside glistening with goodness and a buttery inside ready to march the rest of your dinner across your taste buds. You can use it to scoop up a mouthful of collards and dredge up the last of the pinto beans. If you do it right, you barely even got to wash the dishes. It might be named after a sinful woman, but done right, it's heaven. Hell, they both are.

My mama used to pacify me with a hoecake and a green onion. Sat me in the corner of the kitchen with our old one-eared spotted hound. Since he and I were best buddies, we'd take turns gnawing on the hoecake. Dogs can't eat onions, but they sure are partial to cornbread.

I was an only child reared up amidst a pack of cousins. My disposition has always been toward the bright side of life. It's in my bones. Not in every instance, you understand. I've had heartache aplenty, but more often than not, I believe that the hero escapes from the railroad track and the dog gets his girl. What a sad life it would be if you thought different.

But there I go a-rambling. You wanted to hear about baseball, didn't you? Back then, baseball was big down in our part of the country, that being Lee County. By the time I was nine, I was blossoming into one of the best ballplayers around.

There wasn't no TV, or even radio, back in the first decade of that century. Oh, there was newspapers in most counties, but those came out once a week and didn't have enough pictures in them for folks to figure out what was going on. So, by and large, you sort of had to make your own fun whenever you wasn't working. Naturally, we spent most of our time outdoors.

One of the great things in the summer time was when a community would have what they called an ice cream supper. We didn't have ice in the summer, it being hot and all, so they probably should have been called just cream suppers. Everybody from all the farms would come out to Fox's meadow and bring them a picnic meal.

One of my earliest memories is of one of those suppers before I was old enough to play. My daddy was playing, and I was sitting with my mama and her brother, my uncle Stump Dibrell. I don't know where my Aunt Sacagawea was, but I sure don't recall her being there. And she would have figured in the story, too, cause my daddy hit a vicious foul ball that went right off Uncle Stump's wooden foot and bounced hard out past the right fielder. Uncle Stump let out a yelp. It must have stung him, I guess. And he hopped up and took off running around the bases. The crack of that wooden foot sounded just like the crack of the bat, and they come right together. My daddy thought that the ball was fair so he took off toward first base. The ball kept rolling right on into the high grass. Uncle Stump crossed the plate and, without slowing down, run off down the road. Daddy slid into third on his belly just ahead of the throw which skipped past the baseman and allowed my daddy to trot on home.

Well, all hell broke loose. The other team claimed that Uncle Stump's run didn't count because he hadn't been in the game at the time. My daddy's team pointed out that there had never been a rule like that before, since it had never come up, and that you can't just go making up the rules as you go along. I got to agree with that line of thought myself. All the while, nobody has figured out that the ball was foul to begin with, except for me and my Uncle Stump, and he and his wooden foot was half a mile away by that time.

The real trouble started when Daddy begun talking about sleeping in the house. See, women back then would let a man sleep in the bed sometimes after he hit a home run. But as soon as Daddy let on that he's expecting it, mama gets up on her hind legs.

"That was a triple with a throwing error, plain as day, and if you think you're gonna be getting any on account of that, you'd best think again."

"Oh, come on, Butternut." my daddy said.

You see, he told me when I got grown that he'd been in a terrible slump and hadn't homered in several years. So, the scorer's ruling was mighty important to him right at that moment. As luck would have it, the umpire owed my daddy 34 cents, and he sidles over to where my daddy and mama was yelling at each other and says, "Nice Homerun." Mama resigned herself to losing all the way up until Uncle Stump limped back to the house at three o'clock that next morning asking for sandpaper to clean the ball mark off his left foot. Daddy got up and went back to the barn and never said another word about it.

Uncle Stump Dibrell was an interesting fellow. He was my mama's youngest brother; I think I mentioned that. He lost his foot during the Spanish American War. Had something to do with the canned meat scandal.

Now, while my daddy and uncles and cousins had taught me about the game itself, the first I really started learning about the big leagues, you know, got something to set my sights on, was when a bunch of us kids heard tell that there was a copy of Baseball Magazine just there for the looking at, out past Marvell someplace. Well, me and my identical cousins Luke and Vora Hazelett decided that we would pretty near die a premature death if we couldn't get us a peek at that.

When I say identical cousins, by the by, I ain't just making a joke about the old Patty Duke Show. They really was durn near identical cousins. Their daddies was cousins and their mamas was, too. And they lived right next door to one another. To make matters more of a big coincidence, they was born on the same day. Fifth of August, 1902. Folks long speculated that either Luke's daddy or Vora's had come home drunk and wound up in the wrong house one night, but my mouth to Jeff Davis's corncrib, those two younguns looked plumb exactly the same. They was also cousins once removed, but that was a surgical procedure, and don't bear repeating now.

News back then was oft times more gossip than fact, so we heard all sorts of tales from the other boys around those parts about where they had seen that copy of Baseball Magazine. An old witch used it to lure little boys into her tree stump. Spacemen had brought it from Oklahoma City. Wild tales like that. We finally got us a good tip about some old boy that had laid his hands on this gem over to Pine Bluff. Nobody could recollect his name, and I must admit that was to make finding him all the much harder.

We didn't dare tell our folks that we was going on some three day wild goose chase to have a look at magazine pictures. And that was all we could do cause none of us could read even an eye chart back then. In Arkansas in those days, lots of boys didn't learn to read good till they was, oh, about nine or ten.

You see, we had us a one room school house. It was that way everywhere, as far as I knew. The girls would pay attention, but the boys had their minds off someplace else. You know, dipping a ponytail in the ink or putting a skunk sack into the potbellied stove. That trick there would let school out for a day or two certain. So, the teacher taught the girls and otherwise bided time till the boys settled down or run off.

Well, one day when we could stand it no more, we headed down towards the river, asking questions of any soul we happened to see. The river I'm speaking of, of course, is Big River. Marvell was across it and down in Phillips County, I might add. That was the first time I ever went out of county.

So, we walked, and, being three little urchin looking boys, we ate damn good. Every house we passed almost, the woman would be out in the yard sweeping the dirt and look up and say, "My, but you boys look hungry." And we was at first. Then we tried to act hungry, on account of we didn't know how long this generosity would hold up. Then towards the end, we was looking hungry just to be polite. Our bellies was all poking out and the smell of simmering fatback like to make all three of us urp. But we ate it, just the same.

Wash Posey's name first come up when we had stopped to help some widow woman finish off a pot of grits that was left over from the morning. Looking back on that little episode, I think that she wasn't a widow woman at all, but just some lonely lady whose husband had run off. Could have been he just run off since breakfast and would be back in plenty of time for lunch, but he sure wasn't paying no heed to that poor woman.

Anyhoo, this lady says that she herself is a baseball fan. She just loves the Boston Braves because she feels sorry for them. They live up where it's all cold, and they never win a dime. She allows how there is one old boy around there who is a bigger baseball fan than her or anybody else. That is one Wash Posey who lives in a genuine log cabin that backs plumb up to Big River. If you was to open Wash's back door, you'd step right off the threshold and into the water. Only problem was Wash didn't have no backdoor. But if anybody had a copy of Baseball Magazine, that there would be our man.

Maybe I should take a second to explain about Baseball Magazine. It was the best way, and maybe the only way, to get to know things. This magazine would tell you all about the baseball news and have pictures of players and stories about what they did on their time off, and... well, it would capture you like one of those big catalog wish books we used to get. This could take you right to the games, and get you so close to a player you could smell his ten-cent shaving lotion. Just because none of us had ever seen it, didn't mean that we hadn't heard all about it and then some.

Now Wash Posey's place was about another fourteen, fifteen miles from where we was at with the nice woman. That was a good day's walk through the fields and woods, and it was now getting close to eight o'clock in the morning. We'd burned some daylight like John Wayne used to say, and that magazine was the carrot at the end of our stick.

Talking about that, by the way, you know they really used to do that, put a carrot or something on the end of a long pole and put it out in front of the mule. I don't like to speak ill of any living thing, but a mule is one stubborn and none too bright animal, I will tell you that. A lot of them, not all of them now, would go walking after something he wanted if it was just out of reach like that. We had us a mule name of Marcellus who would only plow if you put molasses syrup in front of him. When I was a boy, I made fast friends with old Marcellus, and I'd sneak out to the barn and give him a handful of molasses most every night. If daddy woke up, I'd have to give him half. That was one of the first pets I ever kept. He eventually died of sugar diabetes.

But back to that glorious day. We three walked and run in what we figured was the right direction. When we got to Big River, nobody had heard of Wash Posey, at all. It was starting to get late in the afternoon, and we wanted to see that durn magazine that day, by gum. So, we turned and headed upriver, figuring we'd overshot. We followed that river bank back north for another eight miles I bet. The sun had done dropped down behind the tree tops.

Then we heard a noise. As long as I live, that sound is going to be right here inside my head, and right here, too, inside my heart. It was a crack of wood, real sharp, almost like a rifle. And then another one come, and skipped across the water like a flat rock and echoed off those big sweet gum trees and cypress just as pretty as can be. We three boys looked over to the other side of the river, and there, in a big grassy yard beside this little cabin was some old gray headed lady throwing a ball to some gray headed old man. And every time, he swung real big and hit the ball out to the other side of the yard, and it made that beautiful ringing noise.

You see, not only did Wash Posey have a copy of Baseball Magazine, but he had him a real bat. I mean from a bat factory. See, all the bats that we used back then was sticks that we had whittled smooth. They didn't really taper off at the handle much the way bats are supposed to, and brother, let me tell you, they didn't have that noise when you hit a ball with the fat end.

That there was one of the great fellows I ever met, Wash Posey, and I'd say that goes for his wife, too. Wash knew more about baseball than anybody in the whole state back then, but he was interesting beyond that. He had been a soldier in the Civil War with the 30th Arkansas Infantry. Then he went and got himself captured at Chancellorsville, Virginia.

That in itself is a good story, if you don't mind me heading off again on you. This was back in January of 1863, in what turned out to be Robert E. Lee's greatest victory. Wash Posey and a buddy of his name of Christopher Columbus Branham got sent out to hunt for juniper berries. They had themselves a captain who used to get these terrible headaches, and he was just convinced that juniper berries would cure him.

While Stonewall Jackson was moving around behind the Yankees, old Wash and Christopher Columbus got sent out into the woods. Well, when General Jackson attacked, the Yankees was all playing cards and eating supper. It wasn't long before they took off a running. And do you know which way they run? Right toward where Wash and Christopher Columbus was berry hunting in the woods. They become two of the very few Southern prisoners took at Chancellorsville.

It just so happened that they was captured by some New Jersey boys who sort of scooped them up as they run by. In fact, cause this New Jersey outfit only captured the two of them, and the second lieutenant was the highest ranking officer left standing, they decided to keep these two prisoners for themselves, rather than sending them off to some camp.

They become sort of the house boys and mascots of the outfit, and I'll tell you true, straight out, both of them figured that being house boys was superior to being shot at. Plus, they got full rations from the Union, which was six times better than what the rebels was handing out. New shoes and pants, to boot. But the best part was that these New Jersey fellows spent all their free time, when they wasn't fighting, just playing baseball. Not the town ball or old cat that was common in Arkansas, but honest to goodness baseball.

They say that the modern game of baseball was invented in New Jersey, but whether it was or wasn't, old Wash always swore by how those Yankees played ball. They took Wash and Christopher Columbus under their wings. C. C. become one of the great pitchers in St. Francis County before he died of yellow fever in 1869. And Wash Posey had himself a natural born knack for hitting the ball. All those Union boys wanted him on their team. When the war was over, they asked him to come back up north and play ball, for money no less, but Wash just told them that he had to go back to Arkansas. He had a sweetheart named Claudia waiting there for him. At least he hoped that she was still waiting, and as much as he loved baseball, he missed home.

Back in those times, a woman might just wait for a man. People had a certain honor, I guess you'd call it. Yes sir, it wasn't like today. Course, in this particular case, Claudia had run off with a traveling medicine show and got herself married to a Dr. Leonard Welldigger, the Sultan of Magic Elixir. But that didn't matter one iota, on account of while Wash was walking home from Virginia, he met another girl name of Octavia LaRoot and brought her back to Arkansas and took her as his bride. They'd been married ever since.

Something else that he brung back with him was baseball. I mean the love of baseball, I suppose. He had baseball like a disease. If you stayed around him too long, he'd give it to you, too. He definitely gave it to Octavia. It turns out that what we saw in the yard that particular evening was what that couple did every night. They played ball, just the two of them.

Hang on. I'm starting to get ahead of myself. If I'm gonna tell you this story, then I'd just as soon tell it in order, like it happened. That way you can be as surprised as I was by the way things developed.

What we boys had come to see was that damn magazine, two old folks playing ball notwithstanding. Although seeing them cavorting around the river bank like that was pretty strong evidence that we had found the right place. So, me being the oldest, I yelled out, "Hey! Are you Mr. Wash Posey that has him a copy of the Baseball Magazine?"

"Well, that depends. You gentlemen look like rough characters. Just who are you?"

I knew that we probably did look like ruffians even though we was only six and seven years old. We'd been traveling for three full days, so I tried to sound real nice.

"Mr. Wash Posey, sir, if that's who you are, I'm one of the Wingo boys from further up Lee County, and these boys here are my identical cousins, Luke and Vora."

"Oh, I see. In that case, I reckon that y'all can come on over into my yard."

That was more invitation than we needed, I tell you what. All three of us dove into that river trying to outswim the other two. The water was pretty low, so when we climbed out onto the other side, we was more muddy than wet. Mrs. Posey suggested that she might clean us off a bit before we come into her house.

"So, you boys are baseball rooters?" Wash asked.

"Oh, yes sir. We sure are. We never seen us any pictures of big league ballplayers like they have in Baseball Magazine. That's why we come looking for you."

All of us was kind of talking at once. Wash just stood there patient and nodding while Mrs. Posey wiped us down with a cloth. He said something about a "pilgrimage", although, needless to say, we didn't recognize the word at the time.

After we was scrubbed up, they poured us each a glass of cider right fresh out of the cider mill. And then Wash brought us the magazine. Not just one, but a whole box full of them. He had most every copy of Baseball Magazine you could imagine. They used to have drawings on the cover showing different ballplayers. That was back when drawings were made after a photograph, instead of just using the photograph itself. Kind of a strange thing to do if you ask me, but they didn't ask me. Either way those covers was flat beautiful to my cousins and me.

We looked at pictures of Joe Tinker and Frank Chance and Jack Chesbro, Ed Ruelbach, Fred Tenney, "Wahoo" Sam Crawford, and Mike "Turkey" Donlin who was married to some famous vaudeville actress with a butt you wanted to eat Thanksgiving dinner off of. Maybe that's why he was called "Turkey".

There were lots of others, and we stayed up most of the night looking at all those pictures. Wash and Mrs. Posey sat up reading and talking to us till half past ten, which was awful late to stay up in Arkansas back in those days. Then, after they went to bed, we perused those magazines by moonlight. We must have fell asleep just before sunup because it seemed like no time before Mrs. Posey was prying one copy out of my little mitts and saying, "Get off the floor, you boys, and come eat your breakfast."

When we was done eating, Wash Posey loaded us into the back of a wagon and rode us back home. I'm sure that I can speak for my cousins when I say that my head was just a-spinning. That was a big adventure, right there, boy. I had caught me that case of baseball just like I told you. And I don't reckon that I ever did get over it.

It's funny, but for Luke and Vora, everything wore off in a few days, and they went on to other pursuits. Luke ended up as a greens farmer right there in Lee County. The next year, he turned seven and got married to this divorcee from back on the other side of Crowley's Ridge. They started having babies and never looked back. As far as I know, he didn't ever raise any crop other than greens:

collard or mustard. Every single one of those kids of his had a complexion like a bad stock pond.

Vora, now, he never married. That's because he got him a new pocket knife that Christmas and took up whittling. He could whittle everything imaginable, but his specialty was hogs. Most notable was the way he could carve a Hampshire. Tamworths was good, too, but those Hampshires just looked so lifelike, even if they were made out of cedar. He passed away when a tree fell on him one winter. After he went, people took to calling those wood hogs of his "folk art" and collecting them. Years later, they opened up a shop down in Pine Bluff that only sold Vora's carved hogs. Damn hippies.

I kept going back to Wash Posey's, though. And about the third or fourth visit, he give me one of those Baseball Magazines to keep. That was toward the tail end of the season in 1908, the year of the greatest pennant race of all time, and it just so happened that the one he give me had Iron Man Joe McGinnity on the front. It was a coincidence me getting that particular magazine. See 1908 was Joe's last year in the big leagues.

I said that pennant race was the best ever, and that's no lie. After everybody had tussled through 154 contests, three teams was separated by just one game. See, that was the year of Merkle's boner, they called it. The word luckily having a different connotation back then. Fred Merkle of the Giants, who was a pretty solid ballplayer all things considered, made a baserunning mistake, though some say the umpires just fell for a trick. Anyway, on account of that, a game had to be replayed, which became a playoff of sorts in the last game of the season and which the Giants then lost to the Cubs.

Them losing didn't matter to me one little bit. I had Iron Man Joe McGinnity's picture on a cover of Baseball Magazine, and that made me a Giants fan. From that day forward I dreamed about playing ball in the Polo Grounds. Never made it to that particular stadium. It burned down in 1911, and they built them another Polo Grounds. I spent a good deal of time in that ballpark, though. I tell you what.

Did you ever hear about the Iron Man? I'm sure you did, him being in the Hall of Fame. Joe pitched 466 games in just ten years, and won 247 of them, too.

He threw underhand. The ball took off to the plate and then broke real sharp at the last minute. He was famous for throwing both ends of a doubleheader and winning both. He did that three different times in 1903.

When he retired after that, he moved back down to McAlester in what had just become the state of Oklahoma. See Old Joe had worked in the coal mines down there when he was a kid. In fact, he had almost got killed in a mining accident at Krebs #11 before he ever started playing baseball. The miners had got off their shift and was riding up to the top. Joe was in the third cage, and just as they were getting out, the mine exploded, killing a hundred men or better. That's kind of the way things was back then. Nobody got too worried about blowing up a bunch of poor folks. Guess they figured there was never a danger of running out.

The reason I know that story is that I got to meet Old Joe many years later. I know I wasn't gonna tell things out of order, but I'll make an exception right here. A couple of years after his wife died, Iron Man come up to Brooklyn to live with his daughter, and happened to get an operation of some sort. That was about 1929. The operation didn't take too good, and he was laid up in the hospital.

When I heard that Joe McGinnity was low in the quilts and in New York, see I was living there then, all I could think of was the cover of my Baseball Magazine. I resolved to go visit him.

He wasn't feeling too swift, but he listened to me talk without putting up much of a fuss. Must have liked my stories, so I got in the habit of going to visit him every evening almost. We played day games, so when I was in town, I'd just hop a train out to Brooklyn and chat with Joe. Not many people are lucky enough to spend time with their childhood hero like that. Especially when they can't run off.

One of the greatest things Joe told me was that he had him a big house built down in McAlester at the corner of Seventh and Seneca. I still recall the address. And parts of the interior rooms were made from baseball bats. I bet I made him tell me about that fifteen times.

Joe's operation happened in August of that year. He hung around for a while, not getting any better. The Iron Man finally passed on in November. All his pallbearers were former teammates of his. Before they buried him, his body lay in state right in the big middle of the Elks Lodge up there in Oklahoma. Those folks loved him.

Chapter Two

My school years in Lee County was awful good. What you writers call halcyon days, I think. Of course, I ain't saying that on account of the schooling part. Oh, it was a good thing I got that education. It's just that the education you come away with from a one room school in Arkansas wasn't exactly the best in the world. But like most of my life, I can't honestly tell you that I'd change it.

Most schools only operated about four to six months of the year. You had crops to get out. Still there was a lot of learning to do, and I don't mean in books. I was a slow youngster, I reckon.

My mama used to tell me "You're not a smart boy, Nipper, so be kind."

She also knew that I was maybe the most gullible kiddo in our part of Lee County, so she urged me to keep improving myself. I've tried to learn something new every day, and since I'm now 116, you figure something had to stick.

Now, even the brightest boy of seven or eight or nine years of age still has a mind that'd wander off pretty regular, like I mentioned before. And there was a jillion and one distractions back then.

Did I ever tell you about the time me and Burrell Prewitt snuck his daddy's T-Model Ford out of the barn? Nah, I guess I didn't.

Burrell Prewitt's daddy, huge fellow name of Bilbo Prewitt, was a gambling man. He'd ride horseback from town to town just a-betting while Burrell stayed home by himself. He liked dice or card playing the best, I suppose, but if there wasn't a game, Bilbo Prewitt would bet on whatever he could find.

He'd bet on which bug would scamper past a certain point first. He'd bet on which dog had the most fleas. Or which old woman had a nipple closer to the floor. Although measuring that one likely took a fair amount of sweet talking.

Sometimes he used to bareknuckle fight and bet on that. One time he run up against an old boy who stood six foot eight or thereabouts. Mountain of a fellow who looked like he'd had a goat belly implanted in each of his upper arms. Whatever that means.

Now like I said, Bilbo was pretty good size himself, but just eyeing this other man, he didn't think he could take him.

So, Bilbo sidles up to him and says, "I'll bet you fifty cents that you can beat the living crap out of me."

This gentleman thought about it for a time, and said, "Okay, you're on."

The two commenced to fighting right there on the sidewalk. They was punching and grappling and pretty soon rolled on out to the middle of the street. Like a lot of fights, it started out pretty friendly but turned more angry as it went along.

The big boy drew first blood, and that just made Bilbo Prewitt madder than hell. He started swinging all wild like. Flailing his arms, just furious. He caught the big man right below the ear and caused a trickle of blood to start trailing down the side of his neck. But more important, it set off a loud ringing in the other man's ears. Made it where he couldn't hear a thing. Which was crucial on account of all of the people who knew the big old boy was yelling for him to just lay back and pocket the fifty cents.

Well, sir, with him not hearing right, he went ahead and beat the snot out of Bilbo Prewitt. Left him knocked out colder than an east coast bride. Caused twenty-six permanent scars, but Bilbo won his bet. And that's the kind of thinking that led to him getting ahold of the T-model Ford.

This must have been about nineteen hundred and ten; Burrell and I being around nine years of age. Burrell's daddy was off betting someplace way up north, maybe Paragould County. He got on a bad streak. Just losing something terrible.

I'm not a gambling man myself, never have been, but I've heard the tales of when nothing you do will go right. And that's sure enough how it was at that moment with Bilbo Prewitt.

He'd get him a straight flush, and someone else would lay down a straight flush that was a card higher. He'd roll eleven and the other guy would roll twelve. He'd say the left one was at least a quarter inch lower than the right, and the building would have foundation trouble. You see how it was.

In the midst of all this losing, Bilbo runs across a Yankee insurance salesman having dinner in a little roadhouse. The old boy was wearing a string tie on a Tuesday of all things, so old Bilbo just had to know more.

"Whereabouts you from?" Bilbo opens up with.

"Well, sir, I was born in the river town of Madison, Indiana. But since that time, I have called twenty-three different hamlets and municipalities as my own is my best approximation. Won't you join me, sir?"

Now I'd be willing to lay odds, keeping with the theme here, that Bilbo Prewitt hadn't never been called "sir" in that fashion by a grown-up in his whole life, let alone twice in one minute. So, all flattered, he sat down.

It was a rare occasion when a Yankee showed up around home back then. People didn't travel about like they do now. And most folks around home was so poor that Northern people had no reason to come down there. Us having nothing to take, you see.

What I'm getting at is that right from the outset, Bilbo is sort of fascinated. Plus, this fellow was a bona fide salesman with lots of experience and multi-syllable words. All put together that made him seem slicker than goose shit to a country boy like Bilbo Prewitt. Before you could say boo, his guard was down.

Anyhow, this old Northern boy was an insurance peddler, like I told you, so naturally the first thing he starts to do is size up his potential client. They talk for damn nigh half an hour. The salesman craftily asking questions about Bilbo's family and property and whatnot. But after that 30 minutes is up, it becomes sort of evident that Bilbo Prewitt just flat don't have anything that needs insuring. His farm was rented from his late wife's uncle-in-law, and all Bilbo can tell him about his boy is that he's outgrowing his trousers last time he saw him and that his name starts with a "B". Not much of a family man, I guess.

Now, in my mind the two marks of a good salesman is having a fallback position and being filled with an unbending confidence that you could make a sale to anybody you can get to sit down with you. And this old boy was good, to be sure.

See, there wasn't no big car dealerships out in the country in those days. No showrooms at all. Salesmen had these metal and wood models of the car about a foot or so high. You'd look at that, tell them what you wanted on it, and order the car delivered to you.

I say tell them what you wanted, but the truth is, since we're talking about T-Model Fords, they only come in one color. Black. So, there wasn't really much to choose.

Well now, this drummer, by which I mean salesman, tells Bilbo to sit tight.

"I have something for your perusal, Mr. Prewitt. If you would kindly excuse me, sir, I shall return post haste."

Not understanding the half of it, Bilbo just stares at the old boy, with his jaw hanging limp. The salesman took that as a yes and went out the back door.

It wasn't an instant before he come back, just like he said. And he plops one of them model Model-Ts right down on the table.

"Mr. Prewitt, sir, allow me to present the epitome of modern automobile industrialization. The pinnacle of the transportation arts. Yes sir, the T-Model from Henry Ford's Motor Company can be assembled in a scant 93 minutes, not including the body, which is fabricated from the finest metals available. This spanking new automobile was only first offered to the buying public three short years hence in nineteen hundred and eight."

Bilbo narrowed his eyes and looked from the car to the salesman then back to the car. The salesman, sensing that Bilbo wasn't yet sold, continued.

"As you can plainly see, the wheels are covered by tires of India rubber, which present the passenger or motor enthusiast with the most cushioned ride imaginable. It can easily glide atop the muddiest of country roads."

Bilbo cocked his head to one side and his eyes got even narrower. The salesman took a deep breath.

"I sense by your wardrobe that you are a mechanically inclined man. Let me assure you that the most modern improvements have been incorporated into this machine. It starts with the flick of a wrist against the front crank, and it boasts gears that will convey one either forward or backward."

With that the salesman tugged on a tiny lever inside the passenger compartment of the model and rolled the thing forward then backward on the table. Bilbo scratched at a particular spot on his forehead then followed that up by digging in one ear with his little finger and flicking it at the floor without ever taking his eyes off the car. The salesman was starting to sweat, figuring that he must have run up on the hardest-to-please country boy of his entire career. It became a kind of quest of his just to get Bilbo to ask a durn question at that point.

"I should also mention that the plant of this machine is mechanically oiled and can generate thirty-five horse-power."

Bilbo started on his other ear.

"That is to say the power of thirty-five horses... if they were tethered as a group." The salesman was dying.

"I hesitate to impugn a competitor," the salesman said all conspiratorial and whatnot. "But the Hupmobile or Paige is but rectal effluvia compared to the stability of a Ford."

Finally, after a silence that must have seemed like an eternity, Bilbo raised one of his thick, dirty fingers to the steering wheel on that model car and said, "Kinda small, ain't it?"

The salesman practically knocked his chair over in his rush to stand up.

"Mr. Prewitt, I can assure you that the T-Model Ford is a comfortable sized automobile, even for a gentleman of your stature. Why it's almost sixty-five percent the size of a National or a Peerless. And at a price less than a third of those behemoths. If you'd accompany me into the alley behind this establishment, I'd be glad to demonstrate first hand."

Now old Bilbo may not have been the most book learned fellow you'd ever hope to meet, but he had what the kids call street smarts. Common sense. And his common sense had told him that you don't just walk out into a back alley with a slick talking stranger no matter how big you are.

"Mister, if'n you don't mind, I'd rather not go with you into that alley."

"But I have a full sized automobile out there, sir. How else can I fully demonstrate her comforts? You can't very well ask of me to bring her inside." The salesman was awful perplexed by this development.

"Well, that may be true," Bilbo pondered slowly. "But I've only knew you for about an hour and a half. What if you were just aiming to knock me in the head or shoot me and take all my worldly goods?"

The Yankee wondered for a moment what goods Bilbo might be talking about.

"Or what if you had you some sort of sidekick out there hoping to waylay me?"

The more Bilbo talked, the more worked up he was starting to get, and about this point he took a step closer to the salesman, standing toe to toe, and breathing down at him, all red in the face.

"How the hell do I know that you ain't part of some mean-ass Yankee spy ring that takes big Southern boys off into white slavery? That'd make sense to me."

Well, the little salesman was all of a sudden a bit afraid for his well-being, especially cause the few other folks in the café had now turned to get a look at him. I'm guessing that the first thought he had was to excuse himself, get into that car, and drive on to the next town. But he'd already spent several days getting himself known around this one, and the peak of his sales there, insurance, car and, otherwise, was still to come. Now, any good salesman has to be more than a little bit arrogant, and that's the part of him that kicked in right about then.

"I'll tell you what, Mr. Prewitt." He made one of those big wide gestures to all the other folks. "Even though I'm certain that the good people of this burgh would gladly vouch for the unwavering honesty and the good character which I have shown in the course of the past four days, I shall be most sanguine about remaining with them indoors while you step into the alley unencumbered and try on the T-Model Ford to your heart's content."

Now the salesman was starting to enjoy this new approach. Yes sir, he started preaching.

"Please sink back in the padded driver's chair and let go a deep breath. I implore you to look over your head at the perfect machine stitching of the canvas hood. Luxuriate in the feel of the steering wheel against your calloused hands. Imagine all those horses at your disposal. Why, turn the magneto, and listen to the purr of the motor. Yes, Mr. Prewitt, by all means, take all the time you desire."

The salesman gave a big smile and a slight bow to the folks in the restaurant. Two of them actually applauded. And Bilbo Prewitt slipped on out the back door. He may not have picked up on some of them fancy words, but he sure as shootin' knew the meaning of "take all the time you desire".

Well, I guess it was about seven or eight months after that, me and Burrell was playing with that car out in the broken down barn where Bilbo had been keeping it. Said he needed to keep the elements off of it since it was only borrowed.

We had taken the thing on drives around the barnyard but never had ventured too far. Mostly on account of one of the meanest old roosters you ever seen in your life had decided that the back seat of that T-Model Ford was about the dandiest roost he'd seen yet. He allowed a hen to jump up there every so often, for flirting sake you understand. But most beings, poultry or otherwise, didn't venture too close to this rooster who we always called Old Snack. I reckon that was in anticipation of when he got older and slower.

I should tell you an interesting fact about Old Snack that figures large in this story, too. He was a Leghorn that had a sort of red and brown mottled look to him, but that wasn't the odd thing. The weird part was that Old Snack had a pet hog name of Rose.

Rose was a just a little slip of a shoat when she became an orphan. Both of her folks passed in what we'll call an accident just before Easter dinner of 1909, and they left Rose as the only youngster in the hog lot. Well, as you'd imagine, she mostly got pushed aside when slop time rolled around. The big sows would root out most of the good bits of food before Rose could slip up to the trough.

Now, son, I don't know what experience you ever had on a farm, but I will tell you that while some animals can be dumber than a South Carolina welder, there's also some that you'd swear are downright human. Or at least that they can show some characteristics that only your humans generally get credit for. And that's the way it was with Old Snack, I'm a guessing.

Being the only youngun on the lot, it wasn't long before Rose started crying real loud on account of being hungry. Burrell and me used to sit and listen to her, but being dumb kids, we thought she was singing. Not that she had much of a voice. Sounded sort of like that Beatle's wife.

But that rooster knew what she was saying, and he must have took pity on the little thing cause he took to jumping up on the trough at slop time and pecking at those sows, and even a barrow or two, until they stepped back enough for little Rose to get a hold of some of the decent table scraps. I swear to you I ain't making that up, neither. He watched out for that pig like she was his own flesh and blood all the way up until she weighed close to 160 pounds or more, I'd bet.

For her part, Rose grew damned attached to Old Snack. She'd follow him around that barnyard night and day. He might as well have had that hog on a leash. And once Bilbo Prewitt put that Ford in the barn, Rose started sleeping in the back seat. Just behind Snack's tufted leather roost.

Then one day, me and Burrell Prewitt was looking for something to do, that being our normal summer activity. We'd done wandered around the barnyard for a piece when we noticed Old Snack sitting up over the chicken coop. All at once, it occurred to us that if Old Snack was up there, the T-Model Ford was left unprotected.

We made us a beeline for the barn. Burrell jumped behind the wheel while I cranked that magneto. She caught on the fourth turn, and I hopped in beside him. Yes sir, we was going for a drive.

Well, looking back on it, I'd say we made it about three-quarters of a mile before I heard some squawking coming up behind us. Old Snack had been a chasing us once he seen that we had driven off with his roost. So, I tell Burrell to give her some more gas or else we'd get pecked to death sure as shooting.

He opened the throttle all the way up, probably got that old car headed up towards 35 miles an hour, and Old Snack started getting smaller behind us. We started down a low grade and picked up even more speed. We was in hog heaven.

And I say hog heaven for a reason. You see in our hasty escape from the barn, we hadn't realized that Rose was asleep in the back seat. When she heard her guardian rooster yelling and then felt the breeze in her hair, she got a mite scared. The way we found out she was there is when she made a kind of leap from the back seat into the front. All 210 pounds of her at that point.

She hit Burrell on the right side and me on the left. Then she gave a little twist and pushed the each of us right out the doors of that Ford. Now, what you had left then was a hog named Rose driving a T-Model about 40 miles an hour down an incline, and I don't need to tell you that the factory don't recommend that.

We just sat there on our significantly bruised bottoms and watched that poor car miss the turn in the road and plow right through Old Widow Jacquet's corn, then her corn crib, and finally come to a halt about halfway through her back porch.

Now the widow was a very religious bible thumping sort of woman, to be sure. Chances was solid that she had been sitting there at that very minute praying for something. It could have even been that she was praying for a young hog to come driving up in a Model-T. At any rate, that's what she got.

We naturally did what any pair of young boys would do in that situation. We ran like hell in the opposite direction. My hindsight tells me that if we'd gone up to her right then and explained the thing, she might not have kept the car. But we was pretty scared and had only a modicum of skin left on our butts.

After Bilbo Prewitt come back to town, we had even less skin on our butts.

He went down to the Widow Jacquet and tried to tell her that the car was his, or at least that he had borrowed it for an extended period, but she had already got it in her head that the Good Lord had sent that Ford right to her back porch as an offering for her continued piety, and that was the end of that.

Rose eventually made her way back home. As part of the punishment for losing the car his daddy had took, Burrell had to give Rose and Snack his room. But you probably saw that coming.

It was along about the time I was turning fourteen that I had my first experience with women. Or I should say woman, since there was only the one. It was a dark haired cutie who had started to develop at a somewhat early age, if you follow my meaning. Her name was Jeannie Grace Higginbotham, a year my senior, and I wasn't the only boy from the neighborhood who had started to notice her perky, womanly protuberances.

Fact is, I recall her having a goodly passel of boys trailing after her just about every place she went. At that age, we wasn't near as subtle as we thought we was being. When that girl would take a stroll around the school yard, I'll bet you that all twelve of the older boys at our school would start doing something to impress her. Picking a fight, yelling loud, whistling a song that we'd heard, chasing a rooster. For her part, she'd keep this happy sort of expression on her face like she knew where her mama hid the snuff. She was above it all, and acting like she didn't notice.

That went on most of the fall of 1915. She'd come back from spending the summer with her grandma, and her newly acquired accoutrements had caught all us boys plumb off guard. We all kept embarrassing ourselves in the hope that she'd take a shine to one of us in particular.

I'm still not sure to this day how everything come about exactly, but one cold afternoon in December, I was lucky enough to get Jeannie Grace all to myself.

I guess it started on account of me having one of the better ideas that might have come to me up to that point in my life. See, Christmas was coming up in about ten days or thereabouts, and I got the notion that if I got a present for Jeannie Grace, that I just might manage to position myself a little bit out in front of the pack of those other neighborhood boys.

You need to understand that Christmas in Arkansas in 1915 was one far cry from the commercial feeding frenzy that it has become today. Why, most families could have put everything they got into one big sock hung over the kitchen stove. There were exceptions. Some of the better off around the county, and that is a relative term there, let me tell you, they would get something special for Christmas once in that proverbial blue moon. When we were about five or six, Brownie Dawson got him a store bought tricycle with wide metal wheels. Not a speck of rubber tire on it. Looking back, I'll bet you that Brownie's mama must have saved up her money darn near since he'd been born so she could buy him that tricycle.

You know that was one smart woman. Around about the year after the tricycle, Old Ms. Dawson talked her husband into renting out their farm and opening a store over toward the ridge. They didn't exactly get rich, but they done all right for themselves, I'll say that.

Us boys took turns riding that three wheeler over dirt and mud and rocks till two of those wheels wore completely damn through. Most of us was big enough by then that we looked mighty foolish on a little tricycle anyway.

But here I am going off in the wrong direction. I was talking about Jeannie Grace Higginbotham, and that's a hard topic to get away from, that being my first time.

I managed to take some money I'd earned moving rocks and buy a couple of big oranges. You probably heard stories about how oranges was a regular Christmastime treat back in those days, and that's the honest truth. It was something special for the season.

Funny thing, but here lately I've read me a couple three of those feel good stories about Christmas oranges that folks write for God knows what reason. They come in a whole collection of crap that people keep giving me on account of me being old. They think me reading about what happened to other poor folks a long time ago is supposed to make me feel better. Hell, I lived it all myself. You want make me feel better, give me a new TV or a bottle of top notch whiskey like I got last Christmas.

Just for the record, when I used to tell kids about being happy to get an orange for Christmas, they'd roll their eyes and leave the room. I suppose if you live long enough, your boring stories become history, don't they? I mean, you're here. Not that I ain't pleased to talk to you. Having somebody to listen to your own stories is a damn site better than just reading other people's.

Where were we?

Oh yeah. Jeannie Grace.

I was too scared to give her a present right to her face, you understand, so I left those two oranges on the sill of her bedroom window. It was cold and all, but she left her window cracked just enough for me to slip those oranges underneath so's they'd be the first thing she saw the next morning. I ran all the way back home and got all tight under the covers and did not sleep one iota. I kept imagining what kind of look she'd have on her face when she blinked her eyes at the sunshine and saw them there, sitting on my note. That note was a doozie, too. It said "Happy Christmas." I did at least remember to print out my name.

Well, next day at school, I couldn't look at her. Or nobody else for that matter. I had got the idea that she'd done told everyone else she could find, and they was all laughing at me. Every time I heard a noise, it sounded like somebody snickering or whispering my name. What on Earth could I have been thinking, giving a present to the prettiest girl in the whole neighborhood?

For several hours, my heart thumped louder than the back porch when a hunting dog gets his belly scratched, and I didn't make eye contact with anything but a doodle bug all day. By the end of recess, I was just sitting at the back of the school planning my move out of the county. When we was finally dismissed from the longest damn day of school in modern history, I slipped out the door in front of everyone else, and had made that three miles back home before you could say Warren G. Harding.

I was out in the barn doing my chores, after school milking to be exact, when Jeannie Grace strolled through the side door bigger than you please. When she pulled it closed behind her, I like to passed out cold. Even though I couldn't have consciously told you what she meant by pulling the door closed that way, I guess there's some feral instinct that remains among men folk that was saying to me, "You're about to get some."

She had this voice that even then was soft and low and sultry. Stirred my young blood. When she got older, it might have sounded like some chain-smoking bull dyke version of Camille, but at the time it was sexy as hell.

She took a few steps toward me and cast her eyes down at the straw on the ground and said, "Thanks for the oranges. They was right good."

I felt my knees getting wobbly.

She brought her eyes up to meet mine, but without ever lifting her chin, so she was sort of peeking out under her hair which had fallen perfectly across her smooth forehead. It felt like it took her a week to walk the rest of the way to where I was standing next to that cow. I sure wasn't moving toward her since I was frozen like a statue, afraid that if I moved, she'd get scared and run off. It was kind of like hunting your first deer. The musk scent was similar, too.

She took one hand, with her soft little glove on it, and touched my cheek as light as angels. Then she gave me a kiss, and I'm not sure I felt that either. I don't know if it was the second kiss, or the third one or ten or twelve after that, but at some point I regained feeling. Not just in my lips. I felt the front of my overalls straining in a pain that I had not known until then. The little feller I barely knew was durn ready to bust out of the barn and run around the chicken yard. So to speak. I mean, I didn't really want to leave the barn, you understand.

Without letting our lips ever come apart, we half laid and half fell on top of a feed sack. Almost immediately I commenced to grappling for a way to reach up under her petticoats or her slip or whatever underthings she was wearing. My older cousin, Ricky, had told me all about those. I didn't exactly know what I was after, but I had a pretty good idea of what neighborhood it lived in.

I got to tell you that the exact sequence of what took place next is still somewhat of a mystery to me even after all these years. I'm sure you recall yourself how the physical side of a boy just shy of turning fifteen had a way of over-riding the conversation that you might be having in your brain.

In my mind, I was running down a list of specific business that needed to be taken care of, I'm sure; trying to recollect details of the blue print that Ricky had talked up.

But the rest of my body seemed to have requisitioned just about every ounce of blood I had. I was getting light-headed. Good thing we was laying down, cause I don't see that I would've been too much of a success at standing up right then.

Jeannie Grace was a lovely vision, I told you that. But looking back on it, she just may have been a little less pure than the November snowflake we all thought she was. See, she was sixteen already, and judging by her actions, she must have had a smarter older cousin than I did. That little gloved hand of hers popped two brass buttons on the side of my overalls and slid right inside. My first thought was that it was awful cold that day, and she was looking to warm up, but the fact is that she found my little rascal faster than I could've myself after sneaking two pitchers of sweet tea.

For one or two seconds every hair on my body stood straight on end, as if I'd seen a ghost. My whole being shook like I'd grabbed onto a power line. Felt like it went on for a long time. What snapped me out of it was hearing Jeannie Grace giggling.

It was the kind of laugh that could make a man fall instantly in love except for the fact that you knew it was directed at you, not with you. She kissed my mouth one more time and gave me another one of those direct looks but with her head turned to the side.

"Next time, don't be in such a hurry," she whispered in my ear.

She giggled a little bit more as she smoothed down her skirt, and then she was gone, wiping that little glove off on whatever she passed.

I stayed in a heap next to the milk cow for the better part of half an hour. The words "next time" kept rattling around in my skull, no doubt taking the space of the blood that was slow to return there. Jeannie Grace Higginbotham was my girlfriend!

Well, you're a man of the world. You probably know already that there was no next time. Never happened again. Sure, there was some flirtations, lots of them. But that one December afternoon marked the beginning and the end of my relations with Jeannie Grace.

I learned the hard way that sometimes the toughest part of love is explaining to your daddy why a ladies' cotton glove is stuck to the mule's back.

Chapter Three

We continued to play ball any chance we got in those days. Naturally, all the boys around my age was expected to put in a full six days of work except for any time we spent down at the schoolhouse. But if we could figure out a way to slip in a little bit of ball playing, we sure as shoot done it. We played a lot of catch, and sometimes we played barn ball, which you could also play with just two boys, but you got to bat. That one required a ball with some bounce to it, the best ones being made from bull nads, hair ribbon and a corset cup.

There is one afternoon of catch that sticks out in mind. Not because the baseball was out of the ordinary. It wasn't. It was just the same bunch of boys snatching a little play time between school and chores, whatever we thought we could get away with, but it was an afternoon that brought a little change to our piece of delta nonetheless.

You might guess that I've picked up a lot in my hundred and something years, and one thing that I can tell you with nary a reservation is that old Darwin was right. Pretty much all aspects of life develop a natural pecking order. You give it time, and it sorts itself out. Now, I know Darwin was looking at what folks like to call the big picture, but the same holds true among any group of living beings, and that includes those living in Lee County.

We had us a bully for a brief time when I was growing up. Everyplace does. And I suppose most bullies end up with a couple of fellows who like to tag along behind him, the sort of folks who end up working for a medical insurance company as brown nosing "yes men" because that's exactly what they were cut out to be.

To paint you the full picture, I should start with myself. I was always one of the bigger boys in the neighborhood, but not the biggest. Fast enough, but not the fastest, and I sure as shooting weren't the smartest, but I got by. I never wanted for much in relations amongst the young folks of Lee County.

When I was just about getting pimples, fuzz, and a crackly voice, I had me a growth spurt, too. Almost overnight I went from being amongst the bigger boys at my little school to being the flat durn biggest. It took me awhile to get used to it, and I kept breaking flimsy things or banging my head. I reckon it was a good source of grins for my classmates.

There was one particular fellow around the neighborhood who still had me by a few inches and likely thirty pounds. He was kind of fat, looking back on it, but by any measure he was just plumb large. Freckled-faced, dull-eyed and big, and his name was Rusty Pye.

Some bullies will lord over you through their intelligence, but Rusty Pye could only rely on his size. If he ever got in a thinking contest with a June bug, it would have been too close to call. He had been giving the schoolhouse a wide berth for several years. I only heard him say anything remotely nimble once, and that was the day he got pulled off his perch.

Well, this particular afternoon, Rusty must have been bored. I think that was when he generally got the urge to come around and rattle a cage or two. He was a good three or four years older than I was, so other than being some possums to poke at from time to time, we didn't hold much allure for him.

I never had too many run-ins with Rusty myself. We got tangled up over some slight a year or two before, and I ended up with a bloody nose and split lip, and I skinned my knuckles up giving back. That might have discouraged him a little. Like most bullies, Rusty preferred his targets in the medium to small range.

When he come walking into the middle of our baseball tossing that day, he had two sidekicks with him, Tommy Cloywell, who I knew from school, and some wall-eyed fellow who everybody called by the name of Pickle. The first thing Rusty did was slap one of Burrell Prewitt's throws out of mid-air and yell, "Foul ball, Prewitt."

Then he laughed and laughed.

Burrell was nigh on a year younger than me, still a little fellow, but feisty. He puffed up to Rusty and said, "Leave us alone, you fat fruit."

Rusty come back with, "Kiss my low-hanging ass, and I'll show you where the fruit grows."

Like lightning, Burrell Prewitt reared back and punched him right in the chestnuts for all he was worth. When big old Rusty hit the ground, I think it took Burrell by surprise, but he didn't waste a good deal of time ruminating on it. He jumped right down on top of him, just a windmilling and left hooking and gouging to beat the band, or in this case to beat Rusty Pye.

Tommy Cloywell started to step forward, being one of the "yes men", but I got behind him and put him in a big old bear hug until he got the point that this tussle was to be between Rusty and Burrell, and Burrell kept right on like a little hurricane.

After what seemed like a long time to all of us, but probably wasn't more than six or seven minutes worth of dead set ass kicking, Burrell stood up. He was plumb out of breath from beating on Rusty who for his part was curled up in the dirt covered with spit and snot and blood and who knows what else, whimpering and trying to ignore his own tears of embarrassment.

Tommy Cloywell was the first to get tired of staring at him, all mewling there like that, and he just walked on home without saying a word or offering a hand. Gradually Tommy come around to running with our bunch, and most of Rusty's other followers found someone else to follow.

Rusty finally pulled himself to his feet, wiped his eyes, both of which had started to swell shut, and squinted in the general direction of Burrell.

"That hurt," he said.

And that was the one time I ever heard the boy say anything that I particularly agreed with.

Sometimes getting rid of something bad is not that easy, but Rusty left us alone for the most part after that. I figure that part of him knew that he could still whip any one of us, but another part of him still couldn't reckon why he'd lost so bad, and not being able to answer that, he just picked out an easier direction to face.

Burrell Prewitt didn't give the rest of us a chance at Rusty that day, even though most everyone present wouldn't have had a minute's hesitation to settle a grievance of their own. You didn't pile on, though. That ain't right. My ownself, I made a note to catch up with him one of those days, but I never got around to it.

Rusty Pye met his end not three years hence. He had took to drink by that time, and the liquor tended to unlearn any lessons Burrell Prewitt might have taught him. Rusty tried to jump on top of this little Black gal name of Blanchola Dillard up by Mud Lake, and she stabbed him. Twenty-seven times, I believe. Anyhow, that particular afternoon, Burrell Prewitt punched him in the chestnuts, and then we all went back to our game of catch.

Whenever we could, though, we tried to scare up something closer to a real game. Now, we didn't have anywhere close to no eighteen players. There wasn't even that many boys in the whole school, so we had to improvise. You probably did this when you was a kid, and thought you invented it.

The first thing to go was hitting to the opposite field. If a right handed batter stepped in, then right field was closed. The other way round on a leftie. Kids expected you to pull the ball. Next thing we'd do was make a team pitch to itself. If we had an odd number, you took turns being catcher for both teams. Or you played up against a wall and got rid of the catcher all together. Sometimes you threw a batted ball back to the pitcher, not having a first baseman, and that would get you down to a real game with only twelve boys.

If there was fewer than that, which there normally was, then we played rotation where everybody moved one position over until it was your turn to come in and bat. You got ten outs before you went back to right field and started over again. I'll bet you could go to the middle of Tajikistan and find those same rules.

That was the game we happened to be playing when little Otis Musgrave put on one of the best displays of hitting I ever did see.

Now I ought to say that part of the reason that afternoon was so impressive was on account of Otis not being a very good hitter to begin with. His real name was Fenton Musgrave, but sometime before the bunch of us started school, the neighborhood had settled on calling him Otis. His daddy was one of the local barbers which I wish I'd realized before I tucked into a plate of his mama's homemade cookies. The name Whiskerdoodles should've been a clue.

Otis was also the tiniest boy in that part of the world. If he'd have been a dog, you'd call him the runt of the litter. On top of that, he had him a pair of spectacles, the kind with no wire around the edges, and without those, he couldn't tell his own sister from the back end of a brood mare. Okay, bad example.

Don't get me wrong. Otis was not any kind of little sissy when it come to playing what passed for sports. He tried as hard as any kid I growed up with, but there was no getting around the fact that nobody ever confused him with being athletic. He'd run as hard as he could in a footrace and still not beat anybody but a club-footed fat kid. When we played Harpastum, which was kind of like an Arkansas version of rugby, well, even the fat kids would get the best of him.

When he first stepped into the box that day, and I happened to be standing on first base, I figured that I would be up to bat again lickety split. As fate would have it, nothing could be farther from the truth.

It all started out innocently enough. Otis, who was a lefty, dribbled one just between me and Sam Estill, who was playing second base. Then he put two or three more in the exact same spot. Now, I ain't implying that Sam and me let them go, but all the kids around there liked Otis, so it might have been that we wasn't trying quite as hard as we would have been with one of the big boys who could knock them a country mile. When they come up, getting them out as fast as you could turned into a matter involving some pride.

Sam Estill wasn't exactly a giant himself. Fact is, he was the youngest boy playing that day, a young enough age that we might have used it to keep some other kid out of the game, but Sam had always got himself a pass on account of his family. For me personally, he was my closest neighbor, and therefore my most frequent playmate.

Sam was one of the Negro kids in that neighborhood, that or colored being the terminology back in those days. His grandma and his great-grandma had both been born slaves. They were nice old ladies to all the children around there, but a little distrustful of most White folks, and thinking about where they came from, I can't say I much blamed them.

But their distrust wasn't so big that it kept them from selling sausage. And son, I am talking about the best sausage I have ever had the privilege of putting in my mouth. That was 100 years ago or better, and I've sat down at the kitchen table with Italians and Germans and Czechs and Poles and what have you, but I ain't ever found anything I liked better than that Estill sausage.

Come hog killing time, all sorts of folks would find a little bit of extra meat to take to them Estill women. Sometimes you paid them a nickel or two, and sometimes they got to keep a portion of what you brought them. Now let me explain here, that every family in Lee County had their own smokehouse, and when the weather got cool, you butchered some animals, cut you up some hams and roasts and all, and filled that smokehouse up. You cured them in salt or sugar and left a little fire going. We didn't have no freezer out in the garage.

My point is, that in spite of that, this sausage was so well known that it become a sort of delicacy. It was worth the trouble, you see.

Back then, sausage is what you made with the leftover cuts of meat. And these two old women could perform some kind of spell on them by-products. They made a fresh sausage that would fill your kitchen with sage and pepper for durn near a week after you fried it. Fresh means not smoked, so you ate that right off the bat. And then they had a recipe for spicing smoked sausage that would make a big-headed Frenchman blush.

But the stuff I can still taste to this day is their blood sausage. It was dark and mysterious, just like Sam's sister, Francine. They were using a blend of secret herbs and spices before the Kentucky Colonel could pee standing up.

It's funny, your mind is. My youngest memories don't include much of my daddy. He'd be off working in the field, and I wasn't old enough to go, but some days he would stay longer at the breakfast table, sometimes almost till the dawn was about break. His whole life, he never said more than a sentence or two at a time, but just having him there to look at was important for a boy, and when I think of those mornings, I can still smell that Estill blood sausage frying in a skillet with mushrooms and eggs. Mmmm.

Well, shit, now I've made myself all hungry, and got off the track to boot.

After a half a dozen hits through the hole, Sam and I caught each other's eye. I had my fill of being generous. I was ready to bat, and Sam would be after me, so we stiffened up. But Otis, by God, he had found his rhythm.

If you stay around baseball, you see this sort of thing happen all the time. That's just how hit streaks go. A fella will tell you the ball looks the size of a grapefruit coming up there. You get into a groove, and truth is your mind just can't fathom that there's any way you could not hit it.

Tommy Cloywell was pitching. Now he might not have been the old Big Six with his curveball exactly, but he could sure bring what passed for heat to a bunch of teenaged boys playing with a taped up piece of sawmill lumber.

The boy had no ankles, Tommy didn't. I don't know if you ever run across someone like that, but his durn feet went right up into his calves. Watching him run was sort of like seeing Frankenstein's monster chasing a straw hat through a wind storm, but standing still he could rear back and throw hard enough to raise blisters on a catcher, which in this case was the back side of the Cloywell's barn, and therefore not likely to either swell up or complain.

Thing was though that we could have been playing on the moon and nothing would have gotten by Otis. Every pitch seemed like Tommy would try to throw a little faster than the others, and still Otis would slap those balls through the right side, only now they'd started to get some loft on them.

The right fielder that day was Albert Spurles, red headed boy. He had shifted over from center when the lefty come up. Interesting boy, old Albert was. First thing about him, he had a glove.

I'm sure you wouldn't know nothing about this at your age, but back when I was a youngun out in the country, there wasn't no sporting goods store that sold proper equipment to play ball with. Even if there had been, it'd take you a month of Sundays to save up enough money to buy anything. We didn't have much of a bustling economy.

So, Albert Spurles having him a proper J. C. Higgins baseball glove straight from the Sears and Roebuck catalog of Chicago, Illinois was something worthy of comment, and as you'd expect, a good deal of envy, too.

Albert was a smart boy, ended up going to college and becoming an engineer. That's quite an accomplishment coming from where we was, but not as much of one as I thought it was before I found out he didn't get to wear a striped cap and blow a big whistle. He did build the bridge up to Forrest City, so I guess that's something.

Well, when it come to that glove he was plenty smart enough to use it to his advantage. First year or two he had it, wasn't nobody laying a finger on it. The Lord Almighty could have asked to borrow that glove, and Albert would have just said, "Jesus, it's about time you worked up some calluses."

But along about year number three, it got to where you could do a favor for Albert in return for using his ball glove for an inning or two. Most of it was your typical Tom Sawyer sort of stuff. You could use that glove if you done Albert's chores.

Rent was precious on that thing, too, let me tell you. Milking the Spurles cow would get you the glove for just one batter. The rate for plowing was one inning a half-acre. The one and only time I ever got to use it was when I painted three-quarters of the Baptist Church after Albert's daddy had told the preacher that his boy would be more than happy to spruce the place up with some white-wash.

On top of that, part of the deal was that Old Man Herman Spurles couldn't find out that you was doing his boy, Albert's, work for him. Like most any father, Mr. Spurles wanted to think he had him a hard working young man out there busting his tail for the family good.

That's why I only painted three of the four sides of that church building. Albert did the front himself in case anybody happened to ride by. For all that painting, which took most of a hot Saturday, I got to wear that glove for seven whole batters.

Now, Otis kept plunking singles out in front of Albert Spurles right through supper and on till dark and then all through the night since Otis didn't want to lose his groove. He kept hitting on into the next morning. If Albert played in, Otis put it past him down the line. If he shaded toward the line, Otis just dropped it over the second baseman's head like a pigeon taking aim on a newly washed convertible.

He might have started getting some hunger pangs about half an hour past sunup. Two outs finally.

Otis worked up such a sweat that his glasses kept slipping down his nose, and without those he was blinder than Mr. Magoo in love, but even that didn't slow him down. It was like he just sensed where the ball was going to be and exactly what to do with it to make it land where he wanted it to.

Well, along about dark on that second day of Otis' turn at bat, we began to realize that things was getting desperate. None of us had had anything to eat for well over a day and a half, and we was all starting to get woozy. On top of that, we all would have to be up before the roosters the next morning to start our chores before breakfast.

Albert Spurles finally broke.

"Hey, Otis," he yelled in from right field. "I'll loan you my glove if you'll just ground out eight times."

"For how long?" Otis answers.

I recollect that negotiations continued for about four or five dozen more hits, all while the at bat was still going on. Otis would take a big swing, and then he and Albert would dicker while the ball got throwed back to Tommy Cloywell.

In the end, old Albert parted with his prize J. C. Higgins glove for four months and sixteen days, and that is how the game finally concluded. For his part, I don't think Otis Musgrave took that thing off his hand the whole time, even though it was a right-hander's glove, and he had to wear it backwards. He bathed with it and ate with it and slept with it. Albert said it took another year and a half to get the smell of cheese grits out of the thing.

When that bonehead Bud Selig let the All-Star game end in a tie some years ago, it took my mind back to little Otis Musgrave and the turn at bat that never should have ended.

It was just luck me getting into organized ball, I guess. I was working in the cotton fields over around Brickey's. Well sir, a scout come along one day by the name of Bill Boyle. In those days, there was so many teams, that you never knew where you was likely to find a prospect. Why the Washington Senators found Walter Johnson playing out in some little town in Idaho, of all places. You know they had to promise him train fare back to Idaho if it turned out he didn't like Washington, D.C.. Turns out he liked it good enough to pitch there for 21 years. Of course, that was before lobbyists.

Anyhow, I'll never forget it, old Bill comes driving up next to the fields where I'm bent down picking the little bolls and stuffing them into a big burlap sack. Bill was lost. I have no idea who he was supposed to be looking for, and at that point, neither did he. Bill Boyle was only about a year or two older than I was, but he was littler, too, stood about five foot nine, so that made him look like more of a youngster as I did. I'll admit that I fudged on my age a mite once I found out that he was a ball scout, but I still bet between the two of us we couldn't have ordered a saucer of milk in a cat house.

I was an awful big fellow back then, tall and strong. Bill asked if I'd played much ball. Shoot, that's about all we did back then. The boys down at the cotton gin had them a team, and I was their first baseman. We used to play against all the other little towns around there. I felt no dishonesty in answering that I figured I was about the fourth best player in that part of the county.

Anyways, Bill allows as to how he's gonna look mighty stupid if he don't bring a ballplayer back to St. Louis, so, sight unseen, he says he can get me a tryout.

Now, back then, playing ball was one of the few ways out of those old delta fields, so I laid down my sack, brushed the lint off my trousers, and hopped into that old Ford.

We swung back by the house so I could say so long to my folks. They had been mighty good to me. I realized that, of course, but at the age of fifteen and a half, a boy don't think about sentimentality too much. What I'm saying is that it never crossed my mind that there was any other course of action other than leaving right then and there at the first opportunity, and I didn't reckon a soul on this Earth would feel different.

We pulled up in the yard, and I took off before Bill brought her to a stop. I bet my feet didn't even touch the porch boards. I come a bolting through the screen door just a yelling that I was off to the big leagues, but my folks wasn't no place to be found. I run into all the rooms, but they must have been off tending to the fields.

I'd like to tell you that I had a sharp pang of guilt about taking off without saying a proper goodbye to my mama and daddy and thanking them for all that they'd done to bring me up right, but that would be a durn lie. All I could think of was me hitting a double down the line with two outs and the bases loaded, and all them folks at Sportsman's Park up on their feet yelling my name. So, I grabbed a Big Chief Tablet or something, and scribbled down a note saying that I was off to St Louis, Missouri to be a ballplayer, and that I'd write to them when I got settled in. After all, they'd always be there to thank later, wouldn't they?

Once I left the note, I threw both my clean shirts in a cardboard suitcase and jumped into that car before Bill could change his mind. I had a little money saved up, and I give that to him for gas.

I was some kind of excited, boy, I'll tell you what. I started thanking Bill up one side and down the other, and when I figured that was all covered, I started regaling Bill with my exploits on the ball field. I'll bet you I told him about every hit I'd got since I was three, and when I finished that, I took to telling him about the swings and misses. He must've found it mighty entertaining since he didn't speak a noise the whole time.

I guess we'd only gone about twenty or thirty miles, just crossed the big, new bridge into Tennessee, when I had to go to the bathroom. Bill must have got confused while I was in the loo, cause when I come out, he had driven off with my luggage. And that's how I became equipment manager for the Memphis Chicks.

Chapter Four

MEMPHIS

I found myself a room under the stairs at a boarding house on Gayoso Street near Fourth. I got it in return for a couple dollars a month and doing some odd jobs around the place. It was plenty busy there.

Old lady run it, gal by the name of Kitty. With my level of worldliness, I bet it took me the better part of two weeks to figure out the situation. Nothing but women lived there. Decent lookers, too, most of them. Naturally the place was always filled with gentlemen callers, especially at night. I didn't know what to make of it at first, but I learned quick enough. My perplexion gradually became an education.

To a sixteen year old youngster from Lee County, well, those new housemates of mine were awful exotic. There wasn't a shy one amongst the lot. They was likely to parade around the house in what the older women folk I knew back home would have considered off limits to even talk about. It consumed my thoughts 24/7.

I'm talking about shirt tops hanging by a pair of thin straps and material flimsy enough to read the funny pages through. To this very day, one lady who lived there I can recall simply on account of her stockings. Her name was Lucinda, but the other girls called her Spaniel. I reckon she was a decent looker a few years prior, but by the time I was there, her face had acquired a tiredness that didn't go away, like she was daily disappointed about something.

She always wore these bright red and white striped stockings. Wide stripes that run the length of her legs, top to bottom, and oh what a bottom it was. I dreamed about that hosiery more times than I care to tell you, son. What treasure must have lurked above those stripes. Not to be indelicate, but I think I'd been gone from Memphis a full three years before I stopped getting a stiffy during the national anthem.

That was the first boarding house I ever saw that had its own piano player in the parlor. Hell of a nice guy, too. Little Black fellow named Herbie.

He used to sweep out the rooms and clean up some around the place, occasionally he helped me hammer a nail or rehang a door, but mostly he played that piano. Ragtime and blues, you know. I really love that old blues music. That blues and gospel was the music that I heard right from when I first learned how to listen, and I want to tell you that I had never heard nobody play the blues on a piano like Herbie did. My musical tastes were expanding, as they say.

Herbie become my best friend in those early Memphis days. He had him a room over the stables out back. I liked it better than my room. It was warmer, and the smell reminded me of my cousin Wilma Mae.

Our place was only one block away from Beale Street. When Herbie wasn't playing piano in our boarding house, he was over on Beale at one of the night clubs, most likely sitting in with a jug band, a style of music that was very popular at the time. There was a good deal of drinking that went on around there, and when you emptied a jug, I suppose you instantly became a musician. That's being a good friend of the environment as far as I see it.

Every once in a while, we'd go see us one of the vaudeville shows, but mostly we could only afford to visit the little hole in the wall joints, listen to some music and eat us a hot snoot sandwich. No sir, I couldn't have asked for a better friend in Memphis than Herbie.

My other running buddy during those years was a fellow name of Samuel Coleridge Pequinney who went by S.C. and was four years my senior. When I first met him, less than a year after my arrival in town, he allowed how he was just passing through Memphis and had paused long enough to get him a job and learn the lay of the land.

We first got to chatting at the ball park one afternoon, standing down the right field line where the pitchers warmed up. In those days, though, whoever started a ballgame was expected to finish, so the right field line could get pretty durn quiet. S.C.'s daddy had been a ballplayer, though he'd passed on at a tender age without ever gaining the chance to teach his boy the rudiments of the game. Nonetheless, S.C. was drawn to it, and that's what got the conversation fired up that particular day.

He had left his home in Galveston, Texas with the plan to work odd jobs and see the United States of America, maybe even the world. He figured that eventually something along the way would tell him when it was time to settle down. The employment he'd found in Memphis was as an oyster shucker and bartender at the Acme Saloon off Madison, though they had recently ceased using the name Saloon and would soon vanish altogether. S.C. said the two skills he'd picked up at his uncle's bar, shucking and pouring, used to be a guarantee that he could find work in the wilds of Mongolia, but with all the Prohibition craziness, especially in Tennessee, he was having to scramble of late.

Later in life, I'd say that business about seeing the world captured my imagination, but at the age of 17, the world was a concept I couldn't fully wrap my mind around. Shoot, I thought him being an oyster shucker was glamorous. The only oysters we had in Lee County had come in a tin.

That afternoon at the ballyard we got onto the subject of pitchers. S.C.'s daddy had made it all the way up to Dayton back in 1898, and while he was there, he got to know a catcher name of Tacks Latimer who, in turn, left for time in the big leagues. At the tender age of twenty, Tacks got to warm up Amos Rusie. S.C. figured that put his daddy only a beer and a hand shake away from one of the great fastball tossers in baseball history.

The name of Tacks Latimer stuck in my noggin, too. I'd read that moniker as a youngster on account of him being part of the one of the biggest trades ever concocted. He went from Louisville to Pittsburgh along with Fred Clarke, Tommy Leach, Deacon Phillipe, Rube Waddell, a passel of others, and the great Honus Wagner. Just the thought of it got us both fired up.

Two evenings later, I took S.C. up on his offer to swing by the Acme. I figure it was the highest class joint I'd been into at that point in my life, short of the time I accidently wandered into the lobby of the Peabody Hotel. Sure enough, I drew a few sideways glances from the Acme patrons, too, teenaged kid in a dirty suit and an old apple cap, but I avoided eye contact and kept on a-walking to the back corner of the bar.

With my head down like that, I had a good gander at the tiny white and black tiles all over the floor with the word Acme spelled out near the front door. I snuck a peek at a couple of big mirrors behind the bar and a ten-foot painting of steamboats being loaded on the river. All told, it was more sparkly than anything I'd ever seen, even Spaniel's garters.

Lucky for me, S.C. spotted me right off and welcomed me like long lost kinfolk, otherwise I might have turned on my heel and skedaddled out of such a fine place. The other thing keeping me there was the mouthwatering idea of fresh oysters on the half shell. I'd never tasted such a thing, but my taste buds was raring to have at them, and once the hellos were out of the way, I blurted it out.

"How much are the oysters on the half shell, S.C.? I reckon I can spring for a couple."

S.C. pushed down a smile and shook his head.

"It ain't oyster season, son," he said. "You don't eat them in the summer. They'd make you sick as the dickens."

The disappointment was writ large all over my face.

"I forget not everybody's from Galveston. I got something that'll put the lead in your pencil, though, and it's on the house."

What he brung me was a crab croquette, and he was right, it was unlike anything I'd had before back in Arkansas. Peppery and sweet, crispy and soft, it was a little swallow of heaven. S.C. just stood there in his black vest and clean white shirt, smiling at me like Santa Claus on lithium. His boss man tolerated me nursing a Lemp's lager at the end of the bar until S.C. ended his shift. By that time, it was nothing but backwash and flatter than a nine-year old Swede, so I reckon I was as happy for them to see the backside of me as they was.

Once he hung up his apron, we went off to do our gallivanting, and that's what I'd been saving my few nickels for. We started off by catching the late show over at the Poplar. We later got to where we caught a movie show at least twice a week, me and S.C.. I don't recollect what it was we ogled that night, but I can tell you that a few months later, the two of us sat through five straight runnings of a John Barrymore picture called Raffles, The Amateur Cracksman. It was about a jewel thief on an ocean liner, but the real draw for us was that it also starred Mike Donlin.

I mentioned him before, him being the big hitting star with the Giants who I knew from Baseball Magazine. What I hadn't told you yet was that the very same Mike Donlin had been signed to manage the Memphis Chicks at the start of the 1917 season. That was the first really big baseball star I ever met, I imagine, and damned if I wasn't working for him. I was beside myself, and so was half the other youngsters around the team.

Folks around town loved him at first. He was as big a name as had ever come through those parts of the Mid-South. Women followed him around like un-weaned puppies, and every ball-loving man in Memphis wanted to buy him a whiskey. I can guarantee you Turkey Mike didn't mind either one of them things, neither. It was sad because his beloved wife Mabel, the actress, had died of cancer back in 1912, but his liver was still kicking.

Him being in that Raffles movie wasn't no accident. One of his best drinking buddies was John Barrymore himself. Famous folks like to hang out with each other from what I've seen, and in the case of Donlin and Barrymore, they also liked to try to outdrink each other and sometimes pee for distance. From what I know of it, Donlin and Barrymore remained tight for the rest of their lives. Stayed friends, too.

There was another guy I knew in Memphis in 1917 who would figure out to be a guiding force in my life whether he knew it or not. He was barely a year older than I was, though not likely as green. He was a kid pitcher from Brooklyn name of Waite Hoyt. There had been some wrangling over the rights to him out of high school, but he'd signed with John McGraw and my beloved New York Giants who had sent him to the Chicks.

You'd think us being the two youngest folks around, he would've been one of my running buddies and all, but it didn't work out that way. Waite mostly concentrated on baseball, I guess. Like me, the older fellows got a hoot out of razzing him with those highbrow baseball jokes such as itching powder in the jock strap or putting a dog turd on his pillow.

There was only one time, not long after he got there, that S.C. and I lured him out to the picture show and some libations. His daddy was a comedian in a minstrel show, and Waite told some good jokes that he must've picked up from the old man. I remember one of them was a guy says he envies the birds. His buddy says, "Because they can fly and sing all day?" "No, cause they only have one bill all year." It's funnier after a pint or two.

The kid was a hard thrower with a great curveball, too, but he wanted to strike everybody out. Turkey Mike tried to tell him there was no shame in making a batter hit a bad pitch and letting the other eight fellows out there do their job, but old Mike weren't really all that much of a teaching type. Hoyt stayed about half a year and lost some tough ballgames before they promoted him on to Montreal.

Now, Turkey Mike had done a few months in the pokey for getting all liquored up and taking a public squirt back in Baltimore. Good thing he was a famous ballplayer cause I doubt if that charge would get you much cred in the joint.

"I'm in for armed robbery, what about you?"

"I took a whiz outside the library."

No, sir. It's hard to make that sound tough.

Mike had remarried by the time he landed in Memphis, but this new one wasn't doing much to keep him from pulling the same kind of stunts if the mood and John Barleycorn struck him. She was an actress, too, but not as famous as the first Mrs. Donlin, and though I spied her a time or two, she was no regular in Memphis.

Stories begun to filter back to the ball club about Turkey Mike getting in a bar fight or two, but the baseball cranks surmised that the other fellow had it coming, and they loved him just the same. Even when some bartender had to throw Mike over his shoulder and carry him back to his hotel after a big night out, or when some pretty girl took a swing at him with a parasol, it wasn't nothing more than a fun-loving sport making the most of his time off.

One evening late, me and S.C. was making some rounds. We'd already hit a place or two and had just scarfed down a couple of cracklin' po'boys from a stand this midget couple run back up an alley off of Talbot and South Front Street. Hell of a place that was. They'd built it themselves out of packing crates and tampon boxes, and they fried them cracklins in a sawed-off oil drum. The whole shebang was constructed to be just high enough for a body who was three foot tall or thereabouts. When you ordered your food, you had to bend down and peer in their little window. Herbie had showed me the place, and it was a favorite stop of ours. I'm not one hundred percent sure that S.C. was ever in love with it, but he come along.

Well, we polished off them skin sandwiches, wiped the grease onto our sleeves and strolled into a dim dive called the Jelly. It looked like most of the other joints back then, long and narrow, scuffed wood floors and grimy brick walls, small round tables that hadn't been wiped down since a week ago Tuesday. The attraction at the Jelly was a ragtime piano player name of Limp Eddie Barrileaux. Man, could that dude tickle the ivories.

Now you might think that he was called Limp Eddie on account of something to do with his leg or pre-Viagra woes, but the thing was all about how he played that upright piano. He would pour everything he had into a song. He was "Killer" Jerry Lee Lewis way before such an idea had come to pass. Eddie would approach a song light-like, then a few bars in, it was as if a spirit entered his body. He'd commence to pounding and flourishing, crossing his hands, playing under his legs. He'd jump up, and the round stool he sat on would go flying. I've even seen him leap atop the piano and play hanging upside down, and the whole time that rag music never dropped a note, faster and faster and more complex, sweat flying like Old Man River himself had detoured through the barroom. And when he come to the last note, he went limp as a fresh wash rag. Slumped over and slid to the floor like he's melting. Whoever was sitting nearby would haul the stool back over, help Limp Eddie onto it, and after a deep breath and a slug of whiskey, he'd launch into the next melody.

When S.C. and I walked through the door to the Jelly that night, Limp Eddie had just plunked the first notes of one of my favorite tunes, a piece called the Shoe Tickler Rag. I was paying close attention to the music, and when he was done, I clapped my hands till they stung a little. But do you know who picked up the stool and brung it back to Eddie? Turkey Mike Donlin. I never expected to see him at a place like that in two million years.

Like a lot of fellows, when Turkey Mike got past cocktail number twelve or thirteen, he was headed one of two directions: back slapping or jaw punching. Well, Mike recognized me right off, and lucky for us, he was in a large mood. He slurred out a hello, threw an arm around each of us and steered us toward the bar. As usual, neither of us was flush with cash, and Turkey Mike was no doubt more used to being the drink buyee than the buyer. I think S.C. and me exchanged a glance wondering just exactly where this was heading.

Mike was laughing and rambling on about six different stories simultaneously. We couldn't make head or tail out of it, but periodically, he'd pop out with a phrase like "and that was a smell you never forget" or maybe "I swear to God fellas, I never saw a donkey happier." He'd pause with a real satisfied look, and S.C. and I would go to hoo-rahing right on cue.

I'll guarantee you that none of us intended for Saturday night to last until Sunday breakfast, but that's just what occurred. I stumbled back to my little room, and I reckon S.C. did, too. But when I saw Turkey Mike at the ballpark before the game the next afternoon, it was clear that he hadn't found the notion of a fried egg and a few hours of sleep nearly as appealing.

Not only did it look like he had kept right on guzzling, but his whole countenance told that he was now in a vile frame of mind. He stunk to high heaven.

When I passed by him, he didn't even shoot me a glance. It was like he'd never seen me before in all his days, and I knew enough to keep my profile low.

Roy Fentress was pitching for the Chicks that day against Birmingham. Fentress was a Missouri boy who had just come over from the Fort Worth Panthers that year. Pretty good chunker. He'd win 19 for us that season, but none of those was that Sunday.

I'd seen worse outings, but Turkey Mike Donlin was having none of it. He stormed out there, cussing poor Roy up one side and down the other, snatched the pill out of his hand and announced to the umpire that the new hurler was none other than Turkey Mike hisself. Putting it mildly, we was shocked.

Now you might think that having an ex-Major Leaguer pitching is a good thing, but Turkey Mike was an infielder, not a pitcher. That'd be kind of like getting excited that you got a heart surgeon to do your bathroom plumbing. On top of that, Donlin was old, drunk, and madder than a penguin on Casual Friday.

You recollect that scene from the movie where the pitcher knocks out the mascot. Well, sir, old Mike's first pitch went about a foot back of the batter and plunked a scorecard vendor clean in the noggin. Laid him out flat, it did. The one after that was a 58 footer that kicked gravel all up in the backstop's grill. That was when you started to hear the grumblings from the bleachers. It was all downhill from there.

Even those Chicks players who had been Turkey Mike's most steadfast supporters found little to do but stare at their shoe tops. In scarce 14 hours, I'd watched him go from Mike Donlin, impeccably dressed toast of the Great White Way who was ever ready with a quip for all he met, to Mike Donlin, the angry Irish orphan who was grasping for publicity on the way to city lockup. He and the Memphis ball club parted ways soon thereafter. Old Mike ended his days back in California, scouting players, taking bit parts in movies, but mostly running up debts and perfecting his skills with the bottle. Though it sounds like a sad tale to me when I tell it, I have no doubt that it was mostly a glorious ride for Turkey Mike.

CHAPTER FIVE

Herbie and me got in the habit of going to see the Memphis Black ball team when the Chicks were on the road. The famous Union Giants had fallen on hard times, but A.P. Martin, who owned a Black barber college, put together the Barber Boys, and they rented Russwood Park. There were others: Curve's Wonders, the Pelgram Giants, but they were of a lesser tier. There was a time before my birth where players of different races might play ball with or against one another, but by the late teens, there were no mixed race teams in our part of the world. There would still be a White versus Black exhibition here and there, but that was an event, not common.

The Barber Boys had some nice players. No question that two or three of them, at least, could've played for the Chicks. The best of the lot was a fast center fielder, long and lean, named Smoky Hayes. More than once I saw him bunt for a single then steal three bases to score. One of those times he pulled all three swipes while the same batter was at the plate. Octavius Taylor, who went by the name of Mongoose, had been around for a while, but he could still snatch up any ball that come within a half-mile of third base. Cannon arm, too. Mongoose sipped the shine with Herbie and me a time or two. As for poor Smoky Hayes, he joined the 372nd Infantry and fought under French command at the Argonne. In October 1918, at a village called Somme-Bionne, he got blown apart by a German shell that even he couldn't outrun.

Just a few years later, A.P. Martin combined his team with another, added a few more talented players and formed the Memphis Red Sox. It was a respectable franchise for almost four decades, but I was not around to see it blossom.

Now, S.C. told me the first day I met him that Memphis was to be a temporary stop for him, so when he decided it was time to move on to the next notch on his quest, we dreamed us up as grand a going away party as six dollars could buy. We bar hopped, then, as money dwindled, dive hopped. It didn't matter none about a level of fancy. We laughed at each other's jokes like it was the first time we heard them, and got the cold shoulder from a gal or ten.

That great evening ended up with S.C. coming back to my boarding house, but not to see me. He wanted to get a proper Memphis goodbye from one of the girls, and he settled on a petite red-head, saucy and freckle-faced, who I knew as Angeline. Red-heads have never been my bailiwick, but I must say that Angeline was just about the most popular lady who lived on Gayoso, and I suppose that S.C. figured that knowing exactly why would give him something to think about till he got to wherever he landed next.

The two of them disappeared upstairs. By then, I'd been around that block enough to know that ten minutes or fifteen, and a body would expect to see the gentleman returning to the parlor, but the clock ticked and there was no sign of S.C.. The lady would remain in her room for a mite, freshen her person and her wits, but the gent generally descended like clockwork. Half an hour went by, and Kitty was just about to ask me to go check on things when here come Angeline down the stairs, straining and dragging S.C. by an arm. His clothes were buttoned up all helter-skelter, and he was passed out cold, head bouncing down the steps like a castanet slinky.

Angeline, who had a syrupy South Carolina accent was sweating, gasping, shaking her head and mumbling loud.

"Soft dick. Too much whiskey. Like trying to stack a bowl of Hoppin John."

All the fellows in the parlor, and truth be told, me along with them, started guffawing till our faces hurt. I reckon it wasn't the proud and heroic moment he had envisioned, but that sure was a memorable send off for my friend S.C..

By that time, I had begun to sneak up to Spaniel's room on occasion. It was usually of a late morning before the parlor started filling with gentlemen and when Kitty, who had cautioned me against such things, was still snoring under the quilts.

Spaniel wasn't the type of girl who would entertain a fellow without expecting something in return, but she and me worked us out a bit of a barter system. It took me a while to settle on a balance to her liking. My initial thought was that I could sneak her some of the foul line chalk to use as face powder, but she found that to be insufficient.

Those mornings with Spaniel give me great pleasure and let me start my day with a spring in my step, I tell you what. I reckon because there was no further business pressing her, Spaniel liked to burrow her head into my chest when I got done with my carnal ministrations. Snuggling, I'd call it, and though it made my young mind restless at first, I grew to accept it as part of our arrangement. We'd lay like that for ten, twenty minutes. Never once during those moments did a word pass between us.

In 1917, and for a good time after, segregation was the way things were in the United States, not just the South, but everywhere. Of course, that's all people focus on these days. Like the North was some happy Shangri-La. Some few white folks thought about the situation, but most didn't. The most liberal Americans might have occasionally muttered that things was unfair, but it would've been the rare bird that tried to do anything about it. And if and when they did their muttering over dinner, it was in a Whites only restaurant.

I bring that up on account of going places with S.C. that Herbie couldn't go. The movies was a case in point. When S.C. and I set our mind to see a certain picture, we just went, but Herbie was only allowed in certain of the movie houses, or confined to a separate section. If I wanted to go to the flickers with Herbie, we was generally obliged to stick to the Lincoln or the Daisy on Beale. It didn't bother me much, though I wasn't always made to feel completely welcome in the

Black businesses, either. A few places flat turned me away for being White. It was not until some years later that I wondered how much it bothered Herbie.

Old S.C. never said nothing particularly nasty to Herbie within my hearing, but he didn't cotton too much to hanging around with him neither. For his part, Herbie never said a word. He was generally there when I was craving a snoot sandwich and some slide guitar music, and he and I stayed friends as good as ever.

Maybe it was our slight years, but for the first long time that Herbie and I knew each other, we never really talked much about where we was from. Never even thought about it maybe.

It all come out one night, at least Herbie's side of it did, while we were sipping on a quart of shine and toe tapping to some blues music.

"I got word my mama died," he blurted out.

That'll tamp down a good mood.

"I'm sorry to hear it, Herbie."

I was caught without anything too meaningful to say.

"It ain't nothing," Herbie said as he took him another sip of squeezings. "She was just a whore. Didn't want nothing to do with me. I hadn't laid eyes on her in better than six years."

I had nothing to add to that, but I couldn't help myself.

"A girl like at Kitty's?"

"Naw. She lived in a shack down in Mississippi. Worn out shack and a worn out path been trod down by every man with two bits from Indianola to Moorhead."

"That's ironic."

"I spent my first 13 years running through them woods night and day, maybe fishing, but most likely just sitting on a log someplace, waiting for some red-eyed drunk to quit rutting in her so I could crawl back onto my pallet and go back to sleep. Sometimes by myself, sometimes having to trail my little brother or sister on with me. I am the middle of five, and not a one from the same daddy. Every one of us took off for someplace else soon as we figured to earn a living on our own. Ain't no future in being the child of the Sunflower County whore."

We sat listening to music for a mite longer.

"Is she the one who taught you music?"

'Naw. I learned all my music from an old man in Clarksdale who had the barbeque café and beer joint where I first landed. John Randle. Had me slopping out everything needed cleaning, but Old John could play that guitar. Wouldn't let nobody touch it but him, though, so he taught me piano."

Herbie shook his head and let out a low chuckle, thinking of some moment he wasn't looking to share. I took an extra sip off the shine without passing it over. Finally, Herbie took it from me, and for just a beat or two, looked me in the eye.

"I think I recollect her singing to me when I was a baby. Can't be sure, though."

There ain't no nostalgia to be found in a teenaged boy, but looking back much later, I'd suppose that Herbie was my first real, grown-up friend in this life. That kind of closeness where you never think twice about opening up your inner thoughts and spreading them across the table.

My first great adventure in this life turned out to be with Herbie right after our season was over in 1919. He had decided to go up to Chicago to see a cousin of his that had started playing music in some of the clubs there. It all sounded real high class to us.

That was right before Prohibition come in, by the way, so you'd think we was still drinking store-bought liquor, but what a lot of folks don't recall is that most states had already gone dry. They'd quit making whiskey and beer all over the country. Then in July of that very year, those fat-headed Congressmen had passed some law making it illegal to sell any strong drink at all, even though there wasn't no Prohibition amendment yet. They called it a wartime act, which I always found odd since the War had ended almost a year earlier. Then again, Congress is generally the last ones to know what's going on in the country.

Anyhow, once I got to thinking about going with Herbie, it was an easy decision. The major league season was still going on, and I decided to tag along and see some of the World Series. I'd never been north of Memphis, or to a bigger city, and I had sure never been to a World Series.

As usual, Herbie and me didn't have much money, so we caught us a freight train. That was about the only way we could travel together anyway, me not being a Black man and all.

We got thrown off the train a time or two, I guess. The railroads back then had guards to keep away the freeloaders. Really they was just hoboes getting paid thirty-five cents a day and wearing a railroad hat, but they sure could be mean when they turned on one of their own. That's what happens when a man gets an inkling of power over them who reminds him of himself.

Other folks was real nice to us, though. We ate some meals for free, or for trade really. Herbie would play piano in the restaurant for an hour or so, and I would rub horse liniment on the proprietor's thigh.

We got into Chicago on Wednesday, October the first, arriving at the Union Stockyards about three thirty in the afternoon. Most folks traveling into town preferred to arrive at one of the passenger stations, but our situation and budget only allowed for the more fragrant terminal. Truth be told, we sort of rolled out from under a cattle car about three hundred yards before we got to the Stockyards since we didn't want to meet up with any of them burly railroad detectives.

Now, I had growed up around livestock my whole life, and I thought I knew every smell you might find coming out of any part of a pig or a cow. Grown quite fond of some of them since they couldn't help but remind me of home. But I'm here to tell you that neither Herbie nor myself had ever experienced anything that come close to the stench that welcomed us to the City of Big Shoulders.

We had secured ourselves a prime spot on the rails of that cattle car the previous evening in Effingham, Illinois. Except for digestion and gravity, it was pretty comfortable. Herbie could actually sleep like a baby on those rails. The rocking of the train was like a hand on the cradle to him. Me, I was always afraid that I'd toss and turn myself right onto the track and under one of those wheels, so the most I could do was catnap. I'm saying this on account of we had both dozed off a bit, and the smell from those Stockyards was what woke us up in time to jump off.

It was like the giant hand of stink had reared back and sucker punched the both of us right in the choppers. I don't know if a smell can grab you by the throat, but it sure seemed like this one did, grabbed you by the throat and lifted you plumb up off the ground. It was blood and rotten water and enough burning hair to make you think a herd of Serbian women was walking too fast.

We dropped to the ground and lit out in the direction of where we was staying. We wanted to get settled in and see the sights before the World Series come back to town on Friday. And I'd bet you it took the whole two days before that smell got cleared out of my nose.

That cousin of Herbie's was playing at a jumping little place in the heart of the South Side. We went down there that first night in town and most every night thereafter. Though the highbrow hostelry was downtown, this place was near Comiskey's Park, and was one of the nicest watering holes in that part of the city. Lots of high-rollers, real important fellows, hung around the saloon, as we used to call it. Course, there was some politicians, too.

I kept running into one old boy there who was an ex-boxer. He cottoned to me mostly because I was involved with baseball, I reckon. He didn't mind buying me drinks, which I took to be a real plus, and eventually, he got to trust me enough to run an errand for him. He had me take a whole bunch of money over to Hap Felsch and Chick Gandil. Naturally I was happy to do it since it would be a chance to meet my first active big league ballplayers.

Hap Felsch lived at a rooming house, not much of one compared to mine, if you ask me. It didn't have a lick of red velvet, was all men and smelled nothing like oil. Anyhow, I went to his room and give him the sack of money. Long as I was there, I introduced myself, too. I explained that I was employed by the Memphis Chicks, said that I wasn't from Memphis originally, of course, I was from just outside of Rondo, Arkansas. I told him that made me one of the Rondo Wingos, not related real close to some of my cousins that lived over toward DeValls Bluff, they being a little bit on the uppity side and all, even though that was most likely my Aunt Ridalia's fault, and she was only a Wingo by marriage.

Old Hap shut the door before I could tell him about Uncle Agamemnon's chronic bladder troubles. In my youthful naivete, I remember thinking that was because he had a big game the next day.

The player I most I wanted to meet up with was Dickie Kerr, even though I can't say I knew much about him prior to that Friday. He was a twenty-five year old rookie southpaw for the Sox that year. Threw him a three-hit shutout in Game Three of the Series, and that was the first Major League ballgame I ever saw. Charley Comiskey had bought him that year from the Milwaukee Brewers of the American Association, and word was that he also used to earn money as a boxer up there. He only weighed about a hundred and a half, fought as a bantamweight, I think. But he sure was something out there on the mound that afternoon.

When we first got to the ballyard, we had some trouble getting in. The main drawbacks being no tickets and no money. To state the obvious about the times, Herbie's race wasn't a big help to us neither. You got to understand that Comiskey Park in 1919 looked a whole lot different than it did in 1990 when it closed up. It was baseball's palace, a fantastic place to visit for fans that were used to wooden grandstands set up along the sides of the grounds. I always loved that old ballyard. It had every bit as much character as Wrigley Field did across town, and that's all the worse because the White Sox' new place is a flat piece of crap.

Back at the time I first laid eyes on Comiskey Park, the outfield was just open bleachers sitting atop big wooden fences with advertising signs on them. Out beyond that was the Bridgeport neighborhood with houses and businesses sticking up everywhere.

Herbie was the one which came up with the idea for getting us past the turnstiles. It was the first time I learned the universal value of a clipboard. There were two sitting on the tailgate of an unattended grocery delivery truck that was parked by a big rolled up garage door. Herbie snatched them up, handed one to me along with a stray cap, and told me to hoist a box to my shoulder. We disappeared into that ballyard crowd like butter on a hot griddle.

We only stayed in Chicago for two weeks or so on that trip, but we sure got around. Herbie's cousin played the coronet at the saloon on the South Side, like I told you. That was a pretty good gig as they used to say. It was primarily a White joint except for the musicians and their entourage. Management preferred Herbie stay at a back corner table, and mostly I stuck with him, though I did venture into conversations at the bar. Every night, after his cousin Stitch quit playing there, he packed up that horn and took the train down to a little place on 39th called Mr. Red's. That's where I met one of their kitchen help, a woman named Pearl.

Pearl was from Arkansas, too. In addition to her job at Mr. Red's, she baked pies out of her apartment. Always smelled like yams, Pearl did. Just the thing I needed to clear the Stockyards out of my nostrils. As long as we're being totally honest, the two things that I first noticed about the woman were her shapely breasts, but it would grow to be more.

I liked Pearl an awful lot from the get go. The entrée to the relationship for me was her cooking at first. You hear that the way to a man's heart is through his stomach. Whoever coined that one sure knew what they were talking about.

Pearl cooked the kind of homemade meals that I like to think my mama would have, if she'd known how. Mama never was much of a cook. They say everybody is good at certain things and not so good at others, and the kitchen just wasn't my mama's natural habitat, I guess. She kind of reminded me of that Ellie Mae girl on the Beverly Hillbillies television program. Her pancakes being real heavy and all. My mama's rope belt would have been a damn sight longer than old Ellie Mae's, though. Nope, mama couldn't cook worth a damn, but when it come to killing mosquitoes with tobacco spit...well, I suppose that's not something you want near your cooking anyway.

But let me tell you more about Pearl before I forget. People back then, nobody had a good deal, so you learned to make do with what you could find, and Pearl was just a doggone wizard when it come to changing skimpy meat or ragged looking vegetables into a good meal. I know Jesus spoke at the Mount of Olives, but when it come time to feed everybody with that lone fish, you can't tell me that Pearl wasn't back there at the stove.

She started making my favorite dishes for me, once she found out what they were. Pork chops that couldn't been any bigger than your little finger before she started, but Pearl would put them in some kind of sauce till they swelled up thick and juicy, broad as the back of your hand. I don't even need to tell you that you could cut them with a fork. They had that little brown sheen to them, kind of like rusty chocolate.

And Lord, the greens. Spinach was the best, but they were all good: collards, poke, turnip greens, even the leafy part of celery, if that was all she could get a hold of. Cooked it in the same black iron skillet that the pork chops had been in, little of the grease left at the bottom. Cut up a big yellow onion in there, too. Mm mmm.

Dessert was the thing, though. Sweet potato pie. I think I mentioned a little while ago that Pearl always smelled like yams. That was because she was famous for her sweet potato pie, and folks wouldn't leave her alone about it. She must have baked close to fifty pies a day. Could have cooked a hundred, I guess, if she'd have wanted to. Those pies are what financed her into her own apartment, rough as it might have been. They were that good.

Anyhow, Herbie and his cousin and me was all staying in a room above Mr. Red's place. Long about midnight, that cafe would fill up with people so you couldn't move, and all the best musicians in Chicago would play the blues and the new jazz music until the sun come up the next morning. I wasn't used to sleeping anyhow, so I just tapped my foot and drank, what was by then, bootleg whiskey.

I guess I should mention that most everybody there was Black. I don't mind telling you that things was even worse for their people back in 1919. Naturally, most of them had started out in the South since that's where their ancestors was stole off to, but back in the early years of my life, tens of thousands of them started to feel that the South didn't have a good deal to offer Black folks. They'd work seventy hours a week and not come close to getting ahead of anything. If they did get something worth a duck squat, some jealous redneck was likely to get after them for being uppity. Nope, it wasn't much fun for Africans down there. So, a big bunch of them had started to move up to the North.

I guess it was a little better in that there were jobs to be had sometimes, but if they were thinking it'd be a hot dog welcome, they was plumb wrong. Fact is there was a big race riot in July of that very year, thirty-eight killed in Chicago. The South Side where they called Bronzeville. You'd think such an occurrence would have made things all tense with me being one of the few White boys there, but I didn't ever feel much but good will. A couple of the fellers might have put up with me grudgingly, but there wasn't no trouble. That could be on account of I was a friend of Herbie's, but I like to think they was just nice folks.

Now, I've run across lots of prejudiced people in my day, more out of baseball than in it, and I always hoped that they just don't know better. A man's life is awful sad if he has the time to hate somebody he never met. Shoot, down in Lee County my family was sharecroppers, and far from the best of even that lot. Like I said before, lots of Black families in the same boat we were. In one or two cases, like Sam Estill, I found a close friend among a group of people that some pitiful souls would tell me I wasn't supposed to respect. It wasn't everybody's experience, but it happened to be mine.

My daddy, the old socialist man that he was, taught me to get along with everybody, cause you never knew who might turn out to be that friend when you needed one. Many times, he used to look me in the eye and say, "Son, Black or White, we're all poor, so we ought to stick together. Now go boil your socks, I'm craving stew."

No doubt my daddy was in the minority with his views about race, but he was far from alone. He and his own papa had been part of the Farmers Alliance some 15 or 20 years afore I came along, and a good rasher of those farmers of the people had organized an integrated union. It didn't stick, but they tried.

There's one other thing I'd like to point out, even though I damn sure know that you ain't here for me to expound about race and philosophy. At least back in my corner of the woods, the White folks who talked the worst about Black folks, and kept things stirred up, was the ones with a little bit of money. Like that son of a bitch Ty Cobb, who was the town doctor's boy. In other words, the ones who was taught that Black folks was only there to serve White folks needs.

Ask that kind of person about their feelings today, and they'll blame it on social conventions of the time, saying society just wouldn't allow them to associate with other races back then. Well, that's a bunch of bullshit. They didn't want to know anybody who was different than them or anything about them. Didn't care one iota about poor folks in general. I do believe it's true that nobody latches on to hate as an excuse for their troubles like the poor masses do, but the seed of it is given to them by the rich. Oh, well.

Around the time that I was born, the country folks' music was either from church or it was the blues. Oh, there was all that barbershop quartet sort of thing that you could sing next to the parlor piano, but where we lived, nobody had a parlor or a piano. We made our music with a tub, a washboard, harmonica, comb and tissue paper, and the lucky ones had guitars strung with cat gut. My Uncle Loomus had a two-string mandolin strung with cat hair. Sounded better than you might think, but for twenty minutes after he played, he laid at the edge of the porch and coughed things up.

Most of the songs that people made up was about the hard life that we had. It was sort of an escape, I guess. We sang about working in the fields, eating day old biscuits, and doing chores around the house.

Don't want to wipe off my grandma.

I had to do it yesterday.

Don't want to wipe off my grandma.

I had to do it yesterday.

Please don't make me wipe off grandma

Long as she still smells that way.

That was one of my early favorites. Same kind of music they played in the bars in Memphis. They call it Delta Blues now, back then it was just music.

The brand of music that I heard those nights at Mr. Red's place in 1919 was something else. You could hear the blues and ragtime all mixed together. Those players sure felt good about what they were doing, you could tell that. Everybody was just plain having fun and challenging one another. A few White musicians come in there most every night.

Now, let me explain something else about a place like Lee County, Arkansas. None of those people ever went anyplace. I'll bet that half of them lived their whole lives without ever crossing the county line, and that's the truth. So, when a body did go someplace exotic, they was obliged to keep telling the stories about it over and over when they got back home. Folks figured they'd never get to go to that place themselves, so they might as well get to recall it real good third hand.

One of the favorite places I ever went in those stories when I was a little boy growing up was to the big Chicago World's Columbian Exposition of 1893. That was a neighbor of ours, Randolph Mott, that used to take me there. I bet I made old Randolph tell that story a hundred times or better. He couldn't leave out one tiny detail without me stopping him and saying, "You forgot the part about the Chinese Hoodah." or something like that. That was some place to conjure for a little boy from Lee County.

Randolph Mott was probably close to thirty years older than me. Ordinarily, that would oblige somebody the age I was then to call him Mr. Mott or Mr. Randolph. But he just didn't seem like the Mister type. Long as I knew him, he was just like another one of us boys, only bigger. That made him a remarkable figure to the rest of us.

He had his own house, all to himself. Bushes and honeysuckle grew up all around it, and it never had a lick of paint on it, as far as I recall. I guess his folks had died off before I was born, but he never talked about them. And he collected things. Had the whole yard all the way around that little house filled with stacks of wagon wheels, piles of bottles of all shapes and color, and, best of all, seemed like dozens of bicycles. There were those old timey ones with the big wheel in front and the little one in back. You had to stand on the porch to climb onto those. There were the three wheel ones with no rubber tires, just metal rims. Shoot, there was even a couple of old wooden ones, and one that said Philadelphia on the side of it with no pedals at all that you had to push with your own feet. Randolph would ride those things all over the county and then some.

That was how he come to go to the Chicago World's Columbian Exposition of 1893 in the first place. Randolph Mott loved to get into things. A sense of adventure I guess you'd call it. Things every boy wanted to do, but would most likely get a whipping if he tried.

The way the story goes, Randolph had got his hands on a brand new bicycle. At least new to him. He'd never had one like it before, and he sure did like the way it rode. Saddle on it sat real comfortable. So, he decided that he would ride it all the way to the state capitol in Little Rock. That was better than a hundred miles away, and getting there would be no easy feat since there wasn't no super highway of any sort, just a glorified trail mostly.

Off he went. Folks in Lee County, who thought Randolph was a few beans on the light side of a bushel anyhow, figured they had seen the last of him. And, for almost a year, they had at that.

For his part, Randolph Mott pedaled that bicycle, best one he ever owned, he said, until the balls of his feet blistered up. You know what he done then? Kept pedaling. Took him four days, but he got over those rutted, bumpy roads all the way to the state capitol in Little Rock. When he got there, he took in the sights since it was the biggest town he'd known.

People in Little Rock didn't look more than twice at Randolph Mott. A whole bunch of people there had bicycles, too. One old country boy added to the number didn't make much difference. But, as luck would have it, an old country boy was just what this one cattleman from Texas was looking for. Seems he had a few train cars full of cows and whatnot that he had sold and had to deliver. Problem was some hands that he brought along had took sick with the measles. He reckoned that he needed one more strong boy to help him out, so, he asked Randolph if he would like to earn a few dollars and ride along to Chicago, Illinois.

Well, that was an even bigger adventure than riding a bicycle to Little Rock, so Randolph didn't hesitate one lick. He took that bicycle and threw it into one of the cattle cars, and shook that Texan's hand. He was on his way to Chicago.

I don't think that I even need to mention that a place like Chicago in 1893 was just pure magic for a body from those old Arkansas deltas, even more than it was for me in 1919. After they made it to the stockyards and got their pay all drew out, he wandered around that big city taking in everything he could, determined to spend every last penny before he headed home.

From the time he showed up, all he was hearing about was the White City. That's what folks called the fair, either on account of all the buildings was painted white or because of that architect Stanford White who run around with pale show girls.

And what buildings they were. Giant palaces all situated around lakes and canals like the Greeks or Romans with statues and fountains and lights that run off of electricity. One building would be for just showing off machines and another for just fish, and there was one that had trains inside of it, and you entered it by walking right through this huge golden archway door. Can you imagine? Trains inside of a building. And my mama throwed a hissy when I had that gopher living in my clothes drawer.

Boy howdy, it didn't stop there neither. Did you know that some of the first long distance telephone calls was made right there at the World's Columbian Exposition? The telephone was pretty new back then, and at first it was only used to call people in the next room or so, which is why folks weren't all buying it up too fast. They figured that a body could just get up off their hind ends and walk into the next room as soon as call somebody on the telephone. Plus, you saved on directory assistance.

But here at the fair, you could make a telephone call all the way from Chicago to New York or Boston. Problem was, if you knew somebody in New York or Boston, chances were that they didn't have a phone. So, you had to talk to strangers and say, "Are you in Boston?" and then they'd say, "Yep, are you in

Chicago?" and you'd say, "Uh huh. So long." Needless to say, that lost its bloom after thirty or forty times.

One of my favorite things at that fair of 1893 was the Thomas Edison peepshow. As you know, that Edison invented damn near everything, and he was working on the moving picture at that time. He had a little box you looked into with one eye, and you could see an actual movie. Only one person at a time could see it, so I always figured that the odds of some loudmouth spoiling the ending was even greater back then.

Before long, Randolph Mott run out of money. Even better than 100 years ago, places like fairs would plumb eat up your money. So, he walked into the Chicago World Columbian Exposition employment office and talked his way right into a job. Could have been a problem understanding his Arkansas accent, but when he walked out, old Randolph was a gondolier, as in one of those fellows that stands on a long boat in Italy and hits people in the back of the head with a pole.

And you know what? The work suited him just fine. He poled folks all over those lakes at that fair just like he was born to it. The best part was he got to spend the rest of his time exploring all around the place and seeing everything. That was because he found himself a spot to sleep up on the roof of one of the Ferris wheel cars.

Oh, hold onto the tether there a minute. I forgot to tell you that part, and durned if it wasn't the most famous thing about the whole event. That fair in Chicago in 1893 was where they had the first Ferris wheel ever. I used to make Randolph tell me about that thing over and over. I'll bet I still know all the numbers.

It had 36 cars that held up to 60 people each. It cost 50 cents to ride. That bought you two times around. And it took 20 minutes. Yes sir, I still recall. Sixty people in one car! That's no lie.

Randolph said that the view from up on top was something that a country boy could not fathom. You could see the whole fair and half of Lake Michigan. He'd lay in his bed up there and drift off to sleep with the smell of strange food and the sound of foreign music rising all the way up to him. One drawback was if you woke up late for work, you might have to wait till your car come down to the bottom before you could leave the house.

Well, I'll quit talking about this, I guess. Shoot, it was only my recollection second hand anyway. But there is one more thing you might want to hear. There was another first at that exposition. The first hootchy-cootchy dance. A beautiful girl name of Little Egypt. And, true enough, she stepped right into Randolph's boat one day and asked for a ride. She was all dressed up in veils and flimsy scarves, and a man could see all of her womanly curves just poking through.

My friend started poling out across the lagoon and Little Egypt takes a liking to him and begins to shimmy about. Randolph gets all discombobulated and commenced to row in circles. They must have been out there about eight hours cause a fierce crowd gathered on the shore watching them. All the while, he was telling her about his bicycle and Arkansas and whatnot, and she was real gracious.

Finally, the wind shifted and blew them over by the bank. Little Egypt, she promised to keep in touch, but she never did. When the World's Columbian Exposition ended, Randolph Mott rode his bicycle back to Lee County and waited for that hootchy-cootchy dancer for the rest of his life.

Naturally, when we got to Chicago in 1919, one of the main things on my mind was to head out to the old grounds of the World Columbian Exposition. I finally got the chance to do it on an off day for the World Series. Herbie was inclined to go to a shoe hospital with his cousin, but, since doctors scared me, even back then, I took the streetcar down to Jackson Park, which was where the big fair had been 26 years prior.

I had been keeping the whole experience of that fair in my mind since I was little bitty. It was my favorite place I'd never been, and I knew just what to expect. I was going to walk around through those fine white buildings and pretend that all the visitors was still there by the thousands. I figured I knew my way around just by the stories that Randolph Mott had shared with me till they become a part of my past, too.

Well sir, I got off that car and walked toward the park, all the while knowing that just around the next bend in the street the old fair was waiting. I walked into the park and circled a little pond or two and kept going all the way down to Lake Michigan where some sailboats were tied up, but there was no White City. One, maybe two structures sat at far corners of the place, and I didn't have one whit of a clue as to what they might have been. The great Statue of the Republic was still standing, though in pigeon daubed glory. I looked her over for fifteen minutes or so. It was a fine looking statue, but it felt different to see her presiding over nothing. I was sure there must be more.

Then I turned back to the south again and sure enough, there all by herself was the Atwood Palace of Fine Arts. I knew it right off. I reckon that I was almost at a run heading over to it. It was a handsome building, true enough, but it seemed lonely out there all by itself. I went around the outside of it three times and then headed in the door.

Not much to speak of inside of it from my mind. Real dingy and dark. They called it a museum, but it was mostly pictures and statues just kind of piled about. They closed it up the next year, as it turned out, small wonder since I don't recall anybody but me and a couple of janitors being in there that time.

And that was all there was of the great Chicago World Columbian Exposition of 1893. Well, I was mighty disappointed. My old jaws begun to ache with a kind of sadness. Don't make much sense me getting nostalgic for some place I never saw to begin with, but there it was. I walked over that park some more, looking at folks having their cold picnics and old ladies strolling under umbrellas.

At some point I guess I crossed a little bridge because suddenly I found myself all alone on what I knew was the Wooded Island that had been right there in the midst of that whole fairgrounds. Then, lo and behold, right before my eyes was the Hoodah or whatever that Japanese building was called. I went up to it real slow so it didn't disappear or nothing.

But it was real. There wasn't a damn thing inside of it, but that didn't make a difference at all. It was the most strange and exciting place I had ever seen. There were three buildings all close in a row. The walls were thin like paper. Every so often around the sides, a spot of color stood out plain against the white. It was faded, but I could tell it had been a bright red or green at one time, and the roof was something else, boy. All curled up on the corners like nobody's business.

I plopped down in the grass opposite of it and stared at it for a long time. I could just imagine those people in the Far East passing in and out of the place. I sat there on that quiet little island and I listened real close, and I heard the streetcar and automobile engines and maybe a train locomotive far off someplace, and they sounded just like the engines that Randolph Mott had heard in 1893. After all, one engine sounds just like any other one, don't it?

Then I heard voices of people talking out there in the park, and they all jumbled together, and I couldn't even tell if it was English. The smell of food was out there, too. Something that I couldn't recognize, but it wasn't salt pork, that's for certain. Then, above it all, come floating in some kind of music and the sound of folks laughing. It probably was from one of those apartments around there, but it might have been noise left over from the Midway, just as easy.

Before I knew it, it was pitch dark. I had sat there all afternoon. I took one more deep breath of that park air and headed on back to Pearl's. If you had asked me that day, I'd have told you that I had a pretty doggone good visit to the Chicago World Exposition.

Like I said, we was only up there that trip for two weeks or so, but along about the tenth day or there about, I started getting the idea that Pearl might be sweet on me. She kept trying to stick food in me, not that I was putting up much of a fuss. I sure did like that pie.

Now, I was a little bit shy of nineteen years of age, and, though people may laugh at me nowadays, I had never been with a full grown woman aside from those who did that sort of thing for a living. I was raised to believe that proper women were virtuous. My mama had said that they didn't do the deed, as they say, until they were good and married, sometimes married a year or two. Jeannie Grace did make me question that notion, I must admit.

Pearl was not what most men would have considered a beauty, but, maybe I didn't go in for your normal beauty anyhow. Pearl had a face that grew on you the more you got to know her. After you'd eat her cooking for a spell, heard her true laughter, and smelled that yam musk, she become dadgum attractive.

What I'm saying is that Pearl may have been sort of plain looking to some folks, but she was nice looking to me. She was always happy it seemed like, and her eyes had this sparkle to them, like they were reflecting some bright light that only they could see. There was a girl down in Lee County that had that light in her eyes. Then again, she ended up in the state home, but it wasn't like that with Pearl.

One night toward the end of our stay, when all the musicians had gone on their way, Herbie had headed up to bed, and the sun was already thinking about rising, it presented itself that just me and Pearl was sitting downstairs in her kitchen. It was October, you know, and it was starting to get a little chilly, so the stove give off a good warmth. The odor of cloves and cinnamon and wood smoke was thick all around. I guess it wouldn't be too indelicate to tell you that the smell of food has always made me frisky. I don't know if it did before that visit to Chicago, but it sure as shooting did from there on.

Well, Pearl and me was both kicked back in these wooden chairs, had us a good lean on them, too. We'd been taking turns sipping from a bottle of pear wine that some old man in the neighborhood had mixed up in a washtub on his screen porch. Pretty tasty once you strained it through a cheesecloth.

We got to talking about baseball and dogs and the United States of America. I ain't ashamed to tell you that all three of those things will make me misty eyed every time. Hell, I get tore up just thinking about Old Yeller. The funny thing was that Pearl was just the same way. She went to the pie safe and pulled out a picture of this yellow looking mutt of an animal, ugliest dog you ever did see. She said she owned two photographs, that one and one of her brother who had been in the Army over in France.

Her brother only had one first name, which I don't recollect now, but that mutt had two of them, Frederick Douglass. You see, Pearl had that dog when she was a little girl in Arkansas, and he up and died of a broken heart when she moved off to Chicago.

It was a real sad story, and the first time I ever saw that sparkle leave those black eyes of hers. Pearl's daddy fixed up a marriage for her to his third cousin's boy who sent a ticket and brought her sight unseen to Chicago, Illinois. Then when she got up there, he decided he didn't want her, and she was stuck. Nobody would give her a red cent for a train ticket back home.

Now, like I mentioned, Chicago was a durn bit more exciting than Arkansas anyhow, so Pearl decided to stay, but she missed Frederick Douglass and actually thought about saving up the money to get him a train ticket to come up to her. Can you believe that? A dog riding the train. She did save up some money, too, but before she got enough, a letter come from her mama that said that old dog had passed over. After she left, he crawled up under the house and wouldn't come out, even to eat. He held on for close to a month, gnawing on whatever was dumb enough to walk under the house to him, I guess. But when the dumb animals was eat up, he passed on.

Pearl told me that whole story right there in that kitchen, and by the end of it, she had tears just running down her cheeks. Being a gentleman, and by that time, considering myself her friend, I moved over next to her and put my arms around her. She looked up and gave me a big kiss with those soft lips of hers right on my mouth. Well, son, I'd never felt like that in my whole eighteen and three quarter years up to that point. Spaniel and me didn't do a lot of kissing, you see. Maybe with Jeannie Grace, but that was over so fast, I can't be sure.

Still, this was something different. Something that found a tender spot. My whole skin got goose bumps, and then I just felt numb, like when you drink a lot of whiskey real fast on an empty stomach. I started getting hot at the top of my head, and it run clean down to my feet until my socks started giving off odors. That kiss must have lasted half an hour, and when it was done, I was under the covers in Pearl's room upstairs.

She was some woman. I was one lucky man to know her. Even after I got married many years later, I still went to visit Pearl every time we made it to

Chicago. I wouldn't cheat on my wife, you understand, but there was a spot in my heart for Pearl that, well, I just liked to sit and talk with her. We'll leave it at that, at least for now.

Chapter Six

You know, it's just now occurring to me, but I should have said the first big league player I ever run across was Newt Fisher. He had played in about nine games for Philadelphia back in 1898. After that he played for semi-pro and mill teams around Tennessee where he's from, and, for a certain length of time, ended up in Arkansas. When I was ten years old, he must have been getting close to forty, he signed on with the hardware store down in Helena to weigh nails and play ball.

Well, none of us kids had ever laid eyes on somebody who'd been in the National League, so we rode our horses over to the next county to see what he looked like. It was a Saturday, and everybody who lived in those parts was in town. It was the busiest place any of us had ever seen. Rondo only had two streets, so this was big doings. We snuck in through the loading dock of the store, and, sure enough, there he was eating June bugs and telling stories. Son, to us, he must have been ten feet tall.

I'll bet we sat there for four hours while he talked about baseball. That Philadelphia team he was with had Nap Lajoie and Big Ed Delahanty both on it. Hall of Famers, you know.

Naturally, one of the things that I wanted to hear all about was what happened to Big Ed. He died in 1903, you may remember, in the prime of his career. He had led the league in hitting the year before. Stories were real mysterious at the time. Newt dropped his voice to a whisper and told us boys that the inside scoop was that the four other Delahanty brothers was mad at Ed for being the oldest, and one day they were together and all talking bad about him and started thinking mean thoughts that just got meaner and meaner till, three states away, Big Ed Delahanty just plumb spontaneously blew up leaving nothing but scorched underpants and a three fingered glove.

I was pretty sure that story was the greatest thing I'd ever heard at the time. It was probably another nine years before I figured out that when somebody blows up spontaneous like that, their underpants would have burned up, too. It's not like their trousers would go and so would their hiney while the skivvies just got a few toast marks. No, sir.

I did come to find out the real story some years later, by the by. Seems Big Ed was drunk and starting so much trouble on a train that the conductor put him off at Niagara, Canada about one or two o'clock in the morning. He goes to walking back to the United States, and when he gets to the bridge, the night tender says to him that the draw is up. Ed, he manages to get off a few words, none of which are thank you very much, and proceeds to stagger right off into the Niagara River and over the Falls, which was even bigger than Big Ed. He didn't exactly go over in a barrel, but he was pickled, sure enough. And that's the Lord's truth.

But I was talking about my first trip to Chicago, wasn't I? So much happened. That was probably the most eventful two weeks I ever had, except maybe the time I was accidentally locked in Bill Tilden's hall closet. It was sure weeks I love to recall, I know that.

Herbie and I hopped trains on back to Memphis in plenty of time for preparations for the baseball season of 1920. That was a good way for a young man of few cares to travel.

You know, minor league ball has always been slightly magical. In a lot of ways, a ballplayer would be even more special in a little town than he was in a big league city. That's because more people knew you, or had a real chance to try. If they didn't know you proper, then they knew the woman who done your laundry or your barber or the man at the vegetable stand who promised not to tell nobody.

Now, me being the equipment manager, I was very popular. All the little kids wanted to get a hold of some piece of equipment that a real professional ballplayer had used. Baseballs, broken bats, and catcher's cups were the most prized, although not necessarily in that order.

I bring this up cause I'm recollecting a thing from right about that time after I come back from Chicago. I was down at the ballyard one afternoon before the season started, hanging around the tool shed tightening up the opening on the foul line chalker. The owner of the ball club had decided he could save some money if the lines was only an inch and a quarter wide, so he had set me to souping up the machine.

Come to find out that the speed at which you laid them lines down had a good deal to do with how much chalk you was going to use up, too. First month or so of the year, I walked extra careful to make sure those narrower lines was straight. And you know what happened? They got taller. One day one of the Atlanta Crackers bunted a little spinner down the first base line that kept trying to roll foul but couldn't. Ball got to rotating so fast against that line that it kicked up a tiny little tornado that blinded our pitcher and first baseman. By the time the dust settled, the runner had him a bunt triple.

Course, all that was still in the future at that moment. There I was working on the line chalker when I hear a voice calling "Hey, Mister." It was a sweet woman's voice, so naturally, I figured it was some sort of angel. Who else was going to call me "Mister"?

I was almost afraid to turn around since it might make the angel vanish, but when I finally did it was just one of the prettiest young ladies I ever laid eyes on. I figured her for about a year younger than I was. Her hair was that sort of wispy, wavy kind that always reminds me of Spanish moss but finer and without the bugs, and it swept around her face and halfway down her back like a heavenly chestnut cloud that you couldn't help but want to tangle your fingers in.

I stood up all fast like and ripped the cap off my head in one motion. You know how you'll see a beautiful woman, and when you realize that she's talking directly to you it's kind of like there's nobody else around. For just an instant, her big brown eyes lock onto you and all that loveliness was meant to be seen by you alone. You blush a bit, and your heart wants to move up into your throat. At least that's how it gets me.

Most times that happens just before you notice her six foot four husband or boyfriend glaring at you, but that day we was all by ourselves, just the two of us at a quiet ballpark.

"Mister," she said. "I don't have any money."

I wasn't sure why she was telling me that. Shoot, except for the people I worked for, nobody I knew had any money.

"I'm trying to get me a present for my daddy's birthday. He is an awful big baseball krank. I just know that he would like something that has to do with the Chicks. But I can't pay you nothing for it."

She looked down at her toes as she made that last pronouncement. Before that her voice had been clear and high pitched, like a proud little girl when she talked about her daddy.

Now this may have been the prettiest female I had ever laid eyes on up to that time in my life. There had been some cute ones back home, and I'd seen a bunch of lookers in my travels to Chicago, but there was just something about this one. It was like she was a little princess or something, and she had lowered herself to come ask a favor of me. What I'm telling you is that there was no way on Earth that I was about to turn her down.

The trouble was what to give her. I sure wanted to make a good impression, even though she was clearly out of my league, so to speak, but it wasn't like today. Nowadays, a player or ball club don't think twice about handing off a ball or a bat or even a glove or a jersey. They do it all the time. But in the Southern Association in 1920, a ball player only had two uniforms, one for home games and one for the road. And when you left the team, the durn thing went straight to the guy who took your place. Taking somebody's bat, well, that was likely to get you hit over the head with whatever one he had remaining.

To be honest with you, I was also trying to figure out how I could make her stick around a little bit longer. I didn't want to just hand her something and say

"There you go", and watch her skip off on down the road. For a second, I thought about inviting her to take a walk through the clubhouse herself and see if anything caught her eye, but that wouldn't have been proper at all. You can't just run a flamingo through hog shit and expect her to come out pink on the other side.

So, as scared as I was that my little angel would run off before I come back, I asked her to stay right where she was while I went to see what I could find, and with that, I took off running as fast as I ever had.

Once the season started, there would have been all sorts of things to choose from, but it being late winter, that clubhouse was just dark and musty and barely inviting to the mice. I had hosed the place out myself the year before, right before Herbie and I hopped the rails, so I knew that pickings would be slim.

On top of everything else was that a player didn't stay in one town in the minors back then. The clubs wasn't farm teams owned by the bigs, so a man might be in Memphis one season and then hear that Bloomington, up in the Triple-I League, needed a second baseman the next year, and then be playing in Macon down in the Sally League the year after that. So, when a campaign ended, you took what you owned with you.

You ever have magic happen to you? I mean when you know you're just about down to your last dime, and your stomach is fussing at you, and then you reach into your pants pocket, and there's a ten dollar bill that you ain't never seen before. Well, sir, that's kind of what happened that day in Memphis.

I was looking around at all the empty locker stalls, wondering if a hairy bar of soap would impress her daddy, when there they was, staring me in the face like the rear end of a baboon, only less colorful. A pair of size 9C baseball shoes.

I will swear to you to this day that those shoes was not there when I cleaned the place up at the end of the Chicks' season in 1919. It wasn't exactly the Depression, but a new pair of shoes would set you back better than $3 in those days, so it was not likely that some fellow would just walk off and leave his spikes.

Well, I snatched them up before they could disappear before me like a mirage, and I took a whiff of them. Lo and behold, they smelled just about right. Not powerful enough to offend a young lady's sensibilities, but still with enough of a twang to let a bystander know they was the genuine article. Game worn, as they say nowadays.

I wheeled around for the door to get back outside before that beautiful creature changed her mind and took off, but I'll be damned if that girl wasn't standing right there, not six feet away. She had followed me into the clubhouse stealthier than a fart from the preacher's wife.

If there was ever a moment for that lovely vision to shyly cast her eyes down to her toes again, that was it, but she was staring right at me.

"Mister, I'm figuring you's of a mind to give me them baseball shoes, and my daddy sure will prize those. He sure will. But it just wouldn't be right without I give you a proper thank you."

And with that, the angel leapt right at me and stuck her tongue down my throat bigger than Dallas. It was something you might expect from a horny puma, but not a lovely young southern girl with all that wavy hair.

I've known some fast women in my time, but by golly, I can't say I knew what hit me that day at all. By the time I caught my breath, my butt cheeks already had tile impressions. I can almost guarantee you that no body so rare and beauteous as that one ever graced the locker room at that ball park again. That place burned down in April of 1960 after an exhibition game, but I sure as shooting thought it was going to catch fire 40 years earlier.

As for the story of that young lady, I didn't get to brag too long. After floating on air for less than a week, I spotted her at a boarding house not a block and a half from the one I lived at. Turns out my angel was a soiled dove.

I learned two important things from that little incident. One is that having the knowledge of who she was didn't make that afternoon less special by so much as a smidgeon. The other is that even a whore is somebody's daughter.

Those were sure good old days. Back then the equipment manager was a much tougher job than it is today. I had other duties too. I mowed the field, occasionally worked as a vendor, was a kind of trainer, and painted the stadium on off days.

Like I said, the minor leagues was something special back then. For one thing, there was more of them. Every little town seemed like they had a professional ball club. The one in Memphis that I was with was a part of the Southern Association, one of the best leagues in organized ball.

I was with Memphis for about five seasons. You're likely thinking that the Chicks is a dad-gummed odd name for a men's ball club. Some folks say it was named that on account of being short for Chickasaws, like the Indian tribe. but I'm here to tell you it was because the owner insisted on dying all of his players some pastel color around Easter time. That was one of the drawbacks of the pre-free agency days.

That owner, name of Russ Gardner, changed the name of the rickety little ballyard we played in a couple of years before I got there. It had been called Red Elm Field, but he went and named it after himself. He called it Russwood Park. Thought it'd get him laid. I thought it'd been cheaper to change his own damn name to Red Elm, what with Red being much more of a manly name than Russ anyhow. On the other hand, the "wood" part couldn't have hurt.

The way ballparks was back in those days, especially in the minors, the grandstands didn't hold much. I think we held about 6,487 medium size folks at Russwood, slightly fewer if they was Baptists. The seats was made of wood.

Well, sir, it used to get pretty humid and sticky there back in the early twenties, and that didn't do those seats much good. They'd start making their own splinters, in other words. That give me an idea. I took the initiative without asking Mr. Gardner, and set up a splinter pulling concession just behind the third base bleachers.

It was a simple sort of contraption, really. I took me one of the shoe shine stands and cut out the middle of the chair seat. That way a body could drop their trousers, clamber up into the thing and have me roll under them on a creeper wearing a lighted miner's helmet. That's the way the women's doctors do it in West Virginia.

I've always been an idea man. Often thought I could have gone into the advertising business if baseball hadn't of worked out for me. True to form, that splinter pulling stand become a big hit right from the get go.

I took customers of both genders, though men cost a nickel more on account of the extra territory to cover. I don't know if the money was a factor or not, but I started developing an exclusively female clientele. That is with the exception of a doughy old fellow named Crunchy Landrum who ran some apartment house up on Poplar.

The number of women was curious, too, since ballgames back then drew a very heavily male audience. The stands would be filled mostly with fellows wearing suit coats and straw boaters, maybe the occasional derby, but here I was plucking splinters from about a woman an inning.

After a fashion, I begun to figure out that lots of them ladies wasn't even there for the ballgame. They bought a ticket just so they could come to my stand. I guess they must have been picking up their splinters someplace else.

These women fit a pattern I discovered over a few weeks. Not a soul under thirty-five or forty and every one of them more talkative than a drunk lawyer in the next bus seat.

Eventually some of them become regular customers, bringing their own salves, creams and ointments to rub on. Now keep in mind that I was still about nineteen years old at that time, strapping, and not too bad looking a young lad from what folks told me. If you flip things around, you can see why these nice ladies valued the attention. Why a man would be daft not to want a cute little co-ed rubbing Vaseline on his bottom. Am I right?

So, business went along, guns a blazing, for about a month or two in the middle of the summer. A couple of the old girls would make strong suggestions that I swing by their house on the way to the ballpark of a morning cause they had splinters that might need special attention. Being a single boy, I may have gone. I don't recall.

But I sure can't forget the day that my concession idea come to Mr. Gardner's attention.

By then it was getting toward the middle of August of 1920. Now I should say that some of the regulars who climbed onto my stand was more pleasant to deal with than others, and one of the less joyous times was when I'd get a visit from Mrs. Eulala Starr. She was a mighty hefty woman who always kept several handkerchiefs tucked into various folds of her clothing.

I try to always be nice to everybody, but I had to be extra pleasant to old Mrs. Starr since she was the next door neighbor of the John D. Martins. Mr. Martin being the club president of the Chicks, and as of the previous season, the head man of the entire Southern Association.

Mrs. Starr got free tickets to the ballyard any day she pleased, and since her husband had passed on several years prior, she had developed the habit of coming to the park often. I sometimes think that her late husband had the right idea.

Hunting for slivers of wood up under this woman was tricky at best, but that second week in August, it brought about one of the more unfortunate convergences of events in that era of Memphis baseball.

This stately specimen had recently developed the gout, and her doctor had made her cut a good deal of the richness from her menu.

At the exact moment of impact, my head was turned while I deposited a two-inch piece of what I hoped to be spruce into a nearby spittoon. That could be what saved me.

Since I wasn't looking, I can only reconstruct the happenings from a mix of common sense and three or four hideous noises that seemed to come one on top of the other. Suffice it to say that a lit miner's helmet in close proximity to a two-hundred pound woman on an all-vegetable diet is a questionable proposition at best.

Bystanders managed to douse the blaze after the loss of only a small section of grandstand supports, and my hair grew back in nicely by Halloween. If it had been anyone other than Eulala Starr, I'm sure Mr. Martin would have fired me on the spot. As it was, I was strongly encouraged to contribute all my hard-earned profits toward the rebuilding fund, and the bosses kept a closer eye on me, too.

It all worked out in the end, so to speak. Mr. Gardner decided that as long as he had men working on the place, he might as well build her out good. The next season, Russwood boasted seating for right at eleven thousand, and right off the bat, that new park saw one of the best seasons they ever had in Memphis, Tennessee.

It might not be where the saying come from, but it was one lucky turn of the head that kept my hindsight twenty-twenty.

Chapter Seven

S on, if you don't mind, I want to talk for a spell about that season of 1921 because it was a humdinger. A big time for folks down in the mid-south.

You got to understand just how big baseball was back in those days. There wasn't no pro basketball, sure as hell no soccer, and the NFL was just a diaper wearing baby that was only to be found up by the Great Lakes. On top of that, there was only sixteen teams in the big leagues, and none of them were either south or west of St. Louis. Those minor league clubs were anything but minor to a ton of folks, so when the Memphis Chicks commenced to winning 104 games, the all-time record for the Southern Association, the whole city was plumb jumping.

Back then, it was no crime to come back and play in A ball after you'd had a cup of coffee or two in the Show. Ball players wasn't making much, so a paycheck fielding grounders sounded a whole mess better than a ten hour day in some mill. Most of those old boys would play ball any place that'd pay them until they got run off.

The Chicks had them a few of those Big Leaguers. There was Gloomy Gus Williams and Howie "Red" Camp who was on their way down, and a pitcher, Paul Zahniser, and a shortstop, Andy High, who was on their way up. Little Andy High made it the next year and stuck around the bigs for thirteen seasons. I say "little" because he was only five foot six, even in his cleats.

But the one who had everything fall into place for him that year was a first baseman named Polly McLarry. Word was he had been named after a neighbor's parrot. He'd had a handful of at bats for the White Sox in 1912 and several more handfuls for the Cubs in 1915 when he compiled the lofty average of .197. If there had been any justice, a man named Polly would have played for the Pirates, but he didn't.

Polly was already thirty years old that season, so on days when he felt like being honest with himself, he must have known that he'd be playing out the rest of his string in the minors. But it didn't seem to bother him much.

He come from a little town called Leonard, Texas, up there not too far from Oklahoma. He broke into organized ball in 1911 with the Beeville Orange Growers of the Southwest Texas League.

Now, it shouldn't surprise you that the stint in Beeville was what first made me seek out Polly McLarry. You see, bees have always fascinated me, even since I was a wee youngun'. Did you know that a honey bee can fly up to six miles without taking a rest? Yep. That's the God's truth.

There was an old boy back in Lee County name of Barton Ownsby, a carpenter by trade, and a widower. I say he was a carpenter, but I sure can't say that he was a very good one. By the time I first knew him, Old Bart was down to seven fingers, and I recall a couple more getting whittled away when I was a kiddo. And remember, all this was in the years before power tools. A body has to be pretty liquored up to miss the fact that you're taking off your pinkie with a backsaw, though it is the only way to get a good angle.

It seemed like losing that fifth one took all the fight out of Bart. Up to that time, he must have figured that his digits were still winning, but cutting off that last middle one made it a tie.

Well, he moped around for a few months. You'd see him every now and then down by the river poking through the bushes, trying to scare up some critter for supper, and that's where he made friends with the bees. They renewed old Barton's life, I reckon.

Before long, he started dropping by folks' porches just to tell them that bees had five eyes, or he'd corner some fellow to say how many times he counted their little sets of wings flapping in one second. Most of the time, he was pretty well covered with welts, but he seemed happy. If he got stung in the right spot, well, it kind of looked like a finger might be growing back.

The year he turned fifty-two was when he decided to start the Bee Lover's Honey Cult. At that time, Barton Ownsby weighed in north of 240 and had a scraggly beard that grew in a mite heavier on his left side than his right. One side started up around his eye socket and the other down around his ear hole.

In spite of those physical handicaps, he set out to suggesting to some of the more experienced single ladies around the neighborhood that they ought to start a-hanging around his place and following the behavior of the hive. By that, he meant that your male bees existed for one purpose only, that being to make more bees. Shoot, the male honey bee didn't even have a stinger. If they was anything like old Bart, they likely sawed the durn thing off.

Female bees, on the other hand, did all the work, except for the queen, who stayed at home laying as many as 2500 eggs a day. Even a teenaged oyster shucker in the back of the Blockbuster Video can't keep up with that pace.

Far as I know, the Bee Lover's Honey Cult never did threaten to outdo the Methodists or anything, but we young boys did notice some regular coming and going around the Ownsby place, including common appearances by Lenora Garmint, who my Uncle Stump Dibrell always counted as perky in spite of her wandering eye. Nope, there wasn't a lot of women, but Old Bart did scare up a handful, or at least on his terms.

Well, when I found out about Beeville and Polly McLarry, it sure did catch my fancy. I mean, there being so many bees there that they named the whole town after them. I sure wanted to know more.

When I tried to explain about the Bee Lover's Honey Cult to Polly, he carried on like I was speaking a foreign language. I assumed that was on account of him having had his own version of some old lady with a wandering eye that he'd been pollinating back in Beeville. I played along and kept it as our little secret.

Recalling all about the bees got me to thinking, though. I mentioned it to Cissy, one of the girls back at the rooming house who was kind of sweet on me, and the next time I saw her, she handed me a bowlful of what she called honey custard. It was delicious. I had moved on from Kitty's to a place around the corner where the rent was lower in exchange for more of my handyman abilities.

Cissy and I didn't get to spend time together often what with me having ballgames every day and her working every night, but she figured she could keep me interested by plying me with pudding. Thing was, a man can only eat so much creamy goodness, so I got into the habit of taking the rest of it down to the clubhouse, and I bet you can guess who thought it was the best thing he'd ever passed over his gums. That's right. Polly McLarry. Every afternoon, he'd clean that dish and ask for more.

The other fellow who started begging for me to bring more was a Cuban pitcher we had named of Oscar Tuero. Oscar had been up in the bigs, too. He'd come to the Chicks the season before.

Oscar begged and begged for that pudding. He said it reminded him of a girl back home name of Chinchilla or Conchita or something. I sometimes thought the gal's name changed with each telling. He showed me a photograph, and I think I'd have begged for more myself.

Before you know it, Cissy, the girl back at the boarding house was earning an extra fifty cents a day by rising a little early and whipping up three big bowls of honey custard. Then it was four bowls, and eventually nine bowls with half the team chipping in. Polly McLarry would eat his before batting practice then come back and lick the bowl, and Oscar Tuero would eat 90% of his and pour the rest down his sanitary sock. I'm not here to judge.

What was remarkable about the whole thing was the way we started winning. Everybody on the team was doing good. We moved into first place on Opening Day and never looked back. We beat the New Orleans Pelicans by seven and a half games.

Polly McLarry hit .353 and led the league in RBIs. Oscar Tuero won 27 games, more than any other season in his long career, and he pitched until he was 48 years old. At the end of the year, he paid Cissy $35 for her recipe for honey custard. I heard tell that whatever town he wound up in, he'd give it to some local woman and have pudding delivered to the ballpark whether he was pitching or not.

That would turn out to be my last full year in Memphis. Everybody fell back to Earth the following season, but the first time I ever had flan in a Mexican restaurant, well, I bet I'm one of the only guys alive who could say it reminded him of the 1921 Memphis Chicks.

My friend Herbie and I still palled around like before, but the tone of things had changed in America. Black soldiers had fought in the war and expected a fair shake when they come home from France. The NAACP was a decade old or more, and some of those soldiers joined up to push for the cause. It sparked a nasty backlash that turned into a rise of the Klan.

I've heard old White people say that the Klan was just a social organization, that they meant no more harm than the Rotary Club. Well, I'm here to tell you that a fried chicken and Cole slaw picnic is not acceptable cover for beating Jews and Catholics to a bloody pulp and lynching Black people in the dark of night. The Klan did not deserve the name human.

The movies and books will have you believe that the 1920s was all about bob hairdos, hiked up skirts and bootleg hooch, but it was also the heyday of vile hate, anti-immigrant crusading, and sour-stomached conservatism. When I walked the streets with Herbie, there was no denying that Memphis sometimes had a different feel to it.

It was mostly words, name calling that I could usually melt away with a withering look. I was 20 years old and was a sturdy youngster, topped out well above six foot. Not many wanted to tempt me, even though I was quite the peaceable fellow. But there were exceptions.

One still and sweaty night has never left me. It was a Monday, most likely, things being real slow at my rooming house. Herbie and me was headed out to scare us up some music. He had stopped by for a couple slugs of cheap whiskey up in my room prior to being forced to pay for them. It was a money saver. We had just stepped out the back door. I generally used it out of habit, but Herbie was obliged to. Seeing a Black man come out the front door of a joy house just wouldn't do in Memphis.

There was a festering knot of White boys hanging around the street end of the alley. I reckon they had come downtown to buy some time with the girls only to find the prices outweighed their pocketbooks. I made them at about our age or a couple years younger. Their clothes said manual labor, but they had tried to clean up. Before the door even shut behind us, they had marked Herbie and me as the substitute entertainment.

"Why is some Black buck coming out of a White whore house?"

That was from a fellow as big as me, and there were five more with him.

Herbie spoke up before I could.

"Gentlemen, I'm no customer. I work here."

Another one pushed forward.

"You better be the cheapest fuck in the place."

That drew a big round of laughter.

"He's the piano player, and I'm the handyman," I told them, reverting to our 1917 biographies. "We ain't looking for trouble."

"We is."

With that they set upon us. Three of them held each of us while they took turns punching and kicking. I'd like to tell you that we give a good accounting of ourselves, but I think that'd be untrue. We were outnumbered. All the while they never let up with a stream of every insulting word for a Black man that ever got said.

I use the word us, but the beatings were far from equal. Once they had me down on the ground and bleeding heavy from a cut over my eye, they mostly just sat on me while the others kept pounding poor Herbie. One of them that had me pinned was taunting me the whole time.

"You got no business keeping company with monkeys," I recollect him saying. That was one of the nicer things.

I could see his ugly mug through one eye and smell his stinking breath, but he had my arms locked tight, and another one was kneeling on my legs. After what seemed a good while, they ground my face into the alley dirt and went laughing down the street, straightening their cheap secondhand suit coats as they went.

Herbie wasn't moving, but I could hear rough breathing, so I knew he was still among the living. A fellow we called Old Dave ran a shoe shine stand out on the street, and he come hustling around to help me get Herbie up to my room. The sad fact is that some of the girls were used to tending to wounds like that, albeit not as many blows at once. A couple of them served as nurses, but there was no doctor. You could see his nose was broken, and there was a big gash under one eye from a boot toe. The broken ribs was the worst of it all for him, made it hard to breathe, let alone walk or dress yourself. Herbie knew to protect his hands since that was his living, so he had tucked them hard under his body, and tried to curl up in as tight a ball as he could.

The discussion about finding a policeman was short lived. Memphis coppers didn't give four shits about a Black man getting beat, and Miss Belle who owned the joint knew that every call to the polis was another excuse to shake her down for cash. Healing was the end of the matter.

By the time the Chicks come back from the road, all I had was a cut and enough bruises to take some ribbing from the boys. Herbie was laid up for two weeks before he could go back to work, and that was that. Except for the fact that my friend was more scarce for the next few months. We never talked about it, but years later I realized that the whole thing was a reminder that, no matter how much we personally weren't bothered about our friendship, our realities were not the same.

There was a telephone at the boarding house there in Memphis, but I'd never had cause to use it much. I'd have called my folks from time to time as money allowed, but they didn't have a phone, so it was a surprise to hear Miss Belle tell me that I had a call.

It's funny. When you're young and everything is going good, most people don't give it a second's worth of thought. Counting your blessings is for old folks, I imagine. As the 1921 season ended for the Chicks, there was no doubt that I was on top of the world, and that's when things have a way of knocking you off your perch. At least some of the time. That phone call was one of them.

The voice on the other end of the line was my Aunt Sacagawea. I took to asking her questions a mile a minute.

"Did you and Uncle Stump get you a telephone?"

"No," she allowed. "I've come all the way out to Dawson's Store to borrow theirs."

"Well, that's just about the nicest thing I've heard of. Is everybody there? I reckon y'all are calling to congratulate me on us winning the league. It sure was exciting."

The season had only ended a couple days previous, and I just figured the whole world was as dotty as I was over it.

She let me run on for a spell, and then, in a quiet voice, she said, "Nipper, your daddy's gone."

I guess that stopped me in my tracks.

Have you ever heard bad news and a part of your brain understands it right away, but another part ain't willing to accept it? That's the best way I can describe what was happening in my head right at that moment. What eventually come out of my mouth was a stupid-ass question.

"What do you mean?" I asked, hoping I didn't understand her.

"He's passed over, Nipper. His heart give out."

There was a long minute of silence. The ache in my jaws wasn't allowing any more words to come out.

"Well, I reckon this here phone is about to ask for more money than I got, sweetie," she said. "You'd best come on home. Your mama needs you."

And the call was over.

I thumbed my way back down to Lee County that afternoon. That was the first time I dealt with dying close up, and it was the first time I'd seen somebody's empty eyes. At least it was the first time I'd paid heed to it. Mama let on that things would be all right, that these things was part of life and had to be handled, but even at that young age, I thought she looked lost in the woods.

The only thing we ever said between us about it was when she handed me daddy's Henry Clay cigar box of treasures. She made sure my grip was firm around it, and then she put her rough little hands atop and beneath my own.

"Son, your daddy was a better man than most, I suppose. This here belongs to you to do with as you please, but I hope you won't discard them without some thought. Supper'll be ready at the usual time."

And that was it. That was the extent of our family support.

I suppose you're curious as to what was in the cigar box. It was an old box even then, but to my imagination, at least, it still smelled of tobacco and cow barn, which meant it smelled of my daddy.

The box contained his razor and shaving brush. A sliver of soap. A piece of watch chain without a watch or a fob, a Third Grade report card, a letter that Uncle Stump had sent from Tampa, Florida during the Spanish American War and a faded campaign ribbon urging people to vote for Alton B. Parker, a bald man with a mighty fine moustache.

I stayed at home with my mama and the rest of the Lee County folks for over two months, making sure the tail end of the harvest got done and things got buttoned up for the winter. We planted a few fall vegetables so mama didn't go hungry. I went back to Memphis right before Christmas on account of nobody felt much like celebrating, and I suppose even at twenty years of age, I knew my life had moved on.

Chapter Eight

New York City

It was halfway through May of '22 that I heard about the big equipment manager's convention up at the Polo Grounds. I thought it was kind of odd, being in the middle of the season and all, but I went anyway. Naturally, by the time I got there, I'd figured out the whole thing had been a practical joke. Oh, those Memphis boys. Turned out I stayed in New York for the next twenty some odd years, though. Funny how things end up. It was time for my next chapter anyway.

The boys on the team had chipped in for that ticket. Or at least the one up there. We were always playing jokes on one another. I'm sure I had pulled off an embarrassing doozer against one of them, so they had responded in kind. I must admit it was well played, but when I stepped off that train at Pennsylvania Station, my pockets felt emptier than a bill collector's heart.

I figured that I'd find a way to get me a train ticket back home lickety split, but at that instant I had about a dollar thirty-seven, so if I was going to make the best of my unexpected adventure, I knew I'd best hit the sidewalks.

Thinking back, it probably took me an hour to get out of the train station, that being a space like none other that I had ever seen. If you never experienced the great hall at Penn Station, you missed out, son. That was a pure cathedral to transportation, I tell you. Glorious ceilings billowing like huge, clean sheets on a clothesline hung 150 feet in the air. It was as grand as anything ever done by the Romans or the Frenchies for gods or kings. It's just that American gods are usually things like railroads.

Once I hit the street, my sense of awe began to wear off. It was nice being in a new place and all, but you got to remember that I'd been to Chicago and traveled to cities all over the South and then some, so New York City wasn't going to impress me on account of it being a little bigger. I just tugged down my hat and asked the nearest policeman the way to the Polo Grounds.

Now it wasn't the first policeman I asked, mind you. The first one was a wee Irish fellow who didn't seem interested in the least at how ball players down in West Tennessee loved to get a leg up on equipment managers. Neither did the one after that, or the Italian-looking one who called me a hillbilly even after I explained that Lee County, Arkansas was pure old delta, and that you had to go all darn near to Bald Knob before you start to get even a whiff of rolling terrain.

Then I met Officer Ramsey, and he was friendlier than all the rest of New York's finest put together. Fact is, he talked to me first, and that gave me a good feeling. He looked to be wearing the same floweredy bathing cap that my Uncle Earl was partial to. I wouldn't have even known he was a policeman if he hadn't told me.

I allowed as how I was looking to go to the Polo Grounds to watch John McGraw and the New York Giants. The first thing he told me was that I shouldn't be in no hurry. Back in those days, the Giants wasn't the only team that played at the Polo Grounds. In that season of 1922, they shared the joint with the American League Yankees, and that happened to be who was in town on the day I arrived. The Giants wasn't due home for another week.

Now, I didn't put a great deal of stock in the American League at that time, and being from Lee County, anything named Yankees put a bur down my shorts. On the other hand, I wasn't about to pass on a chance to see a big league baseball game.

On top of that, New York City, or I should say the Polo Grounds, was the top of the world in 1922. Not only did my beloved Giants and the evil Yankees both play there, but they had met each other in the World Series the year before. The whole durn thing played right there at the same ballpark. Nothing like that had ever happened before, and I was ready to catch some of that conjury.

In spite of my dire financial situation, it wasn't too tough for me to decide on a course of action. Shoot, even if I didn't give a whit about baseball, I had only heard of two or three places in New York, so I bid Officer Ramsey a large thank you and said the Yankees would do just fine. Just making that little decision altered my whole outlook. I reckon that right there was the moment I decided to make my mark on the world, though the concept was completely unknown to me at the time.

I thought about walking the 150 blocks up to the Polo Grounds and save my nickel, but truth is that I wanted to ride that subway that people was talking about. I wasn't sure when I'd get a chance to do that again, so I hitched up my pants, looked up at all the big buildings, and swallowed hard cause that is a feeling that'll make the juices rise up your gullet. Not the skyline itself, mind you. No sir, the feeling I mean is being in any metropolis, which is always less friendly than some small burg, and knowing that after breakfast the next morning, you'll be plumb broke. Tap city. That's when you learn to be resourceful.

Since I had a little time to kill, the game not being for a few more hours, I reckoned it would be a crime if I didn't see the Woolworth Building, so I set off to the south, that being the opposite direction of the Polo Grounds, but then what is an adventure for.

One of the things that was hard to miss that first time I walked through the streets of New York was the smell. It wasn't a single smell, no, sir. It was a hundred of them all mixed one on top of the other. Chocolate and fresh cut meat, food cooking from every place imaginable and cat pee, lots of cat pee.

Finally, up ahead, I could see the Woolworth Building rising. Even though I had some more distance to go, it got your attention. Now, 57 stories might not sound like much to you, and I've been in taller buildings since, but that was 1922, and the Woolworth Building was the tallest structure in the world. Me being a tourist, feeling like I was on vacation, I was obliged to stick my head inside the big front doors, and it was the second time that day that I could have stood there drooling. I almost imagined being in some palace of Constantinople. By the time I took a gander at the big City Hall around the corner, it was hard to keep from being impressed by all of the finery. Then I headed to the subway, and it got even worse.

The subway station at City Hall was one of the strangest places I'd ever seen that you could go into for free. Not glittery like the Woolworth Building, not overwhelming like Penn Station, but little and artsy with more than a whiff of underarm. It was a cross between one of those painted country churches and a fancy gas station men's room with a train running along one side. There were little green tiles everywhere and big skylights that let the sun shine below ground, sparkling, like the building's underpants had worn a little thin.

People was bustling about every place you looked, too. Nary a one of them would stop to look you in the eye or give a nod in your direction, neither. You needed a mirror just to be sure you were really there.

Riding the subway, now that was something else. It'd come to be as natural as breathing by the time I'd been there some years, but that day was another matter altogether.

Funny that I should use the word breathing, cause that wasn't something that come easy on the subway in those days. It might not have been as hot as Lee County, but August in New York was still summer, and there was no such thing as air conditioning back then. And let me tell you, I'm convinced that folks call New York City the big melting pot because that's how you felt on the subway in the summer.

I tell you that not to complain, because I was still as fired up about my arrival in the big city as I had been at Pennsylvania Station some hours prior. I just want you to have a picture of how I looked when I got to the Polo Grounds. I was something between wet and damp. I'd been sleeping on straight backed depot benches for three days running, but my personal humidity had started to steam some of the wrinkles out. As for odor, well, I'd have to describe it as a wolverine dipped in curry.

So that was me, suitcase in hand, who walked up to the player's entrance to the Polo Grounds on the late morning of May 16, 1922. The Yanks were facing Cleveland that day, but it was still too early for the teams or workers to be there, so I strolled right on through the open gate and started to wander the tunnels.

Well, sir, I was just a-looking. Taking it all in. When all of a sudden I heard a voice right behind me.

"Hey, pal, right here."

"Scuse me?" I said.

"You walked right past me. I'm the one who ordered the two slices with double anchovies. Hell, I smelled 'em through the door."

Turned out to be Waite Hoyt who was scheduled to start, and even though I knew he'd hooked on with the Yankees, it still took me by surprise to see him. He said he'd had a rough night, and salty fish always calmed his nerves. I took that to mean that it helped his hangover, as any fool could see that his eyes were redder than Big Bill Haywood.

I had to tell him that it was most likely my undershirt he caught a whiff of, and the closest I had to salty fish was a half bottle of Eau du Racine toilet water from Kresge's which I was pretty dang certain contained a dash of Blue Gill. Waite nodded and took him a swig. Then he scrunched up his face and took him another.

After the second gulp, he squinted a little and looked at me hard in the face.

"Don't you remember me from Memphis? I was assistant equipment manager, and you and me and S.C. Pequinney went out on the town and seen us a baseball picture with Harold Lloyd and Bebe Daniels and had us a beer or four at a place called Pete's where they'd serve pretty much anybody had them a nickel."

"Nope, But I might if you give me one more swallow."

It had been a long time, I reckon.

We'd been teenagers when he'd been throwing for the Chicks, Hoyt fresh out of high school. That day I saw him again at the Polo Grounds, he was all of 22, and still about 16 months my senior. In spite of being older, folks called Hoyt by the nickname of Schoolboy. When it come to drinking, old Waite done things kind of backwards. He drank the whole time he was pitching, and then quit not long after he retired. Shoot, seems to me that the time to get liquored up is when you don't have to be anyplace.

Well, the pitching matchup that day was Hoyt against Stan Covaleski. Both future Hall of Famers, and both of them went the distance. Old Stan only give up six hits, but the kid got the better of him. New York won it 3 to zip, and after the ball game, who do you think Waite Hoyt come looking for?

"That hooch of yours must've fixed me up, kid. I felt pretty solid out there."

"Yes, sir, I reckon for dime store toilet water it's right tasty."

The Yankees were coming off a great season. The two years before, their star player, George Hermann Ruth, had put up the best numbers in the history of baseball. As good as 1920 was for the Babe, 1921 put even more shine on the kettle. Nobody had ever seen anything like it. Fifty-nine home runs, batted .378 and had him a slugging percentage of .840-something for the second year in a row.

But 1922 wasn't starting off real good. No, sir. You see the Babe had put together a barnstorming tour after the prior season. That's what players did back at that time to earn extra money. Fact is that a few of the big ones made more money playing exhibitions around the hinterlands than they got under contract from those skinflints that owned the ball clubs.

Everybody did it, too. Old Man Connie Mack, who was a durn owner, used to personally take his boys on barnstorming runs after the regular season. These would last through November and even all the way up to Christmas some times.

Trouble had arrived not long before, though, in the form of Judge Kenesaw Mountain Landis which is one of the strangest names ever pinned onto a youngster. Of course, Judge Landis had probably looked like a scary old man ever since he was 11. His daddy named him after the spot in Georgia where he'd got shot during the Civil War. Story was that he told the doctor he was naming his boy for the place he got wounded, and if not for a friendly records clerk willing to issue a second certificate, the Judge would have been Buttocks Landis from here to eternity.

Well, old Buttocks had put in a rule eliminating any barnstorming once the season was over. The owners wanted their ballplayers to stay hungry, you see. So, he had suspended the Babe and Bob Muesel for the start of the season.

They come back to play on May 20th, just four days after I showed up.

In the meantime, Waite Hoyt, who now luckily remembered me, decided to help me out. He saw that I was more than a step or two down the pathway to being hungry and broke, and he allowed as how there could be a position open as third assistant to the club house man at the Polo Grounds. By that time, a telegram had arrived offering me a return fare to Memphis, but this New York job sounded like a dream come true.

Son, do you know who was the superintendent of the Polo Grounds, the fellow who had to give me the a-okay? Amos Rusie, the great fastballer. Mr. McGraw had give him a job while he was down on hard times. He was a big fellow, about my size, with a bulldog mouth and a jacket that looked like he just pulled it out of his back pocket.

Once I told him that I had known a fellow whose daddy played at Dayton with Tacks Latimer, I was as good as in. I come to find out in later years, though, that my understanding of the moment was a little different than Rusie's, but it worked out all the same.

When I told him my story about my old pal S.C., Rusie squinted at me and said in a loud voice, "Who?"

"Why, Frank Pequinney, Mr. Rusie. His boy S.C., which is short for Samuel Coleridge, was an acquaintance of mine back in Memphis. They come from Galveston, Texas, or at least S.C. did. His daddy had played there and took a liking to the place on account of the warm salt air, though it weren't always so tranquil. That might be just what done his daddy in according to S.C.. There never was nothing like the great storm of ..."

"All right," he interrupted me. "You got the job."

I was in hog heaven. I was so excited that I didn't even pick up on the fact that Amos Rusie was drunker than a skunk on a rope. On top of that, he was about deaf in one ear. Truth was that Rusie had asked "Who?" as soon as I started my story and dropped him the name of Tacks Latimer. For the first two years I worked at the Polo Grounds, that's who he thought I was, and it bothered him something fierce that I looked even younger than I had back in 1898. All that mattered to me, though, was that I was in the big leagues.

My immediate boss, the clubhouse man at the Polo Grounds was a dandy fellow named Fred Logan who was pretty much as old as Rusie. Big league jobs like that didn't come along too often, so when a fellow got one by the tail, he hung on like the dickens.

Old Fred loved to tell the story of how the great John Montgomery Ward had once tipped him a full fifteen cents to run down the street and grab him a roast beef sandwich. That meant that I was in touch with the very roots of professional baseball. Yes, sirree.

I settled into my job, and it wasn't a wink before I come to understand that big leaguers was nothing more than minor leaguers with a better eye. I worked for the Yankees when they was in town, and my beloved Giants the other half of the time, and I took note of the big surroundings most every day. I have always been a trusting soul, but I reckon those early days provided a leap in my life's education.

The old books will tell you that Miller Huggins stood about 5 foot six inches, but I'm here to tell you that is one piebald lie. He stood maybe a slug's hair taller than five foot, and weighed maybe a buck and a quarter. I could have wadded him up like a chewing gum wrapper. I don't know if that runtiness give him such a sour disposition, but on the best of days, you would've described him as businesslike.

The one thing about Huggins that there was no denying was that he was smart as a tack and twice as flat headed. He had studied law, from William Howard Taft, no less, and been a successful infielder who got by on wits and cajónes. He somehow understood what kind of a handful the Babe would be pretty much from the day he met him. He give him a lot of rope figuring a happy slugger was the best thing for the ball club, but just the same, he wasn't no fool, and that was where I come in. The day before the Bambino was due to come back in May 1922, Huggins motioned me aside and explained that he wanted me to kind of become the Babe's keeper for the rest of the season.

"Don't let on to him that I gave you an assignment," he told me. "Just behave like the big kid you are and tag along. Keep him out of trouble and report back to me."

I'd love to tell you that he said it with a smile, but I'm pretty sure Huggins wasn't familiar with that motion. If he'd have tried to grin, he'd have pulled enough muscles to land him on the disabled list.

I can't say I learned to like Huggins, but I reckon I learned to respect him. Every off season, the newspaper men would write about how Huggins was going to be given the heave ho, and every year he'd be back. For the most part, he got more out of a ballplayer than anyone. Except a smart hooker. I've seen them clean out a player till he squeaked.

Anyhoo, I took Huggins' instructions and started tagging around behind the Babe when I could. He got it in his head that I was there to run his errands and be his gopher, and after that, I was an accepted part of his world.

Chapter Nine

In spite of me getting to know the Yankees first, I don't want to neglect that I had plenty of friendships among some of the Giants. There was a passel of upstanding fellows on that squad.

It's tough to describe what I'm about to tell you. Just about all baseball had a real hard-bitten feel to it back then, but the Giants was particularly tough. I suppose they reflected their manager, McGraw. It's not that there was much of an age difference between the two ball clubs cause there wasn't, and as I just laid out, Miller Huggins, the Yankees manager sure was a far cry from Captain Kangaroo, but McGraw was just a particular kind of son of a bitch. I suppose it couldn't help but leak down among his charges.

If you believe in psychology even a little, it ain't hard to figure out the why of it all. McGraw's mama and three of his sisters died during an epidemic when he was but 12, and his lush of a daddy beat him so hard that the boy moved in with the widow woman across the street. Far as I can tell, nobody ever asked for him back. During his years in baseball, he scrapped, cheated, tripped, belittled, and did anything else that might give him an edge over the other guy. As one of his own coaches put it, "McGraw ate gunpowder for breakfast and washed it down with warm blood."

Boy, those Giants could hit. They had seven of the eight position starters who topped .300 that season. Seven of eight. Ain't that something? They were who I'd come to see, of course, and they were the ones who turned from idols to flesh and blood. Highpockets Kelly. Frankie Frisch. Dave Bancroft. Casey Stengel. It's an odd feeling to learn that your heroes are just men, but satisfying in a way.

Now Stengel, everybody knows that he was a character, all right. You know the sparrow in the cap story. I saw him pull that one more than once. It become one of his best gags, to tip his hat to the crowd and have a little birdie fly out.

Most folks don't recollect that he was a damned good player, too. He hit .368 for the Giants in 1922, mostly in the second half, and led the league in getting plunked by the ball in order to reach base. Course he was a part time outfielder by then, cursed by legs that stayed bunged up most of the time. Still, he was a showman, and easy enough to get along with.

Not long after I got settled in, a chance arose to see Shoeless Joe Jackson play baseball, though he wasn't shoeless at all. There was a promoter of semi-pro ball name of Eddie Phelan, and he wanted to start a team over in Brooklyn with Shoeless Joe and Buck Weaver at the heart of the lineup. He was drumming up publicity by touring Joe around upstate and over to New Jersey. Every place he went, he'd pass around a petition to get Jackson and Weaver reinstated in organized ball.

Well, me and Aaron Ward headed over to Hackensack with the word that Joe was to be playing. Wardy was from Arkansas just like me, and though he was a college boy, he sometimes lowered himself to pal around out of respect for the home state. Then again, it was only a Baptist college.

Joe Jackson wasn't as big as I was, but he was bigger than most. Had a sleek look about him, deep set eyes and a long nose like a greyhound. What struck me was how long his neck was. It give him an ostrich-like quality when he swung that black bat of his.

Shoeless Joe was 35 years old in 1922, but man alive, he could still hit. He swung the bat hard at a time when most were punchers. The Babe flat out said that he copied Jackson's swing. Even then, the world knew that Joe Jackson was what you'd call a superstar. That day was the only time I saw him play ball, and I classify that as a great shame.

I believe there is at least a scrap of good in every dog and most human beings, but every now and again, you run across one in which the positive part is buried too deep to make the looking worthwhile. One such person was Carl Mays. For several years after the Great War, there wasn't a pitcher in baseball not named Walter Johnson who was more effective than Carl Mays. You'd think that would make people happy to have him as a teammate, but I could name nary a soul who felt that way.

You probably know that it was Mays who killed a man pitching him up and in, but Mays was known for that. He hit more batters than anybody in the league most years. One game he threw at Ty Cobb every time the bastard come to the plate. Mays had thrown into the stands at spectators, and if any of his own fielders made an error, he would cuss them as loud as he could right there on the diamond. He had no friends nor was he looking to add any.

A few of the Yanks had warned me to keep my distance lest I get an ass-chewing of my own, and I tried to keep that in mind. My story telling about Shoeless Joe wasn't intended to have anything to do with Carl Mays, but he sure as hell made it his own.

The Yanks had the park this particular week, and during a rain delay, Aaron Ward was sitting on the stool in front of his locker and regaling the boys with his observations on Joe Jackson. I was standing off to the side punctuating things with regular "yeps" and perhaps a "That's the God's honest truth." I suppose I was pushing a little to be considered one of the guys.

When I got a chance to get a longer word in, something that didn't always come up in a baseball clubhouse, I jumped.

"Y'all knew all them Black Sox. Do you really think every one of them would throw a World Series like that, even for money?"

Well, sir, Carl Mays, who per usual wasn't seeming to pay anyone a lick of attention, come up off his stool so fast that it shot into two others like a durned jet-powered bowling ball.

"You fucking half-wit shitbag!" he screamed at me with his right arm pulled back and balled up. "You shut your goddamned mouth talking about things you don't know. Every one of you bastards. I'll pop any one of you like a goddamned flea."

He was all red around the edges, and that sure didn't help to make his natural sneer any more attractive. The fellows who'd been listening just all sat there for a stunned minute. Finally Frank Baker said, "Crawl back under your rock, Mays." After a parting epithet or two, Mays stomped off.

The sore spot, I come to find out was that a whole passel of folks suspected that Mays had took money to throw a World Series game or two himself just the previous October. Captain Huston even said as much to the press, by golly. I reckon if you don't have any friends, it's nigh impossible to sell them out.

Huggins tried to trade Mays a few times, but couldn't find any takers. Eventually they sold him off to Cincinnati. You know, it may have been that getting threatened by that son of a bitch is what made some of the fellows start to accept me. I guess a little good comes from all things, don't it?

I've been talking mostly about the Yankees so far, I reckon. Most of the Giants players did me right, though. In fact, I even met a young lady soon after I arrived there thanks to Pep Youngs. Him and Pancho Snyder had both come from San Antonio. A nice town. And a girl third cousin of his had just arrived in New York to become an actress. Pep's Aunt Marie had told her to make sure she looked up her famous kinfolk so he could grease the skids. On the day she hit the Big Apple, though, it was an off day, and Pep was scheduled to play golf. He was a mighty serious golfer, you know, so he asked me to keep an eye on her since I was right near the same age.

Her name was Christine MacCamie, and even though she was from South Texas, she was as alabaster as a mime in milk. It was as if the hot sun had shone on every Texan but her. She had long, straight, shiny blonde hair and the kind of pouty mouth that would make your toes curl. Her voice was sweet as a songbird but still managed to bare a hint of a sultry growl. In short, there wasn't a man in New York that wouldn't have drunk her bathwater.

I think most men tend to think of young blondes as a little naïve and virginal while a darker hued girl might have found her way around the block once or twice. It's stupid as hell, really, but looking back on it I see that it was that way for me. Christine was likely the first blonde that opened my eyes to the error of those thoughts, a learning moment which you might say was a step from boy to grown up. Hard to pinpoint what made me take notice. It might have been the mischief in her blue eyes, or something fascinating in the depth of her dinner conversation, or it might have been when she went down on me in the back of that taxicab. Tough to say.

Nothing long term came from our dating, but it did allow me to meet the fellow who became one of the best buddies I ever had. Long about the time that I started getting attached to the fair Christine, things come to an abrupt termination. One day I was meeting her at a little plain door saloon following the ball game. It was one of those prohibition joints where anybody could knock on the door and get a drink as long as you weren't the chief of police. He had his own joint.

Well, as soon as I cleared the front door, I spotted this curly looking little fellow just a-chatting up Christine to beat the band. He was working it hard, leaning into her, elbowing other would be suitors out of the way like a big power forward protecting the lane. Instantly, I got it in my head that I needed to come down hard and protect my claim. I made a beeline for the little worm with one thing on my mind, marking my territory.

Now, in case you didn't know it, doing something like this in front of a sophisticated young woman can be a delicate operation. Sure, there are some who get a thrill from seeing their boyfriend haul off and punch some fellow for no good reason, but the better women don't go for that. They know that some ill-tempered barroom brute is liable to turn out to be less than a bargain in the long run. So, you have to be a mite subtle.

I slipped my arm around Christine's waist and pulled her close for a smooch.

"Hi, honey. Sorry I'm late," I said extra loud so that any guy within ear shot could see what's what. Then I give a quick shot of the stink eye at the curly haired fellow.

Christine kissed me light, one of those half mouth and half cheek sort of affairs, then she wriggled a little daylight between us. She passed an aw shucks look at all the men folk, and most of them slinked away, but the curly headed one stepped right up and stuck out his hand.

"Chrissy said she was waiting on her beau. Nice to meet you. I'm Paul Flinkenberg."

He seemed like a real stand up sort of person, and that'll take the puff right out of your chest when it comes to marking territory. He was from Lafayette, Indiana and had been in New York only a few months longer than I had, but things were going great guns. He had just gotten divorced back home, and was now finding his fortune as a baggage man for the new United States Lines, a steamship company. They operated big ocean liners that went back and forth to Europe. To make the acquaintance of some fellow sending luggage on important journeys like that, well, whatever lingering pangs of jealousy I might be harboring jumped right out that barroom window. Not that the joint had windows, you understand.

We played us some billiards, bought each other nickel beers and swapped stories for the rest of the night. At some point along the way, the fair Christine turned her attention to one of the bartenders, the same chap she left me for about three weeks later. But by the time we said our goodnights, Paul and me were fast friends.

You ever have a girl step out on you? I guess we all have. I'd have to say that some instances are more painful than others. You see, life has a lot of moving parts, and I suppose that in the summer of 1922, things were going too good for me to get down on account of some girl, no matter how winsome, shapely and obliging she might be. It never occurred to me that there wasn't another one even better who was just fixing to step around the corner.

Tough to say how long it took me to figure out about Christine and that bar keep. Being a first timer to the cuckold game, I wasn't as attuned to those non-answers that you get to your questions. After you've been through it a few times, those little things stand out like a hairy ballerina.

"Hi, honey," you say when you finally get her on the telephone. "I come by to pick you up at 8 like we planned, but you wasn't there. Where were you?"

"Oh, posh. Why would you ask that?"

After about three weeks of me thinking things were hunky-dory, we was getting all cuddly when I picked up a strong smell of cigar on one of her negligees. Now, I might not be the quickest fellow on the uptake, but I knew I didn't smoke. I also knew that actress or not, a woman didn't wear a see-through kimono to a speakeasy in 1922.

Christine fessed right up.

"Sweetie," she said, stroking me on the cheek. "I guess this new fellow has plumb turned my head. I'm really sorry. But we did have some fun, didn't we?"

It's one thing to forgive a girl for a little lapse in judgment. But when they're lapsing six or seven times a week, and bright-eyed about it, it's definitely time to move on.

After a going away romp, I started walking back to the ball park, and damned if I didn't see Paul Flinkenberg heading into that same bar where I'd met him before. Turns out that on top of being a good story teller, he also knew how to help a fellow cry in his beer.

I should mention that we were knocking back real honest to God brew, too. During Prohibition, all the breweries started making near beer with less than one percent alcohol. Miller had Vivo, and Schlitz had Fame-O. There was Juvo and Luxo, Pabst made Pablo, which was not a Mexican beer, and the Budweiser folks make Bevo. I reckon they all ended with that letter cause after one sip, you said "Oh, shit, this ain't real beer." What's the point in getting all the peeing, bloating and farting but none of the buzz?

That night was good, though. Within two hours, I was laughing tears at a story of his younger brother, a lad of about 15, getting caught by the game warden with a backpack full of drunk possums. See, he'd a hidden a quart of shine in the compost pile out to their rear of their property, but before he could get back to drinking it, an extended family of possums got into it. The critters was soon so high that they thought they was squirrels. A whole pack of them, must've been nigh on two dozen, commenced to chasing each other through the trees, playful as all get out. When they got winded, they took to eating acorns, eventually nodding off on the branches and then dropping out of the trees like overripe kumquats. Oh, me.

Paul's brother gathered them all up, every last one, and stuffed them into the Boy Scouts of America knapsack he carried with him. He headed back up to the house to start dispatching the critters with an eye toward possum stew. Well, he hadn't like to made it more than 100 yards when he caught a glimpse of the county game warden heading down the path his way.

In a flash, things started occurring to the boy. He wasn't sure whether there was a season on possums in Indiana or not, but he reckoned getting them liquored up was not likely to be a legal hunting technique. So, Paul's brother ripped off his backpack and flung it up over his head, lodging it in a tree.

The game warden wandered right up to him.

"How you faring, young Master Flinkenberg?" he asked.

"Fair to middling, sir."

"What are you up to out in the woods?"

"Um. Hunting, sir."

The game warden rubbed his chin.

"You don't have a gun, son."

"Ah. Well, that's why I was heading back to the house."

By that point, the possums had wriggled around enough to loosen up the string on the backpack, and I'll be damned if one of them didn't fall from the sky with a pronounced plop. The game warden jumped a mite and looked over to see a possum slowly staggering away. He looked back at Paul's brother all big-eyed.

Plunk. Here come another one. The game warden was slack jawed while the young feller just stared past him into the trees, refusing to make eye contact.

Plinkety plunk plop plop. The bag was open and slaphappy possums took to falling everywhere. Likely wearing paper hats and singing sea shanties, they was. Finally, a particularly husky one landed smack on the game warden's noggin, knocking his cap askew. Paul's little brother looked at him for a beat then finally opened his mouth.

"I don't know about you, mister, but if it's going to keep raining drunk possums, I'm a mind to head back to the house for a slicker or an umbersol."

Oh, me, but if that don't make me laugh to this day. Paul's brother come to a tragic finish about a decade after that. Met his demise when he farted on a heating pad. Now, now. Don't fret. They are perfectly safe nowadays, but this was an older model. Powered by coal. Boom. They never found nothing but feet and a hat.

Chapter Ten

There wasn't much time to stew over lost love anyhow. Less than a month later, the Polo Grounds was once again the center of the universe. The Giants had been the class of the league for some time, and they wrapped up the pennant with a week to spare, but the Yanks was in a tooth and nail two-team race with the St. Louis Browns. Those guys had six fellows top .300, and one of them, George Sisler, posted .420.

The guy who was catching everybody's eye that year was a gawky, scarecrow-looking outfielder name of Ken Williams. When he stood on the top dugout step, he looked like a meerkat in a flannel jersey. He put up more home runs and RBIs than the Babe did that year, though he had him a six-week head start thanks to Buttocks Landis. Hell, Williams knocked three dingers in one game that year, something nobody in the league had ever done before. But the one thing the Brownies couldn't do that season was beat the Yankees.

They come close. Because St. Louis was such a long train ride, they spent either a long time at home or a long time on the road, and that September they had the whole month in their own ball park. We went in there at the middle of it with only a half-game lead, and things got ugly. It also happened to be one of the trips where it was my turn to travel with the team. I was pumped.

They had the biggest crowds of the year, standing in roped off sections of the outfield and mighty rowdy. Whitey Witt got knocked plumb out by a beer bottle in the first game. We took that first one anyhow, then they took the second, so we knew that next one could make or break us.

Now, Williams used a heavy bat. Forty-eight ounces. To look at him, you wondered how he could even lift the durn thing. He was like a six-foot ant.

The Babe come to me in the sixth inning that day with us down a run.

"Kid," he says. "We can't let that stringbean beat us. You got to switch out his lumber. Give me the high sign, and I'll distract him."

I run back into the clubhouse to come up with a plan. See, I had never been much of a jokester back in Lee County, more of the jokee, but I had learned the trade some at Memphis. The way I was looking at things, the Babe was calling on me to maybe save the season.

The clubhouse in St. Louis was pretty much like all of those first concrete parks, bare cement walls, open lockers, the pipes for the showers hanging from the ceiling. I was looking everywhere for something to change Williams' bat, and I might not have thought of the lead pipe at all if I hadn't hit my head on it when I fell off the top of a locker chasing a rat.

I grabbed the hacksaw that Bob Shawkey used to trim his corns, and cut off a piece of pipe about six inches long then split it lengthwise. Then I signaled the Babe and waited for my shot.

In the seventh, Williams doubled and Baby Doll Jacobson, so named for a little teddy he liked to wear next to his sanitaries, sacrificed him to third. That's when the Babe started stripping like a hoochie coochie dancer out in left. Well, sir, when he started flipping his undershirt at some chippie over the ropes, every eyeball in Sportsman's Park was on him. Not a soul noticed when I screwed that lead pipe over the barrel of Ken Williams' bat. When he come around to score right after that, the Browns were celebrating too hard to think about any hijinks.

As luck would have it, we put up a tally in the eighth, and then who but Whitey Witt knocked in two in the ninth. That one was a big surprise after he'd took a Budweiser to the forehead on Saturday. Everybody on the Yankees figured he'd be seeing double, and we couldn't believe Huggins had him in the lineup. Then again, the Babe had hit plenty of times when he was seeing double, so why not?

Sisler was the lead-off hitter in the ninth, and he was looking at his last chance to keep the longest hit streak in American League history alive. No lie. He had reached 41 straight games the day prior. Bullet Joe Bush got him out, and that brought up Williams.

You could see it on his face that something didn't feel right, but he couldn't put his finger on it. He had his head cocked, and he was waggling that bat looking all perplexed. One of the rookies on their bench even yelled to him that he had a piece of lead pipe stuck to his bat, but Williams just hollered "Shut up, Busher" and kept on hacking.

In the end, Bush got Williams, too, and we hung on for a 3-2 win. Everybody in baseball knew the Brownies was through after that day. When we all got back and found eight inches of water in the visitors' clubhouse, I was afraid the shit was fixing to hit the fan. Luckily someone had unplugged the fan on account of the water. Huggins was still plenty mad, though. For some reason, he blamed Lefty O'Doul who hadn't left the bench the whole series, and four days later, O'Doul became the player to be named later in the Joe Dugan trade.

I felt bad about it, but years later, when O'Doul found out what happened, he thanked me for sending him down the path he got. I drank free at his place in San Francisco for three decades.

Though 1922 was my first time to travel with a whole ball club, I got into the swing of things pretty quick. There was a lot of time to kill. Ballplayers did the same things as most people. Card games. Drinking. Eating. Knife fights. Reading the paper. I think story telling was really the biggest pastime for the boys.

Guys would lounge around the hotel lobby or huddle in the aisle of the Pullman, and over the run of a season, you were likely to have heard most every detail of each other's lives, I'll tell you that. From your first girlfriend to your last bowel movement. It was like living in an old folk's home.

The beauty of swapping tales is that the lowliest rookie was on par with the biggest star if he had the gift of gab. And that went for third assistant clubhouse men like me, too.

One of my best, or at least most effective, was the story about Tex James' worst trip to the privy. See, old Tex was a neighbor of ours back in Lee County. Veteran of the Mexican War. North of eighty years old when I knew him, but still shuffling around. He had long since leased his field to a tenant, but Tex still kept him a little garden patch with beets in the summer and chicory in the fall. Always had him a tangle of melons or squash out there, too, and Tex had to shuffle out through his vegetable patch to get to his outhouse.

On the night in question, old Tex was roused out of bed around two in the morning by a powerful need to pee and likely more. Son, a young man would've just had a squirt off the porch, but at his age, and I know this first hand now, you always got to be prepared for a little extra. Hell, at eighty-some odd years old, I reckon his prostate was the size of them Crenshaws he had growing behind the house. So, Tex stumbles through the garden patch, cussing every pebble, bur and bramble between the back door and the one-holer.

He swings open the door, and it's blacker than a miner's lung in there, but Tex backs onto the seat and sure enough, he barely made it. No sooner had the dam opened than a wolf spider the size your hand sank his teeth into the middle of old Tex's ball sack.

Look at it from the spider's point of view. He'd found him a likely spot to catch a juicy moth, and some ingrate firebombs his nest with semi-digested melon and God knows what kind of old man bits that Tex had been storing up in his intestine. You'd bite the shit out of whoever unleashed that hell your damn self.

Well, sir, Tex jumped higher than he had in decades, banged his head on the outhouse wall, and knocked himself colder than a wedge. That's where the sharecropper found him at daybreak, half in and half out of the johnny, face down in the dirt with his nightshirt pulled up under his arms and a bright red scrotum that had swelled up bigger than a nutria rat. He slowly come to, and after a month or so, his plums had shrunk back to normal, but that there was a cautionary tale for every young boy in northeastern Arkansas, I tell you what.

Now, like I said, that was one of my more popular yarns to spin with the boys. They'd request it, just like Yankee Doodle Dandy, but there was one of the Yankees who really took that tale to heart.

Froggy Lippincott his name was, a shavetail little catcher from Staunton, Illinois. Didn't hang around long on account of my story about old Tex James ruined his career. For the first two nights after he heard it, Froggy couldn't sleep at all. Afraid of nightmares. Finally, Chick Fewster, who was rooming with the kid, came back with a sawed-off garden hoe and told Froggy to rattle it around the hotel toilet before he sat down. It seemed to ease the boy's mind until he stepped on the upturned hoe head in the middle of the night and popped himself right in the cods. He swelled up just like old Tex. Sort of a self-fulfilling prophecy. Needless to say, squatting behind the plate was out for a day or two. After the fourth time it happened, Froggy Lippincott had to quit baseball entirely. Last I heard he was singing operetta in Montana. Shame.

You know the Babe sometimes kept a hoe in the bathroom, but she never caused him no trouble.

Captain Huston, the other owner of the Yankees in them days was a bit of a drinker himself, and it wasn't infrequent that he'd take the Babe out on the town. The Captain and Colonel Rupert didn't much get along. One big bone of contention was Huggins. The Colonel had hired him against every objection Captain Huston could throw at him. They weren't the best of friends previous to that, but it was sure a downhill road after.

That always struck me odd how two people who didn't even like each other thought it was a good idea to go into business together. I reckon it happens all the time, but it plumb contradicts common sense, if you ask me.

There was a lumber mill east of Lexa, a fair piece south of where I grew up, and these two old boys had started it together back 30 or more years before I ever come into the world. Barton and Moore were their names. According to the local lore, their daddies had been rivals for the same woman back in the day, a thick waisted redhead with a face full of freckles and one milky eye. She didn't marry either one of them, but the bad blood persisted.

In spite of that, the two gents, who lived in neighboring farms along about where Crooked and Lick Creeks met, decided to partner up in this mill. They took out bank loans together, ordered a big saw blade from Pine Bluff, and built the place with their own four hands. The arguing started almost from the get go. Old Mr. Moore was a short fellow who was balder than a lightning-struck knob. He was quick with a wisecrack, but was also convinced that he held two thirds of the world's knowledge, and was a fast draw on the advice. Jakey Barton was the nicer of the two despite having a mouth that was in a permanent pinch.

Old Jakey was building the mill wheel to fit below the headrace while Charlie Moore was trying to line up the drive machinery. When it come time to marry the two assemblies together, there was a warp. It wouldn't turn true. My daddy, who was a youngster at the time, told me that many of the colorful additions to the vocabulary of the area boys come from observing the construction of the Barton and Moore Sawmill. Some days there was fisticuffs, often a piece of iron got winged from one towards the other, and always there was yelling.

Eventually, everything got adjusted. Well, at least the machinery did. The sawmill was still making boards and money when I was a kid, and the two owners were both there to serve your needs six days a week, but they had not spoken to one another for over two decades.

Jakey Barton was a morning person, I suspect. He got there with the roosters, and the first thing he done, every single day, was pick up Charley Moore's coffee cup from a little square table next to the cold potbellied stove, and wipe his pizzle all the way around the rim. Some mornings, when he was particularly annoyed, he'd rub that little sucker around twice. We boys never tired of laughing at the notion that Old Mr. Charley had been drinking dick coffee since the 1880s and was none the wiser.

You know how kids keep a secret, though. One day, word of the ongoing practice reached back to Charley Moore. Without a mention, he went out into the woods and grabbed up a handful of poison sumac leaves. That Friday night, wearing his work gloves, Charley went back to the mill, crushed those red-stemmed devils and rubbed the oil all around the edge of his own coffee cup. Saturday morning, Charley said his stomach was queasy, and he decided against any coffee. By Sunday, Jakey Barton could barely sit in a church pew, and he limped gingerly two miles to the mill each morning, and two miles home, for more than a month, foregoing the mule he normally rode. For his part, Charley Moore bought a shiny new, blue spotted enamelware mug.

Anytime I heard about Colonel Rupert and Captain Huston, it brought to mind Barton and Moore. I never got invited to the owners' office for a hot beverage, but believe you me, I had a whole satchel full of excuses why I'd have to decline.

As described, I went to my first World Series in 1922, though I guess "went" ain't the right word at all. Once again, the entire thing was played in the Polo Grounds. I didn't even need to leave the building where I slept.

It was a one-sided Series that year. The Giants topped the Yanks four games to none, but there was also a tie in Game Two. Irish Meusel, Silent Bob's brother and fellow left-fielder, banged a three-run bomb in the top of the first. In case you was wondering, it alternated game to game who got to be the home team. The Yankees chipped away and after 10 innings, things was tied at three. George Hildebrand was the plate umpire, and he walked out and called the game on account of darkness. Hildebrand umpired for better than 20 seasons, but it wasn't always smooth sailing. He once got his ass kicked nine ways to Sunday by a manager out in California. I don't know what bone headed hijinks brought that one on, but in October of 1922, it was a bunch of bull dookey.

When Hildebrand called the game, I could still see through a lady's night shirt in a window on St. Nicholas Avenue. It wasn't yet dark, and the fans, over 37,000 of them, kicked up such a ruckus, hollering at anyone who looked the tiniest bit official, that Buttocks Landis announced they would give all the gate money to charity. Whether the money ever got to widows and orphans, well, I couldn't swear to it.

Of course, I didn't miss a twitch, spit or scratch of that Series, it being my first. It was also the only time that I could honestly say that I was personally acquainted with every player on both sides of a World Series. You think about that for a minute.

Frankie Frisch and Heinie Groh each hit the ball good. You know anything about Heinie Groh, young man? Well, you ought to. He was one of the best third basemen ever played the game. If they'd had them back then, his house would've been full of Gold Gloves and All Star Game jerseys. He was a little fellow, like Jose Altuve, and you had to love him. His hands wasn't big enough for a thick handle, so he went to Spalding's store and they come up with a bat that looked like a milk bottle. Big at one end and then lathed down at the other. Naturally, that got the balance off, but he choked up with the best of them. Durnedest thing you ever saw, but it worked.

He was little, but he had muscles like steel. He wasn't afraid to take a ground ball hop off his chest, neither, but a man that size had no chance when the Babe steamrolled right over him at third base. See Ruth's bat had been quieter than a flea humping a hippo that Series. He only managed two piss ant little hits, so he was frustrated. The basepaths were unfamiliar, but still, he blasted into third base standing up and sent Heinie sprawling one way and his cap hanging up in the air like a damn Roadrunner cartoon.

"Kid, the basepath is half mine," Babe tells Heinie as he was dusting himself off.

The fans were on the verge of riot. As much as they liked seeing the Sultan swat the long ball, their memories were short, and the fact of it is that his power numbers was barely half of what they had been the year before. On top of that, he'd missed a month with the suspension, and I'd say there were two Giants fans for every Yankees fan in New York. If Ruth hadn't have been out, we might have had real trouble that day.

Chapter Eleven

With the baseball season ended, and me no longer detailed to watch the Babe whet his appetites, I was faced with a first. Up till that time, I don't guess I'd ever been in a situation of being so completely on my own. With no games, the Giants cut my pay in half. They let me keep my room at the ball yard, though, so I had a few coins to rub together more often than not.

The only real duties I had were chasing trespassing kids out of the place, keeping the rodent population low and seeing that trash didn't blow onto the concourse. The front office people, such as they were, supposedly worked year round, but I can promise you that nobody paid much attention if and when I sneaked out of my little cubby hole under the bleachers.

I had always had dogs back on the farm, and I took the opportunity to adopt a stray terrier. Little brown and white fellow. Him and me stayed together for over a decade. Slept with me every night except when they had me out on the road. Many is the time that I lay awake with a foot cramp because I didn't want to disturb that pooch.

My first big adventure that winter come in mid-October, just a few days after the Series. Paul Flinkenberg left a message at the ball park asking if I wanted to go to Coney Island. I jumped at the chance, even though I wasn't entirely sure what I was signing on for. The subway had just hooked up Coney Island to the rest of the city a few months prior. When we got there, it was a bit of a construction zone. They were still building the boardwalk. A year later, they widened the streets around there and knocked a couple of hundred buildings flatter than Mia Farrow. In spite of all that, it was spectacular.

It was the first time I'd ever seen the ocean. Now that might not sound like much to you, if you grew up by the water, but it sure was something to me. I'd seen Lake Michigan, and that was no doubt remarkable, but at Coney Island there were real waves, breathtaking brown water rolling up onto the tan beach with bubbly beige foam. It all makes you feel kind of small and insignificant. I stood there staring at the horizon and wondering if there was somebody like me looking back from a thousand miles away. Nature has a way of choking you up when you see a little piece of turd wash up, and you say to yourself, "Gee, that could've come from France."

Coney Island was something else in 1922, even though the summer season had ended. Most of the big attractions was still open, just on a shorter schedule. There was a big long pier off Surf Avenue, and we rode the roller coaster, explored the parks, ate the hot dogs, and wasted the proper amount of time so's that our money would last. That wasn't the half of it, though. Once the sun dropped over behind the buildings, there was lights to amaze the eye. There was fun to be had in the daytime, but it was most assuredly one of them places that was truly magical after dark.

Dusk had found us at Steeplechase Park. It was a humdinger, and, when I spotted the midway, I figured I had found the key to maximizing Coney Island. Having my baseball background, I figured I would be a natural at knocking over little milk bottles and winning kewpie dolls to hand out to all the pretty ladies, but try as I might, there was one stubborn little fellow that refused to fall over. Right as my frustration was a-bubbling to its high point, and I was grumbling toward Paul, a short, little man stepped up behind me and whispered, "Save your money. It's nailed down."

"Scuse me?" I said, turning around.

"Shh. Shh. Hold it down," the fellow muttered, and he motioned me and Paul over to a break in the booths.

"You two seem like mensches," The man said.

"Scuse me?" I was starting to repeat myself.

"Regular fellows. Working men," he said. "I hate to see you losing your last few shekels on a rigged come-on when you could use them buying your new friend an egg cream."

It turns out that he had overheard me and Paul Flinkenberg talking about the Yankees in a way that made him curious. He was a ball fan whose cousin, a kid name of Heinie Scheer, had just come up with the Athletics. More than that, he was Jewish and eyeballed Paul as one of his own. Put it all together, and he figured we should be pals. Simple as you please.

Our new found friend was named Izzy Levy, and boy, he had done it all. Loaded folks onto the Wonder Wheel, been a horse puller for the steeplechase ride and wrangled the midget clowns at the Insanitarium. When Paul and I met him, Izzy was working as the hoser at the Dew Drop Slide. We found out Izzy was making $5.50 a week and had been employed at the Steeplechase since he was 10 years old. As much as he might envy my job with the ball clubs, I was a little jealous of a life as exciting as his. Once we got to know him, Coney Island become a regular stop of ours, and at a steep discount.

That next one was a big year for me. I went in to it by having to choose between the Polo Grounds and the Giants or going to work for the Yankees. The more Babe Ruth got famous, the more the Yanks felt like they ought to have their own ball yard where they could keep all the money, and 1923 was when their golden dream was finally going to come true. After a year of working for both clubs, for me, it meant picking one or the other.

I suppose we make choices from the time you first get a chance to crawl off with your brother's cookie, but this was the earliest I recollect a decision being hard. All the ones that come before had felt good. This one was going to feel bad on one side or the other. Looking back, it was the first time I was really called on to think like a grown up.

I wasn't sure I liked being a grown up much, and I made my choice with pure kid-like reasoning as opposed to any adult analysis. I flipped a coin. Yes, sir. I had agonized over it till I felt like I was going to yank out my nose hair and throw up my breakfast, and every time I thought I had more plusses on one side of the ledger, I'd think of something new. So, I pulled out an Indian head nickel, made a pinky swear between my right hand and my left hand, promised to stick to the results and tossed that sucker in the air. When I pulled my hand away, it was tails, and I was a New York Yankee.

I'd made my decision to leave my boyhood idols behind, and though it would still pass through my mind once in a while, it didn't weigh on me. The Polo Grounds grandstand was getting expanded, but the Yankees was finishing up a whole new cavern of a ballpark, and I faced an offseason picking up bent nails. I had hit the big leagues.

In such a fancy ball yard as Yankee Stadium, you'd have thunk that there would be plenty of cubby holes where the club wouldn't mind me staying, but they didn't look at it that way. I was obliged to find myself a place to live again. I scouted around for a house similar to the one where I stayed in Memphis. It was nice having the ladies nearby, but no luck.

What I did find was a room in a boarding house that was pure-D New York, as far as I was concerned. It was a fourth-floor walkup on the alley side of an old tenement building near 187th and Lorillard Place. The manager and super of the joint was a friendly little Italian fellow name of Bingo Tavarozzi. His given name had a few more g's and n's in there, I think, but Bingo made him just as happy. The three things I recollect most about him was that he was a great cook, had more back hair than a yeti, and loved baseball enough to knock three dollars off of my weekly rent.

I had come to enjoy the Italians a good deal. Italian women were generally quite the eyeful, though getting past their brothers was a gauntlet. I already mentioned the best thing: the food. Not only was it delicious, but good damn luck walking past an Italian's apartment flat without someone shoving a forkful of something in your mouth. Seeing as how I was a big and maybe-still-growing boy, it was a match made in belly heaven.

I know I'm spending a lot of time on my first couple of years in New York, but son, they held so many new experiences for me. While I was living in Memphis, I suspected I was a man of the world, but I learned different. The first time I took a bite of Bingo Tavarozzi's lasagna, streetlamps in my brain lit up for the first time ever. The sausage was just shy of the Estill's, but it was held close in the arms of this soft cheese, like nothing that had crossed my tongue before. With the tomato and red pepper flavors, that pasta that I'd come to appreciate and stringy mozzarella on top, whoo, boy. It also opened my eyes to the notion that men could cook, too. Yes, sir. It's a big world out there.

Miller Huggins asked me to continue keeping a little bit of an eye on the Babe from time to time, so I found myself still being the occasional tag-a-long to the Bambino. The first road trip we went on was up to Plymouth, New Hampshire in late January to get the Babe fitted with a new Lucky Dog glove. Most of the big leaguers was using them back at that time, and the Babe was still big stuff in New England. His off season home was up there, and all those Red Sox fans both loved him and hated him at the same time. Within the same block, you'd get both cussed and have the skin worn off your hand from folks shaking it.

The Lucky Dog mitts had a little picture of a hunting dog on it, and that appealed to both me and the Babe. The folks that made them claimed to use elk skin, and that sounded damn exotic, me being just an Arkansas boy. I reckon they had elks in New Hampshire. If we was required to use local leather back home, everybody'd be wearing a possum skin glove. Though it would come with its own pocket already broke in.

Not only did the Babe get him a few new gloves on that journey, but he ended up with an endorsement deal. They paid him a few bucks to slap his signature on an official Babe Ruth model that would become the envy of youths across America. The boss man took note of me, too, and bestowed upon yours truly an Ivy Wingo Lucky Dog catcher's mitt, one of their newest offerings. I started explaining how we wasn't real sure of how me and Ivy was kin, but before I could get to the good part, the Babe decided it was time to explore the crowd of women that had formed outside. I held on to that Wingo mitt for many years.

As the calendar rolled round to spring training, I figured I'd be able to rest up at my place in the Bronx and get ready for the season, but at the last minute, Huggins pulled me aside one day while I was loading duffle bags with sanitary socks and told me I was coming with the team to New Orleans. That was exciting news.

The ball park down there was Pelican Field, and that pleased me to no end. I've always been a big fan of pelicans, you know. Noble bird right there. They soar low over wavetops like an airplane glider, and hold a whole sack full of fish in that pouch of theirs. Yes, sir. Noble bird.

We were staying at the Grunwald Hotel which later became the Roosevelt. No sooner than the train had arrived at the depot, but everybody associated with the team, meaning players, executives, lowly clubhouse and equipment men, dropped their portmanteaus in the room and scurried across Canal Street to shoe leather the French Quarter. It was a warm, muggy day as I recall. Not raining, but moisture seeping up through the pavement to make the streets wet just the same.

Those old bars all had their shutter doors wide open, and the chatter of drinkers and the smell of spilled beer wafted onto the banquettes. Still lots of horse drawn conveyances about the narrow streets, and an uncommon number of nuns all got up in their penguin suits. I wouldn't want to live there, I don't think, but New Orleans can't be beat when you got nothing to do but drink, eat, and ogle.

It was different in the 1920s than what you'd see today, I reckon, and yet it was the same. That feeling of faded glory, but more so. Same buildings, though lots of them were subdivided into little apartments. Sicilians lived in most of them. You'd hear Italian and French as much as English, and you couldn't help but smell good sausage cooking. Another smell you couldn't get away from was bananas. They were hanging every which way you looked. At a place on Jackson Square called Billy Cabildo, they gave you a five course meal for 50 cents, and a bunch of the guys paid another 50 cents to get a quick shag in the bushes from some of the street girls. That's if they didn't feel like walking a few blocks more down to

Storyville which might not have been as wide open as it had been, but was still more than a going concern.

That's where I went off to, of course. Storyville. It reminded me of Memphis. Not for the vamps, but for the music. On Beale Street and in Chicago, Herbie and me had listened to them traveling jazz men go on about the best players in the world being from down there, so I sure was not of a mind to miss my chance to hear them.

Big Eye Nelson was a clarinet man who had got drunk with us between his sets in Memphis one night, and he said the place to go if I ever made New Orleans was the Big 25. Son, he was durn tootin'. I'll be damned if he wasn't one of the fellows blowing there that night. John Robichaux. Albert Glenny on the double bass. Big Eye played with a blues style. One of my favorites of his was "Clarinet Marmalade." And I got introduced to "Eh, la Bas" that night. That's a tune right there. I went back to the Big 25 every night I had in New Orleans that spring, sat and toe-tapped and slurped down illegal Jax Beer. I listened to them folks prattle on in French, not knowing a word they said, but boy that's as much fun as can be had.

Though a handful of the Yankees might have shared my taste in music, nobody went with me to the Big 25. Biggest doings was when three of the boys happened upon a voodoo shop over on Ursuline Street. Hoyt, Joe Dugan, and a rookie outfielder up from the Galveston Sand Crabs named Harvey Hendrick. Nickname of Gink.

Hoyt and Dugan each bought them a gris-gris bag that was supposed to increase their athletic powers. Dugan also picked up some St. John the Conqueror oil that, when you dropped a dash below your belly button, was supposed to make the ladies swoon with uncontrolled passion. Dugan needed the help.

The trouble come with Gink. The fellows thought he decided not to buy anything, but when they got back to the hotel rooms, Gink produced a mojo from his pocket and told Hoyt and Dugan that he swiped it.

"What the living shit were you thinking!" Dugan started just screaming at the kid.

"I figured if I stole it, it would make the magic more powerful."

"You simpering dumbass, you don't jack around with voodoo! Now get out of my room."

Sure enough, Dugan was right. Gink had done brought down a whole barrel of shit on his head. He had started out the spring pretty good, but after that morning, he didn't smell another hit for three days. On the fourth day, he pulled a hamstring so bad he could barely walk. The club sent him packing, but before he could get to the train station, his suitcase fell off the Canal Street car, caught a spark from the overhead wires and busted into flames. When he tried to pat it out, his coat sleeve combusted, then his straw boater. Last anyone with the Yankees heard of him, he was limping down Basin Street, hatless in a one-sleeved sport jacket, muttering to himself loud enough that folks was tossing him spare change. No, sir. You don't jack with voodoo.

There was also a Norwegian kid trying to make the club that year by the name of Oswald Loogevall. He was tall and skinny, I guess the popular word is lanky. He had an unruly shock of blond hair and a nose that made him look like a hawk who just caught a big whiff of bad cheese. He was a shineball pitcher who had spent some time in the Western League with the Sioux City Packers before he found his way to our spring training.

Now alcohol is a funny thing. I like a good drink now and again, still. Lord a 'mighty, I'm probably past the centennial of my first cocktail. Had a couple of glasses of hooch last night while I dozed in front of my programs on the TV, but some fellows just don't mix well with it.

Most of the time, when you hear that so-and-so gave up the sauce, you wonder what took them so damned long. There's a whole mess of mean drunks out there. Then there's others who start having such a good time that they sort of borrow everybody else's fun, and I think Loogie fell into that category. From the first impression, you knew that he was a fellow familiar with the feel of cold porcelain. I sure as hell know he funned himself off the Yankees during spring training of 1923.

The first day he showed up, a couple of the boys give him an invite to hit a bar or two after practice.

Loogie shook his head, cast his eyes down and said, "Aw, fellas, I appreciate it, but I can't drink. I get like a wild Indian."

Well, I didn't know any wild Indians, but I'd heard tales of my great-grandfather, William Flying Pants, and how he could outdrink any man in Lee County. Course, you're always told that Indians can't handle their liquor. Makes them crazy. Fire water and all that. But I'd never seen it happen, certainly not with a Norwegian.

To a ballplayer in those days, hearing a rookie say he didn't want to go drinking with them was about the worst thing that could have happened. They bodily picked the boy up and hauled him to the closest hooch parlor.

As our time in New Orleans went on, Loogie kept staying out later every night, drinking more and more, and having a much better time than the rest of the team by the looks of it. Even Meusel and the Babe would give up and go back to the hotel leaving the kid singing these God awful Norwegian folk songs to some poor, captive bartender.

The most amazing, or embarrassing, night for Loogie come when a split squad of Yanks went down to Houma, Louisiana to get some playing time in against a local semi-pro team of shrimpers and crawfish men. I went along myself to handle the equipment. Truth be told, I asked for the job on account of me thinking that the crawfish men was akin to mermaids, and I sure as hell wanted to get a glimpse of that, boy. It served to be a mite disappointing, though their left fielder did have one hand that was noticeably bigger than the other.

Back then, spring training was mostly just done amongst your teammates. Any games played was against the local minor league outfit. That year, our regulars were scrapping against the New Orleans Pelicans every afternoon, so Huggins arranged for the scrubs to go scrimmage down at Houma for a couple of days. We piled into three touring cars that the ball club hired, a Mercer, a Chevy, and an Oakland, and headed south on one of the most doubtful looking car tracks that you ever did see.

Houma was down in Terrebonne Parish, a pretty forgotten corner of the world in them days. The drive was already pretty spooky with mossy, gnarled trees and stagnant black water, shimmery dragonflies the size of your hand, but when the local boys started telling tales of pirate kings, swamp monsters, and voodoo princesses, some of our boys was ready to go back without ever setting foot on the running board.

Oswald Loogevall was just the opposite. He wanted to hear every tall tale that Houma, Louisiana could offer. If there really was swamp monsters, young Oswald would've paid to wrestle them. He was charged up.

Once we'd finished our first ball game, Loogie and his new Louisiana pals headed straight to the nearest saloon, and he started downing hard boiled eggs and bottles of bootlegged Dixie Beer, matching them one to one. I don't think Prohibition made it to Terrebone Parish, at least not for thirsty members of the New York Yankees, and at least four or five of our boys were whooping and hollering well into the nighttime, surrounded by a whole passel of admiring Cajun folk. I was just there to keep an eye on them, you understand.

I reckon it was about nine o'clock that a dark haired, pretty little Acadian girl come sashaying through the door. I still recall her name, Anastasia Theriot, though folks called her Alligator Annie on account of her arms.

Loogie damn near jumped out his skin when he saw her. That skinny boy was convinced it was love at first sight. He started elbowing any other potential suitors out of the way, slathering on the charm, weaving stories of his ball playing exploits, even bragging that he was some kind of Viking royalty. Annie was having none of it.

If you're familiar with the term three sheets to the wind, Loogie was five sheets, three pillowcases, and a comforter. How he climbed on top of the bar, I couldn't tell you, but he did. At first, he was just singing and doing a Scandinavian folk dance up and down the wooden bar top. Then he started banging two pot lids like cymbals, and that's when most every man there scooped up his drink afore Loogie punted it through the bar mirror.

I'm not sure just how he pulled out his pecker cause I never heard the pot lids miss a beat, but there he was crooning at the top of his lungs, high stepping along the bar, smacking kitchenware, wobbling and teetering over both edges with his johnson swaying to and fro in the breeze. Even Alligator Annie was a slight bit mesmerized.

It might have gone on for an hour, or maybe it was three minutes. Time sort of stopped. What broke the spell was his half gainer off the front of the bar. Some people tried to break his fall. Others was scrambling out of harm's way, and I'll be damned if Loogie didn't end up with his hot rod stuck in a shot glass half full of moonshine whiskey. It must have stung something awful because he went to bucking like a rodeo bull, smashing into chairs and customers and generally clearing empty glassware off the tables like a paraplegic bus boy. His last act in the ballet was pitching through the front plate glass, doing a somersault across the board banquette and coming to rest in a dry horse trough, glass-hatted pecker pointed toward the heavens.

He came to in the Terrebone Parish jail, and try as I might, the laws had no intention of letting that boy go for a few days. Somebody down there had them the idea that the rich New York Yankees could pony up enough to keep everybody in boudin and white lightning for a month or more. If it had been a starting player, they might have been right, but Colonel Rupert wasn't about to part with his earnings over some skinny-ass wannabe bullpen pitcher.

The bar wrecking took place on a Tuesday, and it was Friday when Loogie finally stood before his honor Judge Gaspar Baptiste Porche who was smoking on a cheroot, winking at the court secretary and eating a smoked sausage sandwich.

"Mr. Looginville," the judge said.

"Loogevall," young Oswald corrected him.

"My courtroom. My names, Mr. Looginville," was the answer.

Loogie nodded.

"Why on God's green Earth was you dancing on the bar with your tally whacker hanging out, Mr. Looginville?"

"I was crabbing!" Loogie said.

Well, sir, if there was one answer that would make a Cajun forgive, that was it. The judge and everybody else in there took to giggling then laughing then downright guffawing. Oswald Loogevall was set free by the fine people of Terrebonne Parish, and he and I made a beeline back to New Orleans where the rest of the team had already retreated.

It was one of the smartest answers to a question that I ever did hear, but it wasn't enough for Miller Huggins. That was the end of Oswald Loogevall's big league career, but it did give him a helluva story that he could never tell his grandchildren.

Chapter Twelve

Huggins tabbed Shawkey to pitch the first contest in the new stadium, and he won it with a three-hit complete game. His pitching style was slow for the day, unlike Hoyt and some of the others who'd just as soon zip things along. As long as he pitched, Sailor Bob wore a bright red long sleeved undershirt beneath his uniform. He thought the flapping red sleeves distracted the batter. I suspect some days he felt stronger about that notion than others.

There were over 74,000 people there to watch Shawkey's win. By far the biggest conglomeration of spectators to ever witness a single baseball game. The governor threw out the first pitch, and for good measure, Shawkey himself even scored the first run. It was quite the spectacle. Of course, Babe hit a home run.

Like I said about the gloves, the Babe loved dogs. So did Bob Shawkey, which might be one of the reasons I was such a fan of Sailor Bob. He was one of the biggest outdoorsmen I ever knew, a real expert on the golf course, and he would take the Babe and other teammates out hunting or fishing all the time in the off season. Some of his favorite spots were up in Maine or Quebec, Canada, the real wilderness, I tell you. Every so often, I got to tag along to haul shotguns or bird dog chippies.

Even on a hunt in the backwoods, in a one room cabin, those ballplayers expected a place to dip their wick of an evening. It didn't matter if they spoke English, somehow some local ladies figured that putting out for a big league ballplayer was the thing to do, and my job was to see that they had directions to the cabin.

In October of 1923, just after the Series, Sailor Bob organized a moose hunting trip to New Brunswick for Joe Bush, Fred Hofmann, Sad Sam Jones, and the Babe. Since I had been the Bambino's shadow for most of the season, one of them come up with the notion to bring me along. So, there I was, lugging a trunk full of gin and shells and what have you onto a train that would eventually get us to a little village called Blackville. It was a small collection of shacks that looked like buoys anchored amidst an endless sea of dark old growth forest.

The hunting cabin was a two room affair with bunks enough for the six of us, a ragtag assortment of seating close to the fireplace, and a built-in sink that was served by fetching buckets from a tributary of the Miramichi River that was some 300 yards distant. Additional facilities was known as the woods.

Ball players for the New York Yankees was accustomed to indoor toilets, even in 1923. We stayed in fancy hotels that either had the crapper attached or no further than a few doors down the hall. So, there was some complaining and ribbing of Sailor Bob every time one of the lads was forced to don a jacket just to go relieve himself. It was all good natured, I suspect, but once the hooch started flowing, the boys got either lazy or confused. The first night, in pitch dark and a drunken stupor, Bullet Joe felt a belly-rumbling call of nature. Barely conscious, he started feeling around in the darkness for the hotel loo.

Now Bullet Joe Bush had grown up palling around with Indian guides and true sportsmen, hunting and fishing around central Minnesota. Story was that he honed his fastball winging rotten apples through the crescent vent on local outhouses, so he knew his way around the outdoors. Yet, the hotel life had spoiled him. Somehow, he felt his way to the cold water sink and dropped his long john flap before he woke up enough to realize his mistake. Trying to correct in mid-squat, Joe stumbled backwards and become wedged solid between the sink encasement and the wall. None of us was remotely awake enough to hear him slurring for help. When the rest of the boys started stirring a tad past daybreak, we found Bullet Joe sleeping it off right where he fell. Me and Sailor Bob pulled him loose, and he scampered out the back door to complete the business he had set out to do some hours prior. Ever good natured, Joe came back shivering in his under drawers, bruised on his forehead but with a big grin on his face.

That same trip, Sad Sam found a little pup out in the woods all by his lonesome, and we took him back to New York. Shawkey nursed him back to health and gave him to the Babe since Bob said he was full up on hunting dogs at the moment. I still recollect the scene at the cabin the day the Babe decided to adopt the pooch. The big fellow was sprawled out in an oversized rattan chair getting a hum job from a bob-haired French girl, and he was holding that damned puppy the whole time. Every once in a while, Babe would look down at the top of her head and say, "Give it a little squeeze, sister."

At the time, the Babe was living at the Ansonia Hotel on Broadway at West 73rd. It was some kind of rolling party at that place, too, boy. Babe was the king of the roost. He paraded all over the joint in his bathrobe, even down to the barber shop in the basement. Usually that New Brunswick hound dog padded along in his wake.

Chippies would drop in and out of the big hotel at all hours of the day. The Babe had something to do with it, sure, but the bigger truth is that it was one of those times and places where the younger folks were not at all particular about who they boffed. Seeing a couple of total strangers macking in the elevator lobby was the norm.

I reckon I had my share of fun whilst I was a hanger on there, but not all of it was on the sheets. Once, had to be after midnight on a game day, the party had wound down to the Babe, Long Bob Meusel, myself, and a bob-haired floozie in a tasselly green dress. She had passed out and then rallied to start back on the champagne. As I recall, she had enough makeup smeared on her cheeks by that time to pass for an opera clown, and her left stocking had a run in the thigh that would render it unfit to catch salmon. The party had got real tame. Long Bob was making noises about getting home to his pregnant wife, and I had already said that the tumbler of Scotch in my big paw would be my last.

Suddenly, the Babe tugged on a tweed Ivy cap and announced he wanted to play some golf.

"Babe, it's a mite dark," I pointed out.

He just countered with, "Kid, you work for the ball club, and the ball club wants me to be happy. Right now, what'll make me happy is to play golf."

He had a point, or at least I thought he did at the time. We all four stared at one another for a few long seconds, then I snatched up Ruth's golf bag and headed for the door. Nobody said a word. Finally, Babe stepped into his bedroom and emerged with golf shoes on. Meusel nodded at me, and off we went, as liquored up and unlikely a foursome as ever would grace the links.

I can admit now, that I didn't really have much of a plan until we reached the elevators, but then it all seemed crystal clear. Now, the three of us men all topped six foot by a goodly margin, so as we crowded in, I looked down at the little dude in the blue uniform and just slurred out, "Roof."

While I have not even a suggestion as to what it was like at street level, I swear that I cannot deny the unbridled joy of driving golf balls off the roof of the Ansonia Hotel in the middle of the night. With me teeing balls up on top of match boxes, Bob and Babe took turns knocking them into dim distance. Every once in a while, they'd pause to guzzle, and I would smack one with the mashie niblick. Clearly you will never hit a drive on a real course that will match the length you can get with an 18-story head start.

Even had we been sober, I doubt that we could have heard the screams of those New Yorkers still roaming the Upper West Side at that hour, nor the breaking plate glass, for that matter. I think we may have laughed at squealing tires once, but that was the extent of any realization that our sky-high driving range might be wreaking havoc below. The next day, as I lay in bed with one eye opened, those concerns crept into my noggin for the first time. By the time I got to the Stadium, I had convinced myself that I would be summarily fired for landing the Bambino in jail, but that was not the case. If any authorities ever said word one about our golf outing, I never heard about it.

The Ansonia was filled with artist types and what folks back then called people with a Bohemian lifestyle. That meant they drank a lot, rooted around in each other's sheets, and spent much of the day dodging debt collectors.

There was one old boy who fancied himself a sculptor. Claimed to be a member of the French royal family, and maybe that was so, but he did tend to slip up and use words like "vittles" and "clod-hopper," though with a French accent. On the other hand, when he was drinking, which was most days, he preceded damn near every swallow by screaming out, "Confusion to Napoleon!" I don't know about Napoleon, but it befuddled the beejesus out of me.

His name was Eddie Ardoin. He had long hair that was slicked back like Dracula, and I never saw him out of a smoking jacket the first four months I knew him. I figured he had to be close to 40, but it turned out that he was 27, just a few years older than me.

Now Eddie Ardoin wasn't the kind of man who made friends easy. He would go out of his way to make a bad first impression. You had to want it, that was his motto.

Ardoin loved jazz. Duke Ellington had a band called the Washingtonians that was the house band at the Club Kentucky on 49th and Broadway. Nine pieces in a basement. Jazz was still an evolving thing back then. Ellington had him a song called the *Creeper* that could've been a ragtime number that I heard back in Memphis with my friend Herbie. There was another one name of *East St. Louis Toodle-Oo*, and that was a real toe tapper with those wailing horns. It was like the rough edged jazz I was used to, but becoming more sophisticated all the time.

It was Eddie Ardoin who first took me to the Club Kentucky. I reckon that was how I passed his test. He could see that I wasn't no poseur just trying to impress someone. When I started relating stories of some of the bluesmen I'd swilled suds with down in Memphis, we become fast friends. The second or third time we went, I rang up Paul Flinkenberg to come along, and a trio was born. We would enjoy a lot of adventures over the years.

Try as I might, I couldn't make either one of those boys a Yankees fan. Paul remained loyal to the Cubs who were the closest club to where he grew up in Indiana, and though I managed to introduce Eddie to the game of baseball, he stubbornly decided that since the Giants had been my first love, they should remain so. Thereafter, he announced that he would become a diehard Giants fan on my behalf.

Eddie, in his smoking jacket and carrying a silver hip flask, would sometimes appear at games over at the Polo Grounds, and from what I heard, he quickly become recognized as a colorful character. At least one time, he got colorful enough that I had to bail him out of jail.

That escapade had to do with his fondness for a one-eyed pitcher name of Claude Jonnard. In spite of the fact that Claude, and his twin brother Clarence, was from Nashville, Tennessee, Eddie latched on to him since his name sounded French. He would get liquored up and sit in the right field bleachers singing the Marseillaise and shouting, "Vive, Jonnard!" I don't reckon the Tennessee boy understood a word of it.

Now, Claude had his best year in 1923. He was finishing games, and though there was no such thing as a save back in those days, that's what he was racking up. On the day in question, Jack Bentley was getting banged up by the Pirates in the 7th, and an early Giants lead was hanging by a spider strand. That's when Eddie Ardoin began shouting for McGraw to pull Bentley and bring in Jonnard.

"McGraw, change the pitcher, you badger!" Eddie yelled in that weird French accent.

"McGraw, you are a Spanish cow! Bring on Jonnard!"

"McGraw, you are a dishcloth, you lower than shit!"

Bentley had now loaded the bases and let in two runs, still with only one out, so Eddie decided to take matters into his own hands.

First, he stood on top of his seat and pantomimed pulling a sword from its scabbard. Then he announced to all around him that he was going to make a pitching change.

"Vive Jonnard!" he screamed at the top of his lungs as he vaulted over the fence onto the field. That was about an 18-foot drop, and Eddie allowed later the fall was a bit sobering, but he was committed. Regaining himself, and with his smoking jacket flapping behind him, he started running toward the mound, yelling at McGraw the whole way. It was farther than he anticipated, and he had begun to run out of insults.

"McGraw, you pump for diarrhea, bring on Jonnard!"

Poor Jack Bentley, a nice fellow who happened to be a Quaker, just stood there slack jawed as this out of breath wild man who may have escaped from a drawing room comedy slowly ran toward him on the pitching rubber. Frankie Frisch, who was not a Quaker, was at second base, and clotheslined Eddie when he reached the infield dirt. When I picked him up at the police station that evening, he still had an elbow imprint on his neck.

"What the hell were you thinking?" I asked him.

"I swear I thought someone would stop me before I got that far."

Chapter Thirteen

I made a trip back home for a visit in late winter of 1923. One of the most cheering and elucidating parts of my visit was finding that my boyhood pal Sam Estill was working as an assistant secretary for the Chicago American Giants, Rube Foster's old outfit. He was only 19, being three years younger than me, but he had convinced somebody up there to give him the post. I don't reckon it was coincidence at all. He and I would see each other from time to time even after I moved to Memphis, and I had shared my adventures in Chicago, including meeting Foster, with Sam many a time. He was not in Lee County during my stay, so I didn't get a chance to ask him if he dropped my name to secure that employment, but he might have. I did leave a note with his kinfolks allowing as how it sure would be good to see him again someday.

It was my first trip home since moving to the Big Apple, so I had my little valise stuffed with various souvenirs for my folks. I had a picture postcard folder for Uncle Stump and little soaps from the Ansonia Hotel bathrooms for Aunt Sacagawea. My mama got a milk glass slipper with Coney Island painted on the side, and I handed every one of them a penny that I had carried to the top of the Woolworth Building. All in all, they found the little gimcracks pretty exotic.

I went by and seen my cousin Luke and his green children. Dropped in on some of the other kin. There was time leaning against the porch poles at Dawson's Store, sipping Royal Crown Strawberry Sodas with some of the chaps I'd grown up with. I tried to see everybody, and without exception, they wanted to know about life in the big city. I told them that it sure smelled different, and there were even more crazy folks than we had in Lee County, except that some folks just couldn't learn to leave them alone. They hung on my every word.

I had to take the train in and out of Memphis, so I stopped there for a couple days on my way back north. My hope was that Herbie and me could take in a few musicians, but he was a married man by then, and his new wife wouldn't let him out. She was expecting their first child, and did not feel that her husband would be safe going around with me. Maybe she was right. We sat on the back steps of his apartment house and visited. Herbie seemed happy with his domestic situation, but it wasn't for me.

I asked after Spaniel with a twinkle in my eye, but nobody had seen her of late. I hit Beale Street on my own, but the music didn't sound as exciting as it had just a few years prior. Really, all I got out of the whole stop was a couple of hours drinking homemade wine with Herbie and swapping tall tales. It was the best part of the trip.

Toward the end of the 1924 season, I got a telegram from Sam Estill. That was the way folks communicated back then when you needed to tell a body something right away. Letters moved pretty fast, but they still took a day or two. Not everyone had a telephone, and if you did it was likely one of those things nailed to the wall on the first floor of your rooming house. As for email or texting, well, if you had tried to explain that to somebody in 1924, they would have punched you square in the face and had you committed to the looney bin.

Anyhoo, this telegram come all the way from Chicago letting me know that some of the American Giants was headed to Cuba for the winter and saying that if I could make my way down, there might be a spot open for an equipment man and jack-of-all-trades, as he put it. That started my wheels turning right away.

Needless to say, I'd never been out of the United States before. Hell, I figured that at 23 years of age, I'd done used up all the excitement any boy from Lee County, Arkansas could mark down on his ledger. There was no way in creation

I was going to let an opportunity like this pass me by. I told him that I'd see him there.

Train travel was not all that expensive as long as you'd forego the Pullman berths, so I booked myself a seat on the Carolina-Florida train to Tampa. From there I had a tiny cabin on a steamer to Havana. It was on the lowest deck, tucked under a staircase near the bow. It bounced up and down more than Spaniel's bed, and I had to step into the hall to put on my drawers, but it got me there.

Now, like I told you, I rate the difficulty of getting a drink in New York City, or most populated locales, during Prohibition to be akin to finding used gum under a school desk. In Cuba, though, everything was not only wide open, the art of creating cocktails was thriving. American bartenders were moving there by the hundreds, and bringing their silver shakers with them. You found American bars bundled cheek to jowl as soon as you left the docks. Sloppy Joe's, Donovan's Jig, Dos Hermanos. Sam met me at one called the Gold Dollar, and we spun our newest yarns while drinking Presidentes, these orange-colored concoctions that compelled you to repeat a story four or five times.

Havana was a feast for the senses, like New York but in color. The busiest parts were filled with rich Americans looking to get drunk and laid, but if you walked away from those blocks, and into the neighborhoods where we was staying, you found fellows selling sugar cane off an ox cart, or others standing ready to slice you a fresh pineapple with a machete. I was fascinated by the old ladies smoking cigars on a park bench. On the flip side, our hotel had cockroaches that could bench press canned fruit.

Sam had him a job as a sort of traveling secretary for the American players, being there to help smooth the edges in an unfamiliar land. They relied on him, and he had learned to speak pretty fair Spanish, at least enough that were never left wanting. My job for those weeks was working for Almendares in the Cuban League, and my duties was just as described, a little bit of whatever was needed.

Cuba wasn't as bad as Arkansas or Georgia when it come to the way they treated dark skinned folks, but they sure weren't color blind neither. The bosses were pale, and the best ways for the Afro-Cubans to escape the cane fields or the restaurant bus tubs was to be a famous dancer or guitarist or boxer or pelotero, the latter being a ballplayer. By 1924, there were a handful of players, Dolph Luque, Jose Mendez, Miguel Angel Gonzalez, Cristobal Torriente, and maybe Martin Dihigo, who were full on worshipped. It wouldn't surprise me if they weren't painted on retablos for somebody's bedroom wall.

I drew the straw for Almendares out of pure luck. It was a suburb of Havana, I reckon you'd call it, but lordy, what a group of ballplayers we had. Five of those fellows are in the Hall of Fame, and I could make a good case for two of the others. We had Luque, Andy Cooper, and Bullet Joe Rogan in our rotation. Biz Mackey doing a good deal of the catching. Pop Lloyd and Dick Lundy in the infield, and the best of them all, Oscar Charleston, in center field. I was watching an all-star team every single day. More than once I longed to see them match up with the Yankees club I worked for. It would have been a sight.

After all the decades I spent around baseball, you can probably guess the question I get most often. Who was the greatest player you ever saw? I witnessed more greatness on the diamond than any man alive, I'd wager, but if you're asking who's the best all-around, my answer has leaned the same for many a year: Oscar Charleston. McGraw thought Charleston was the best, too, and said so to the press. Ruth, Ted Williams and others were better hitters, Barry Bonds, though I never once saw a man who could field his position any better than Oscar Charleston. A little faster than Willie Mays, maybe, and sure-handed like glue. He was the package.

Charleston was an all right fellow off the field, I suppose, but he had him a mean streak wider than the butt of that woman at the dollar store, and I guess you might say that he was pre-disposed to thinking that white folks looked at him with evil intents.

Word was that one time he ripped the hood right off a Ku Klux Klan fellow and just stared at him, daring that coward to do something about it.

One story that I saw with my own eyes was when half the Cuban Army run onto the field in Havana on account of them not liking how the game was turning out. It was certainly the most eventful day of that winter. A wholesale riot busted out right there in front of me. As the benches emptied, I found myself in the thick of the melee with the rest of the Almendares boys, duking it out with whatever Cuban Army fellow come close enough. I was holding my own when I heard a whale of a ruckus going on behind me. Or come to think of it, maybe it was the lack of a ruckus. A little spot amongst the otherwise wholesale fisticuffs that was growing quieter than the rest. I turned around and there was Oscar Charleston knocking down Cuban soldiers like bowling pins. I know you'll think I'm off telling tall tales again, but my hand to your mother's skirt, he knocked out a dozen of them fellows. Gradually, everyone else quit their fighting just to watch. They were circled up all around him, and as they closed in, Oscar would throw him a cross and an upper cut and big right hook and three more of them were stretched out on the infield dirt just bigger than an elephant's kidney. I never saw anything like it. Charleston took the wind right out of them soldiers' britches. Slowly, they just tucked tail and strolled off the field. Little groups of them at first, then the whole shebang. That was how the game ended. I assume that we got our portion of the gate receipts cause that night we had us a large time in a cantina.

By that time, us and the Lions were probably the only teams making a profit. The Santa Clara Leopards, the cream of the previous year, was so deep in the hole, that the owners moved them to another town. That game with the soldiers proved to be a metaphor for the whole season. Linares, the big shot who ran the league, just shut everything down, and it was time for all the Americans down there for baseball to head back home.

I sometimes still think about the Almendares Blues getting rowdy drunk in that Havana bar in January 1925. We were back slapping and hugging as winners do, not a care in the world tall enough to reach us on our lofty perch. I wonder if those men ever relived that night in the years after time robbed them of baseball. Dick Lundy died shining shoes in Jacksonville, Florida. Bullet Rogan, who was also with the Buffalo Soldiers in the Philippines, ended up working at the post office in Kansas City. I hope that they still caught a smile from those days when we were invincible.

Me and Sam Estill made us a stop in Lee County on the way back from Cuba, though we weren't allowed to travel together for most of the way, at least not officially. That was nothing new to either one of us. I mentioned earlier that the Estills were our closest neighbors back home, but Sam and his older sister, Francine, had to go to a different one room school. Neither one of those outfits ever topped 25 pupils total. First through eighth grade all sitting in the same room, sometimes with a rug hanging over a clothesline to divide the ages. What they called the colored school was about a mile and a half closer to my house than the one I attended. Both schoolhouses were built by the men who lived close by, but it was unthinkable that the same boys who played together be allowed to learn together.

It was around the middle of February or a little after that we arrived back home. I was still a novelty since most people born in Arkansas in those days did not escape. I made the rounds, which remained a longtime requirement every time I went home.

Sam and me had talked about old times on the trip back, of course, and one of the running gang we wanted to say hey to was Tommy Cloywell. Now, let me say that rural America had always produced a good share of moonshine and bootleg hooch. Folks nowadays seem to figure it was just during Prohibition, but that ain't so. The Cloywells had been in the hooching business since way before I come along. Truth be told, that may have contributed to our shared desire to visit.

By prearrangement, Sam and I showed up at Tommy's farm on a cold Wednesday morning. Icy leaves were crunching under my feet as I pattered through the woods. Amongst those bare trees, a body could hear a twig snap from a quarter mile or more. The Cloywell shine shack was pretty well disguised, half buried in the ground and with chicken coops fronting three sides. Tommy's daddy always told us boys that the heat made the hens lay better, and that might be true.

I knew I had to pass it to get to the house, and sure enough, Boyd Cloywell, the younger brother, was just leaning the shotgun back against the wall by the time I first saw him. He just give me a head nod.

"Tommy's up to the house."

"Sam Estill will be by directly, so don't shoot him none." I told him.

"Obliged."

He was not much of a talker, old Boyd.

Sam showed up about half an hour later, and the three of us commenced to recollecting and passing a jar of Cloywell shine. The tales got taller as we moved down by the creek to do some fishing, and even more so after we'd skillet fried a mess of blue gill for our late afternoon lunch. Bony things, but they eat all right. About dark, either Tommy or Sam brought up the name of Elmo Kenner, and it was the first harsh word of that fine day.

Now, here's the thing about race: if you're looking to find even a fly speck of logic in the whole thing, you might as well be scouring the bayou for alligator feathers. Black people down south, and elsewhere, would spend their whole life trying to avoid trouble, sticking to what was considered their part of town just so they didn't endure the daily indignities of stepping off the sidewalk or bowing their heads or still being called boy at the age of 42. But once a Black person got past a certain age, all of a sudden they gained respectability. Like the mailman dropped off a packet of virtue when they turned 65.

Don't misunderstand me now. I'm not saying respect in the pure sense of the word. The White folks in town still looked down on them and used their derogatory words, but they started calling them Miss or Mister or Uncle or something. With their first names, mind. Miss Esther or Uncle Buck or Mister Jim. If one of those elders was to ever commit an offense or say something considered uppity, well, it sort of got laughed off whereas it would earn a younger man a beating or even worse.

Elmo Kenner had crossed that line.

There was an old white-haired man named Pompey who lived out near Brickeys. He had been born a slave, and even in my youth, he had grown to be called Mister Pompey. After Emancipation, he had managed to save up enough money to buy seven acres, six and three quarters of which he put into cultivation. It was not reliable land since the river put it under water every time it come a frog strangler rain. Still, Mister Pompey was awful proud of it.

Then, not too long before I moved off to Memphis, the MoPac Railroad run a spur line down to the county seat, and it split old Pompey's farm like Solomon's baby. That parcel had been everything he worked for. He'd had two wives die on him already. What kids had lived were long since grown, so from his way of looking at things, that farm was the sole end of his life's blood. Forgetting the amount of land that he just flat lost, those train tracks meant that Mister Pompey couldn't even get his plow over to one side of the place. Afore long, the old man's accommodating disposition was as overgrown and weedy as the three acres that had ended up on the wrong side of the tracks.

Mister Pompey's age was an estimate, but best guess was that by that winter, he was in the range of 78 or 80 years old. He'd sit on his porch, tobacco juice dribbling from his toothless mouth, throwing rocks at the grackles and crows, even though there were no crops for them to be getting into anymore.

Elmo Kenner was running for sheriff in the election coming up the first week in March. Odie Bales had been the law in Lee County for more than 45 years, and had kept the job through piles, boils, a stroke, a gunshot wound, obesity, and hair loss, but just prior to Christmas 1924, he got hit by lightning. The job was wide open, and the men vying for it had been campaigning at every house, barn, and watering hole. They would've literally given a stump speech to a stump, as long as it would sit still.

Bigotry back there was a matter of degrees, I reckon. Whether Elmo Kenner was the worst of the lot, I can't tell you since I never met the man. What I do know is that when he drove up to Mister Pompey's house one dreary February morning and commenced to begging or bribing for a vote, he got himself what he considered a bucket full of backtalk.

"White folk in this county ain't let me vote since the yankee soldiers left," Mister Pompey told him. "So, what you want me to do about it?"

Kenner evidently had a policy for just such an answer.

"Oh, I suspect that we can get you a ballot if you know how to vote. Might even see that you get an extra jar of shine. That's what you people like, ain't it?"

"I don't drink, boy. I am church going folk," Mister Pompey said, all outraged at the mere suggestion. "And unless you know of a colored man running for whatever you're after, then I got no hankering to vote, neither."

Elmo Kenner acted like someone had spit square in his face. He got out of his car, walked up on that old man's front stoop and give him a fierce backhand that knocked him out his rocking chair and right down into the dirt. During the summer, there would have been a patch of begonias there, but that day old Mister Pompey just lay bleeding on the bare, cold ground. Elmo Kenner mounted back into his shabby Davis Touring car and motored off down the lane without speaking another word.

Sam's eyes had grown watery with his telling of the story, and I knew it was more from anger than sentiment. The recounting sure made me boil, too. Mister Pompey was an old man whose life the last several years had turned into a puddle of grub piss, and he was just doing the best he could till his string run to an end.

The three of us sipped and cogitated for a while. As much as our first reflex might be to just shoot the son of a bitch, we weren't murderers. Trying to give back what he'd dished out might work, but chances were good that we'd be the ones to come out on the short end. Eventually, we figured that our best course of action was to see that such a mean-tempered simpleton did not become sheriff of Lee County. Our plan was to collect and destroy every placard, banner, sign and flyer boasting the name of Elmo Kenner. We was going to wipe that stain from the visual record.

It become clear that first night that cleansing the whole county would take more than a few hours. Since Sam and me was just home visiting, the only vehicle we had at our disposal was a 1922 Model TT Ford truck that the Cloywells used for their clandestine activities. Up until 1924, Henry Ford sold you a heavy-duty chassis with a cab on it. The bed or back end or what have you was your own damn business. Most folks put a wood flatbed back there, but some built something that looked like a panel van, and occasionally you'd see those Model TTs turned into a bus. Tommy and Boyd and their daddy had come up with a rectangular contraption that was akin to a regular pickup truck bed, but this one had a hidden storage compartment that run the length and breadth of the whole business. It was five and a half inches tall, just high enough to slide pint Ball jars in there. Accounting for a piece of milled lumber running lengthways for support, it would hold 53 gallons of moonshine all secreted behind slick little doors camouflaged with Arkansas delta mud.

We made good progress the first two nights, and we took great solace knowing that there was no remaining time for the print shop over in Brinkley to run more advertisements, even if Elmo could pay for them. We reckoned two more nights of making our rounds, and Lee County would be a barren place for Elmo Kenner's campaign signage.

The third evening, though, shit got complicated. It was time for a delivery run, so in addition to our well-intentioned vandalism, we had to make drops at little joints and dives up toward Wrightland and Haynes and then various backwoods cribs and flops all the way to South Plains. Easy enough, we figured.

Well, sir, we pulled into this ramshackle shanty that almost certainly had started life as a hay barn and was now being held together with flaking lime whitewash and an assortment of stolen signage and lumber. It was about 300 yards across a fallow cotton field from a crossroads, sitting back in a little catalpa and tallow thicket that had sprung up along the bank of a mostly dry run. There was a weedy track about a quarter inch wider than the Model TT, and no place to turn around. Since it was just a neighborhood joint, most of their finer customers arrived on foot anyhow.

One of the first things we noticed when Tommy pulled into that copse of trees was a ginormous sheet of pine board with Elmo Kenner for County Sheriff painted across it in these big, uneven red letters. Not surprisingly, sheriff was misspelled. We were at a loss.

First things first. We helped Tommy unload about two dozen jars of hooch into an old tomato crate and hauled it inside. There were several knots of patrons in various stages of awareness. A fat man in bib overalls thumping a washtub base was providing the entertainment, and one and a half couples were dancing to it, along with whatever melody they were hearing in their heads. There was no electricity, of course, but it was all lit up with kerosene lamps, and the smoke put a nice mask on the less pleasant odors.

The boss man of the place was a weathered, skinny old bird name of Freeman Bowes. He had four pack a day skin, and he was sweating copiously even on a late night in February. Still, he offered us each a bottle of home brew for only a nickel, so we took him up on it. Seemed the polite thing to do. While we drank, we surveyed the place. Now we had a little buzz going before we set out on that night's adventure, and customers or not, we had done made a solemn pledge to purge Elmo Kenner from Lee County.

Nobody paid much attention to us as we slipped out. We lingered around in the shadows. It was dark as all get out under them trees, but we waited till we made sure nobody was stepping outside after us to steal the rest of the shine or just to take a squirt on our truck tire. With the coast clear, Sam and I threaded a thick piece of hauling rope around the four corners of the campaign board and tied the other end to the front bumper of the Model TT. Our mental picture was of a few quiet pops as we slowly moved away, and nobody would be the wiser. Being such a narrow track, we was obliged to back up all the way to the road, but the clientele in the joint was so pie eyed, that we couldn't imagine that to be a problem.

Well, son, we had not counted on the low quality of effort and construction that Freeman Bowes had put into creating his masterpiece of a saloon. Tommy dropped her into reverse, and we felt a brief mite of tugging, then come some creaking noises, then about two or three gunfire pops. That was followed by a dull thud and a large cloud of dust as the entire west wall of the building fell over. It was like slow motion, and behind it, suddenly flooding the dark night with the glow of a dozen and a half oil lamps, the entire bar and all its foggy customers was suddenly exposed like a footlit tableau at a drunk middle school pageant. They all very gradually lifted their heads and stared at our receding windscreen.

I still recollect Sam Estill's cogent commentary,

"Shit!"

As other parts of that building started to lean precariously, Tommy pressed that gas pedal as far as it would go. If it was a movie scene, the rednecks would've poured from the bar and piled in their pickups to give chase, but this was a bunch of poor, shit faced Arkansans in 1925.

There were no cars, but with a quick response that was rather mystifying, here come Freeman Bowes atop a mule that I later learned bore the moniker Black Ruby. We couldn't see much of anything, mind, but sound let us know that he also had him a shotgun.

My supposition is that we were not the first persons he had chased away from his bar on mule back. That is based on the fact that he had mastered the art of reloading in stride.

The Cloywell's Model TT was only two years old, in good running order and with the basic factory equipment, for the most part. It didn't have a jumbo gearbox or nothing cause there are no hills in the delta, and in 1925 folks in rural Arkansas had not yet learned the finer points of souping up a motor. It was not the moonshiner's vehicle that created NASCAR.

To put a finer point on it, when you purchased a Ford in them days, the dealer told you not to go over 15 miles an hour, but you knew you could easily hit 18 on the back side of a small rise. None of that is true, however, when you are going backwards and towing 10 running foot of pine board as a kedge anchor.

Judging by the noise, Black Ruby appeared to be gaining on us, and we still had another football field of backing to do. Tommy was a fairly bright boy, and using some mental calculations, he reckoned that if he tried to do the three point turn when we got to the road, we would be wading neck deep in shit creek. When we hit the slightly level mud that passed as a county highway, he swung the truck south. Up to then, Freeman and Ruby had been obliged to stay behind us, or in front of us depending on how you want to look at. But once he knew which way we was headed, he cut across the field to get in front. He done it, too. His trouble was, that Sam had a small epiphany. It was like the angel of gearboxes tapped him on the shoulder and whispered in his ear.

"Throw her into first," he yelled, and Tommy did just that.

It was simple genius. Or it would've been if we had not forgotten about the board we was dragging. When he took off forward, it flipped up, smacked the front bumper, then with some banging that was louder than a horny Palestinian grandma, it rolled under the truck. Thanks to the ropes we had tied on, it went just far enough to wedge beneath the back tires, cutting off all contact between our driving wheels and the road.

The only thing that saved us was that Freeman Bowes, who by then had jumped off of Ruby and was standing in the bed of our TT just a banging on the back glass, had run out of shotgun shells. He and Tommy bowed up at one another, while me and Sam, using that as a distraction, sawed through the rope with our Case knives. With Freemen looking a little winded, Tommy stepped to the truck bed, gave it the secret knock, and slid out a pint of shine. He told that skinny old fellow to take a couple of pulls, and then they would recommence to fisticuffing, but as soon as Freeman Bowes let his guard down, the three of us was in the cab, and man and mule was getting smaller in the rear view. If we'd had a rear view, that is.

Ultimately, living on the other side of the county, we might as well have resided on Neptune. Nobody ever come looking for restitution, and we reached the mutual decision that we had pulled and burnt enough campaign material. Elmo Kenner finished eighth in a ten man race for sheriff. I like to think that he eventually got what was coming to him, but I can't be sure since we never heard his name in those parts again.

Chapter Fourteen

John Philip Sousa wrote a song called the National Game in 1925. Old But-tocks Landis asked him to do it. Sousa was one hell of a ball fan, let me tell you. He had played at the opening of Yankee Stadium, and back a few years earlier, he used to have his own Sousa band baseball team. While they were touring the world, they'd pick up a good ball game against the locals wherever they happened to be.

I mention him because in July of 1925, I went with the club on a western trip. That usually meant we did St. Louis, Chicago, Cleveland, and Detroit all in a row. I hadn't been out that way for many a month, and it marked my first time seeing Pearl in six years. We had four days at the White Sox, and I give Pearl a ring from the blower in the hotel lobby as soon as I had dropped my suitcase Friday night. I didn't rightly know what to expect since all we'd had was the occasional letter over the years, but within five minutes of my darkening her door frame, the time fell clean away.

Things had changed in her neighborhood. Pearl was living in a better flat and working in a different kitchen for a little more money. I suspected she had a semi-regular beau, but it didn't come up. We went to one of the joints that had been around back in 1919 and had us a few mugs of bootleg beer, and we swapped stories till almost daybreak. I was the lightest face in the place, but nobody paid me much of a never mind on account of me being with Pearl. I stayed at her place three of the four nights. Give my road roomie a break, which the boys always appreciated.

On Sunday afternoon, Sousa put on a concert afore the ball game, and I snuck Pearl up onto the grandstand roof to watch the show. Comiskey Park was a single decker back in them days, so it was a pretty snazzy seat. I recall enjoying the warm breeze and squeezing Pearl's hand while the band played a song of theirs called "Belle of Chicago." I mean, it's a march, but there is a tender French horn part. Looking at her smooth skin and soaking up the kindness in her face was plenty enough to make you forget your cares, of which I had few to begin with.

The ball game that followed went much less well for the Yankees. Ted Lyons, who was just a big Cajun kid in them days, shut the lineup down with barely a whimper. I say kid, but Lyons had four years of college behind him. Still, he was at the start of a long career with the White Sox, that's for sure. You know, he and George Uhle once pitched a 21-inning game against one another. That's no fooling. Lyons lost. After 21 innings, that's some how do you do, ain't it? He was a good fellow, big prankster, too. He become buddies with Gehrig in later years, and they used to arm wrestle when Ted wasn't pitching.

The White Sox had our number that season, but then so did everybody else, I reckon. That was the year Ruth was sick for so long, and we finished all the way down in 7th place. That club didn't go below .500 for another 40 years, but they sure sucked loud in 1925. Any expectations had long since taken the express train by that July.

Maybe that helped set the tone of relaxation for those four days, but by Tuesday, when we was packing up to head to Cleveland, I was throwing hints to Pearl that maybe I'd come back and stay with her for the off season. She just gave this low-pitched, quiet laugh of hers.

"Oh, honey. Now you know that can't happen," she said while she was brushing my cheek. "But I sure will be looking forward to you coming out west next season or the one after that."

Her mouth was turned up at the edges, but there was a sadness in those black eyes. I know there was in mine. Human beings have amazing and mysterious powers, but self-deception might be their greatest skill. I was having fun in life, so any notion of an empty place in my heart never crossed my mind.

In those years, me and my buddies were bulletproof and inseparable. There wasn't many adventures that we wouldn't tackle. And like most folks in their twenties, I can promise you that we had no idea how lucky we were. Ardoin, Flinkenberg and Wingo. Sounds like a disbarred law firm, don't it? Throw in the times that Izzy Levy hung with us, and we was sketchy as all get out.

There was one time that the three of us was out at McMuffins or O'Fish or one of them Irish bars trying to scare up some strange, and it was nothing doing. That happened a good deal actually, but it never seemed to slow down our fun one smidge. We could make each other laugh recalling stories for days, and when we run out, we just made more stories.

This night I'm thinking of, we had more than a couple of beers and decided we were going to steal a traffic light and take it home. That was pretty new technology in 1925. New York had been experimenting with those signals for a year or two, and believe it or not, at first, they couldn't agree on what the different colors was supposed to mean.

One place might show green to mean go, and four blocks down green might mean stop. Sometimes they flashed, sometimes they were steady. Sometimes only the cars coming one direction could see anything at all. They had yellow and orange and brown and purple. They almost decided never to use red at all on account of every corner they put it on attracted a whole flock of hookers.

But by that night, they had these really fancy towers, less than a dozen of them, and most strung along Fifth Avenue. At first, we were looking to steal the whole tower, but by closing one eye, we discerned that those things was about twenty foot high or better. So, we set our sights on just taking the light part. Hell, if the thing could draw loose women out in the open, just imagine what it'd do for an apartment.

We ended up at 38th Street and Fifth Avenue staring up at this tall, bronze work of art. It was like a triple decker British phone box, all Art Deco-like, and that is what Eddie commenced to climbing. Paul and I give him a boost, but he scrambled on up into the little skybox where the policeman would stand. We didn't stop to ponder why there was no copper inside the box at that moment, and it was a fact that would soon come back to haunt us.

Eddie dropped the sliding window to report that the light mechanism was all wired and bolted in there too good to cut loose with the little screwdriver we had brung along for the job. The good news was that he thought he could liberate the fancy bell that struck on each hour. One of the sometimes perks of inebriation was a total acceptance of improvisation, so Paul and I allowed how that sounded dandy to us.

The first hitch in the plan was that, even in the wee hours, 38th Street was not exactly the boondocks. Before long, a handful of onlookers had gathered, and being true New Yorkers congregating at roughly 3:45 A.M., they were universally urging Eddie along. In hindsight, that may not have been helpful.

Somehow, he managed to uncoil the big bell. As he was doing the loosening, he was hollering down for us to be ready to catch our new prized possession. We were atwitter. One portion of the recent hoopla surrounding the new signals that had somehow escaped our notice, however, was that these bronze bells weighed 350 pounds.

Eddie pulled the final pin, expecting to cradle it down to us. All he managed to accomplish was a severe wrenching of his back while deflecting that behemoth through the glass window. The largest shards of pane fell fortunately between me and Paul, but the smaller pieces of glass covered us like extremely sharp snow. We definitely fared better than the bell. One side of it sustained a major dent and crack, but at least that prevented it from rolling away. To the growing throng, I started slurrily pontificating on the similarity to the Liberty Bell, seeing as how we were liberating this one. They may or may not have been paying rapt attention.

It was the enormously loud clang that brought the absent copper running from a nearby diner where he had adjourned for a coney dog and a squat. He was blowing his whistle and adjusting his trousers, and had about a half block to cover. Paul, me, and every other drunk onlooker took off running up various side streets like kitchen roaches. It brought flashbacks of the famous Elmo Kenner caper that made my butt cheek tingle.

We had not only abandoned our prize in an instant, but we had left poor Eddie dangling about 14 feet up, half in and half out of the tower box. As luck would have it, Eddie's grip gave way just as the policeman looked down to give his zipper a last good tug. He dropped right on top of that poor man, knocking him all woozy. While this sad flatfoot was staggering around in a circle, Eddie Ardoin, one hand holding his aching back, went hobbling west down 38th.

By the time he come to his senses and was filling out his report, most of what that copper knew centered around a badly dented tower bell that was blocking much of the southbound traffic, and the vague memory of a screaming man in a smoking jacket who dropped from the sky and landed on his noggin. We never did go back for another stab at it.

The Yankees had Ruth with his movie star buddies, Hoyt with his vaudeville pals and Benny Bengough with his musicians. Bengough played the saxophone, you know. Me and Paul and Izzy and Eddie ran in similar circles, just a rung or two lower. While the Yanks was hooching it up at Texas Guinan's fancy speakeasy, we were doing the same thing behind some grimy door halfway down an alley where you had to know the overgrown Irishman sitting on the stool out front. Some evenings we'd take the cars out to Coney Island where Izzy Levy would sneak us in the side door at Steeplechase Park to ogle the crowds. We didn't have the riches, but I reckon we still had the lifestyle.

We also avoided some of the trouble when you think about it. Babe Ruth was big with the ladies, as we have already established, but not all the times was squirts and roses. He had been chased through a train by a brunette with a butcher knife, run out of an apartment house in his skivvies by an irate husband, and sued by an extortioner who figured he wouldn't know if he schtupped her or not. Luckily, the Babe called her bluff on that one. Point is, no woman ever even sniffed at the idea of blackmailing my running buddies. There may still have been an irate husband or so. That I'll give you.

You know, that was about the time that Izzy come up with the idea to unionize all the workers at Coney Island. Ticket buyers were lined up thick as Fatty Arbuckle's ankles, but the ones making sure they parted with their coinage and had a good time was working 12 and 14 hours a day, six or seven days a week, and having to scramble for food and lodging.

Izzy enlisted workers from damn near each business on the Brooklyn shore. There was everybody from sauerkraut slingers at Nathan's to roller coaster hosers at the new Thunderbolt. He enlisted two other rabble-rousers as potential union managers. One was an honest to God Russian immigrant who was an usher at the new Shore movie theatre, and the other was a Coney lifer named Lyle. His past endeavors at the shore included lagoon skimmer at Dreamland up until the fire, sideshow mucker, and most recently, as the guy who tarred the concrete and metal joints on the Reigelmann Boardwalk. When I say he was a crusty old fellow, I mean that literally.

The notion was of unionizing then going on strike until management recognized the rights of the workers. There were glorious speeches, lots of illegal hooch hoisted, and then I think the movement fell to pot in about 62 hours. They never even got around to writing slogans or painting banners.

As soon as he heard of it, the assistant manager at Steeplechase Park closeted himself with the bearded lady, with whom he'd been doing the nasty. He slipped her a few bucks, gave her some money, and had her pay off the carneys. Others folded at the first sight of a threat. Loew's gave each of the movie house employees a paper bag of candy corn to drop out. Before long, jealously and discontent had doomed our friend's best laid plans. A few hardliners, like the rounder who welded the midway milk cans together, wanted to keep trying, but the fizzle was too great. On the plus side, at least Izzy never had to eat any of that candy corn.

Chapter Fifteen

I didn't have much truck with writers, but Heywood Broun become interested in me for some reason. We had little in common other than he loved baseball. He missed it, he said. He'd been a sportswriter when I was still down in Memphis, but by the time I got to New York, he was writing a high falutin' column for the *World*. Politics and literature and other things that made less sense to me in those days than a hippopotamus ballet.

He was standing next to me at batting practice one day and just started talking. In hindsight, it might have been to himself.

"For such a laconic fellow, Meusel's bat can produce knocks of uncommon celerity."

I don't know my exact comeback, but I think it was, "Huh?"

"He might not say much, but he can knock it."

"Speaks softly and carries a big stick," I drawled. It wasn't my line, but I was trying to contribute.

It's funny, but after that Broun seemed to trust that I'd be good for a laugh. It was one of those times where I was never sure if a body was laughing with me or at me, but I give him the benefit of the doubt.

Broun was big for a writer, tall but stoop shouldered, and lumpy like an unmade bed. I don't think I ever saw him without a splash of mustard or cigarette ash on his shirt front, but he seemed genuine.

Now, a fair number of the fellows got a bang out of hobnobbing with the writers. Of course, the gang that traveled with us was impossible to escape, but they sure as shootin' didn't go seeking out the third assistant clubbie. That's what made this special to me, if you follow. He was the first writer I got to know, and it built my confidence. I learned I liked scribblers, and I've sought them out ever since.

For such a big city, it really was a small town when it come to the Yankees. All manner of folks wanted to get a piece of baseball, rub shoulders with players, and by that I mean Ruth. If he wasn't available, every once in a great while they'd settle for a fellow who done his laundry. At least that's what I put it down to when Broun invited me to lunch one day.

He told me to meet him at the Algonquin Hotel down in midtown, not the kind of joint I was used to, you know. I didn't have the wardrobe, for one, so I borrowed a sport jacket from the Babe's locker. He didn't know it exactly, but he was such a generous soul, I knew he wouldn't mind.

I got there early so I could ride the elevator, as was my want in those days. Ever since my first lift back in Memphis, I'd been hooked, mesmerized by the little magic levers. You wouldn't know anything about this, but elevator operators tended to be small in stature so they didn't take up too much room. That translated to me being a good foot and a half taller and probably 100 pounds heavier than the dude in the blue and gold uniform that was guiding me up and down, otherwise he might not have shown the patience that he did. As it was, after the 13th circuit, he politely asked me to vacate his cage.

Some of the names around the big table were familiar to me, but most didn't mean any more to me than a bucket of spit. Being the lowest face on the Yankee totem pole, I figured that made us even. All the same, I was nervous, and that must be why I started fidgeting with my hands in my coat pockets. Or I should say Ruth's coat pockets. When I pulled out the first cigar butt and laid it on the table, it didn't cause much of a stir, but by the time the third or fourth one went in front of me, these literary types had commenced staring in my direction. I was obliged to fess up that the jacket wasn't my own but was temporarily purloined from the Bambino's locker.

By the time I finished explaining that the big boy liked to smoke a stogie between each round of busting a nut, they were fascinated. Then, when I started speculating how the Babe had knocked out a four bagger while never shirking his Brooks Brothers sport coat, folks around the table was laughing just as loud as when Franklin P. Adams let fly a verse about Woollcott's little wiener.

It was at this point in the proceedings that Dorothy Parker, who had been slurping gin fizzes like a dipsomaniac camel, reached over and grabbed my johnson. I thought it was a mistake at first, like maybe she'd forgot where she laid her napkin. If I had been slouching, it did cause me to sit bolt upright. A strange woman stroking your goodies will do wonders for your posture.

As squirmy as I was getting, I still figured that it was best not to blurt anything out and call unneeded attention to what she was doing. I admit that I had been stealing some sidelong glances at her in spite of figuring that she was a married woman, waiters calling her Mrs. Parker and all. Still, she had pretty dark eyes and a little cleft in her chin. Turns out I need not have worried about impropriety. She suddenly quit rubbing, put both hands on the table and gave an exaggerated stare down at my lap before she unveiled her latest couplet.

"Tales of the Bambino may make a lady randy,

But all pops up mas fino when she takes the thing in handy."

The assembled writers all laughed uproariously. My johnson was the only one disappointed. It was like her tugging on it was simply part of the creative process.

As much enjoyment as I got that day from famous people laughing at my stories, I never got asked back again. Not my circle to run in, I reckon. The ballplayers had their own round table, making fun of each other and playing clever games. It was just that locker room wordplay generally peaked at comparing somebody's mug to a scrotum.

My only lasting impact on the written record did come in 1927, though instead of a literary column, it was in a box score. Paul and Eddie and I had tumbled into some speakeasy or another down toward Times Square toward the end of July. We was having a grand hoot of it when I noticed that Lizzy Graber, a typesetter I knew at the *New York World*, was standing by his lonesome at the bar.

I have no idea what the man's given name really was, but twenty years previous, an old-timer in his department misheard it and called him Lizzy, and nobody had known anything different since the Taft Administration. Typesetters were an inky lot, and mostly deaf like the pressmen on account of them working around machines all day, but Lizzy was a gentle sort if a mite slow.

Not long after he got to our table, Paul become plumb fascinated with the linotype process. He asked a dozen dozen questions, and they got more leading by the minute. Finally, Paul asked Lizzy if a typesetter could just slip in any old random shit they wanted. In theory, that was so, Lizzy told him.

If Lizzy was a hooked fish, Paul let him run for half an hour before he brought the subject up again.

"Lizzy, I'll bet you that fellow in the mustard plaid jacket relating some story over there at the bar is from the Midwest. It's a skill I have, recognizing accents. Shit, I'll narrow it down even more. He's from Minnesota. I just have this hunch. Minnesota. Now here's the thing, my funds are getting scarce, so if I'm wrong, I'll shine your shoes for you.

"What happens if I lose?"

"Nothing bad. If you lose, I want you to put somebody's name in the Yankees box score tomorrow."

Lizzy's eyes tried to focus.

"I can't put a fake name in the paper. I've worked there 25 years."

"But this will be a real name," Paul assured him. "Nothing fake about it."

"I don't know," Lizzy slurred. "There's lots of people from Minnesota. I still don't like those odds."

"Fair enough."

Paul cocked his ear toward the bar and looked all intent.

"Mankato, Minnesota. Now that's pretty dang specific. I admit that in the past, I might have had a wee bit of a gambling problem, wanting to bet on everything just for the fun of it, but this is harmless fun. What do you say, Lizzy? Be a sport."

"All right. You're on. And I want these shoes shining like a mirror."

Lizzy reared his head back and laughed. He was a good natured man. That was important, too, since the fellow in the plaid sport coat had been working with Paul at the steamship company for three years.

Lizzy hauled himself to his feet and strolled toward the bar.

"Sorry to interrupt, sir, but where are you from?"

The guy eyeballed Lizzy for a few seconds. Paul and Eddie and I just buried our heads or stared off in the other direction. Finally, he pursed his lips a mite and nodded as if he'd answered his internal question. Then he extended his hand.

"Bill Sheeran. I'm from Mankato, Minnesota, but I'm afraid I don't recollect you."

Well, Bill Sheeran soon went back to his conversation, and Lizzy slinked back to our table just a shaking his head.

"Paul, you were not lying. That is an amazing gift. Sure as I'm sitting here, that buzzard at the bar was from Mankato, Minnesota. I couldn't believe it."

"It's all in the vowel sounds, Lizzy."

Paul hadn't cracked a smile in 55 minutes, but me and Eddie was fixing to bust a gut.

"I don't feel right about pulling one over on the paper like this, but a deal's a deal. Whose name do I put in the box score?"

We were still trying our best to hold the laughter when Paul stuck out his hand to a complete stranger at the next table.

"Pardon me, sir. I'm Paul Flinkenberg. What's your name?"

"James McCown."

The stranger looked at all four of us mightily suspicious.

"There you go Lizzy. James McCown. He's as real as you or me."

Willis Hudlin was throwing for Cleveland next day at the Stadium. I know that made the Babe happy since he knocked him around something good. That's who give up his 500th dinger a couple years later. In spite of Babe going 3 for 3, Hudlin got the best of us that afternoon. Cleveland played their starting nine the whole day with nary a substitution, but it didn't stop old Graber from slipping a pinch hit ground out into the box score. The name McCown must have frustrated the dickens out of those baseball historians for decades until one of them compared it to other box scores and got it wiped from the face of the Earth. You're likely the first soul in half a century to know that McCown who topped a slider in the seventh was a typesetter from Midtown.

Late in the season, I managed to get invited on a western swing, which meant a return to Chicago and chance see Pearl. It had been two years, but it seemed like I'd just left there that morning. She had filled out a mite, and I sure did like the new curves. We enjoyed some meals and time together. Pearl still had that scrumptious whiff of sweet potato pie about her. One sad thing did occur. I tried to get her into the lounge at our hotel to watch some music late one night, but the stuck up fellow at the door wouldn't hear of it. Even though much of the kitchen staff was Black folks, we weren't even able to find a place to watch from back there. Pearl took the embarrassment in stride, telling me it was just as well since the cocktails they were smuggling to customers would set you back upwards of six bits a piece.

Herb Pennock walked right past us while I was angling at the maître d' stand and tossed me a nasty look. Most ballplayers stayed very appreciative of the clubbies since they understood how much we were responsible for their game going smoothly, but there were exceptions. The next afternoon at the ball yard, Pennock dropped a snide remark about me staying mindful of the company I keep since I was representing the New York Yankees. Real quiet-like, I reminded him that, aside from my own mother, nobody on the street had the slightest notion who I was or who I worked for. That was about as lippy as I felt I could get without running the risk of losing not just my job, but my return ticket. I didn't forget his nastiness, though.

She never said as much in words, mind you, but I think me taking the lump along with her that night took some of the sting out of the situation. It may have even brought us closer together. I reckon that was the first time in my life that the notion of settling down with a certain someone ever flickered through my head, but it was fleeting. There was no future for a White man with a Black woman in those days, I told myself. Plus, there were buckets more of wild oats that still needed to sow.

That same trip, I did get a memorable musical treat. Detroit was a hell of a town in those days, as good as any place on account of all that automobile money. It was something. The Graystone Ballroom had the Jean Goldkette Band playing there. You ever hear of them? Now, they was one of the best in those days.

That ballroom put me in mind of a Moroccan palace inside. Big painted ceiling with a round crown on top. Balcony running around it, and a polished wood dance floor that could have held two basketball games simultaneously. You get the right clarinet solo, and damned if you wasn't expecting a belly dancer and a snake charmer.

Jean Goldkette was from Europe someplace, but he sure knew his jazz music. Bix Biederbecke played with Goldkette. The Dorsey Brothers were with him for a while. Hoagy Carmichael, too, though, Goldkette himself played the piano. They beat Fletcher Henderson's Orchestra in a battle of the bands around that time.

The evening I saw them in Detroit, they sounded in fine form. I had gone out there by myself, and telling this story might not make me come off in the best light. As you've gathered, I was never a very important person in my entire years of being, so I was not one to name drop for special favors. Shit, there were people I worked with who didn't even know who I was. For some reason, though, I pulled out the New York Yankees card that evening at the Graystone Ballroom. It is highly likely that I was short of funds and was trying to duck the cover charge.

Well, sir, they not only let me in for nothing, but some linen-coated maître d' bowed, led me up front and place a little two top right up on the edge of the stage. Flapped a fresh table cloth, draped it over the top, and fetched me a cup of tea that was anything but. Detroit, being right across the river from Canada, was perhaps the wettest town in America.

It wasn't long before curiosity got the better of some of the gals in there, and three or four of them in a row strolled over and asked me to dance, no doubt convinced that I must be a high roller. Being near flat busted, when I failed to buy them a drink for their trouble, they all quickly excused themselves. That is, all except one.

She was a blonde in a filmy dress of dusty green. Her face came to a sleek point like an Afghan Hound, but I'd have to say it worked for her. I've never been good at guessing ages, and I wasn't fixing to ask. Suffice it to say hers was someplace north of mine.

"My cousin in the kitchen tells me that you are one of the Yankees."

She was trying to make her voice a purr, but those nasally flat Michigan notes was too far up there, poor thing.

"No, ma'am," I told her. "I work for the ballclub, but I ain't one of the players."

She eyed me like she didn't believe me. I could almost see the little wheels turning. She reckoned that a fellow my size who was with a big league ball team just had to be one of the players. Her brain was all clickety clacking to figure out why I'd be lying about it. When she decided, her eyes lit up like a pinball machine, and I swear to Jesus I heard a tiny ding.

"Well, I live close by, and I just love baseball."

"Yes, ma'am. Me, too. How do you feel about jazz music?"

Bless her heart, she sat there with me through two full band sets, rubbing her hand up and down the leg of my suit pants till I feared for the nap. She even bought us a round of drinks, and I returned the favor, breaking even.

When the night was finished, we strolled arm in arm back to her apartment, and she entertained me in at least nine positions, each one accompanied by a question asking if that's the one I played for the Yanks. I must admit, I had her ask me about left field twice. She never did give up on the notion that she was spending the night with a big leaguer, and I don't imagine it slowed her down from gossiping about it to all of her friends. I mean, who was I to cost a lady her dream?

You ever do much thinking about the size of ballplayers back in the day? They weren't all giant, athletic specimens the way most guys are today, the great Altuve notwithstanding. It was pretty common to see little fellows like Arlie Latham and Heinie Groh and Rabbit Maranville. There were hundreds of them.

On the other side of things, some of the boys were surprisingly large. One that shocked me was how big Ty Cobb was. He was like Joe Jackson in that respect. I had grown up in Lee County reading about all of them bases he stole. I guess I was imagining some little water bug skittering across the top of the bases, but no siree. Cobb was taller than Gehrig.

It was the end of Cobb's career in 1928. He was forty-one, and Connie Mack done him in. He'd already retired once, that being tangled up with the news that he'd thrown games for money, but then he come back for a big sack of cashola to play for the Philadelphia A's. Tris Speaker and Eddie Collins was also on that team, a trio of old men, the lot of them past forty.

Mr. Mack, the parsimonious old tight ass, almost never gave his players a day off. If the league had nothing scheduled, Mack would book an exhibition game just to put some extra dough in his suit pockets. That may be fine for youngsters, but it plumb wore the legs off those three old-timers. By July, Cobb was reduced to nothing but pinch hitting. The last time I saw him start a game was early July when Hoyt got the better of Earnshaw at the Stadium, thanks to two dingers from Lazzeri. Cobb had a lone single in five tries. I almost felt sorry for that mean-spirited bastard, wheels hurting, and knees creaking so bad you could hear them from the home dugout. Speaker had already called it quits, and Collins was playing even less than Cobb. Like I said, it almost stirred an inkling of respect, but I couldn't muster it.

The two teams was neck and neck in mid-September when the A's passed through again. They dropped three of four to us, and all we saw of Cobb was one pinch-out pop-up to Koenig on a Tuesday afternoon.

Back during the July visit, the Babe had brainstormed a couple of ideas past me for farewell pranks to get Cobb good one last time. The best one, and the one we finally went with that September, was the notion of setting a honey trap for the old man, but with the bait being a transvestite, the prettiest one we could find.

There was still a Wednesday game, but the A's would be hopping a train early evening, so we got everything set up for that Tuesday night. Ruth invited Cobb to meet him for drinks at Texas Guinan's place on the promise that there were plenty of chippies. Cobb liked to consider himself as good a womanizer as the Bambino, but like the old saying goes, "Chicks dig the long ball." In spite of that, Cobb was as competitive about screwing as he was about base hits. Putting one in the gap, as it were.

My part in the thing was to find the most beauteous crossdresser in the five boroughs. I wracked my little brain, and then, like sometimes happens, a stray word during a random conversation solved my problem. It directed me to a dark little bar in Chelsea with nice ladies who were packing more than a lipstick. It took me a while to find the joint, but I had struck gold.

Not knowing a better way to approach it, I just spilled the beans on our whole plan. Imagine my surprise when a dozen or more of them little fellows volunteered. They liked a good practical joke as much as I did, and the idea of a famous ballplayer really brought it home.

I ended up striking a deal with a comely brunette name of Wanda Jerky. Now, I tell you, she was stellar. This Wanda had long eyelashes, full lips, and barely a whisper of Adam's Apple. She was very tasteful.

Babe lined up one of his occasional companions from the Ansonia set, a flapper name of Suzette, and arranged for her to rendezvous with Wanda prior to dropping into Texas Guinan's. When those two sashayed into the nightclub, a lot of heads turned, though the more sophisticated among them already assumed the ladies were destined for Ruth and Cobb.

The fly in the ointment that night was Ty Cobb's insecurity. You likely know that he never had a lot of friends among the ballplayers. They said when he died, the all-time hits king's funeral was sparsely attended. His weak point was that he liked to see his name in print, so it was not uncommon for Cobb to have a newspaperman in tow. That particular night, unbeknownst to the Babe and me, he had invited Oscar Rollins, a columnist for the *New York Herald*, to join the fun. The cheap ass had even told the scribbler that the whole evening would be on the tab of the great Babe Ruth.

So as our two ladies made their way toward the big back table, that's who was waiting. Ruth and Cobb, Oscar Rollins and yours truly. Other drinkers tried to horn in, of course, but my job was to keep them at bay so our little prank could play out, and it was looking mighty promising, too.

It was dark enough, and the drinks were nice and strong. Suzette was slung over the Babe like a magnet shawl, leaving Cobb no choice but to try to close the deal with Wanda. Trouble was that Oscar Rollins was just as horny. While Cobb drawled on about what a big star he was, Rollins was stuffing two drink umbrellas under his lip like a Polynesian walrus. Cobb shot him a look then proceeded to prattle about a Chalmers automobile he'd won for being batting champion in 1910. Rollins started flipping candied cherries into his mouth with about a four foot arc. It was looking like a standoff.

The party wasn't as exclusive as I'm making it sound. We had half a dozen Yankees boozing it up at a table on the other side of a wall, just waiting for the high sign to come guffaw. Babe had made sure that an *Evening Post* photographer was on hand for the posterity of the occasion, too. I had dropped the word to Paul Flinkenberg, and he and Izzy were lurking near the bar. Why wouldn't they be? How often would the chance arise to see an all-time great tonsil jockeying a drag queen?

We were a gnat's arm hair from pulling the thing off. Cobb finally tired of his own stories, grabbed a handful of Wanda's athletic butt cheek with one of his big paws, and stuck his tongue about a foot and half down her throat. Unsteady as he was, though, Cobb sensed something was off. To this day, I still don't know what made him step back and squint. Might have been the rasp of another man's stubble against his own, but Wanda looked all close shaved to me. Could have been a certain smell, though all that liquor and cigars makes that unlikely. There's no telling.

The Babe didn't see it coming. As soon as they started kissing, he slapped the back wall to signal the photographer, but by the time the flashbulb popped Cobb had come up for air. The picture showed him with closed eyes and Wanda with a dribble of spit in one corner of her mouth. It also shows Oscar Rollins leaning in to take his turn.

Cobb was glassy eyed when the rest of the gang jumped out from the shadows expecting to have the goods on him, but instead of being able to rag on Cobb, they all just stood there with jaws a-hanging watching Wanda all lip locked with the *Herald* reporter. Soon, the unlikely couple untangled and walked a less than straight line to the door. Babe and I just stared at each other and shook our heads.

The most unexpected part of the whole deal was that instead of laughing his ass off at Cobb's expense, Babe spent the next half hour trying to rally the old man from despondency.

"Aw, hell, Cobb, it was a boy. There was no cooch to be had anyway," he said with numerous slaps on the back.

"Well, that's not the point, now is it?"

The next day at the ball yard, there were no at bats coming for Cobb. Mack started him in an exhibition game in Toronto, and he got a couple of non-regulation hits, but when the team moved on to Cleveland for their next series, Cobb didn't bother to go with them. That out to Koenig was his last official at bat, and the last big league tail he ever chased was a dude named Wanda.

Chapter Sixteen

Something else happened in 1928. Poor old Eddie Ardoin got himself into a double pickle that year. There was a dark haired little lady who was a sculptor of what might be termed exotic art. It was the underground stuff that the avant garde may have bought, but it wouldn't be showing up on your granny's coffee table. Her name was Raquel. Eddie and I had both been angling for her, making moderate fools out of ourselves, but he won out. Or at least we thought he did.

She agreed to go out with him, so Eddie made a reservation at a restaurant in Midtown that fellows of our ilk did not normally patronize, and he bought two tickets for a new show at the Cort Theatre called *A Most Immoral Lady*. He didn't give a rat's ass about the subject, but he saw the title as an omen. Trouble was that the morning of their big date, Raquel rang his boarding house and cancelled on him. Eddie had borrowed money from Paul for those theatre tickets with a stipend for cab fare, and he wasn't about to let it all go to waste.

He did what any self-respecting man would do, he scrounged around for another date. After several runs at a variety of women he barely knew, he finally hit pay dirt with a coffee shop waitress called Didi. She was a perky, plump blondish young woman with a big personality. You know how the freshest ingenues will move from the Midwest to New York to become an actress? Well, I'm pretty sure Didi moved there to become a coffee shop waitress.

Eddie Ardoin was a born romantic, though. He showed sweet Didi a fine time. Bought her day old flowers and even sprung for the mid-range wine at dinner. After the show was over, the two of them repaired to Eddie's place since Didi evidently had a whole litter of roommates. He put some Paul Whiteman on the

Victrola, and the pair of them began consummating the evening. Consummating it like bunnies, they was. According to what we heard later, there was moaning and whimpering way out of time with the downbeats.

None of those noises deterred Raquel, though. She showed up about one in the morning drunker than a bag of skunks. Apparently, the guy she stood Eddie up for wouldn't let her stay the night, and she figured she had one more roll in the hay left in her. She started banging on Eddie's door and slurring out "Teddy."

The hot minx didn't even know my buddy's name.

It started soft at first, then got louder. By the time neighbors were telling her to be quiet, she was hollering "Ravage me, Theodore!"

Eddie, who claimed his full name as Edouard, passed it off as being some drunk girl at the wrong door at first. He might have gotten away with it, too, if he hadn't then slipped up and called Didi by the name of Cassandra for no apparent reason in God's creation. Now he had two women pissed off at him.

Piecing it all together from various sources, Didi stayed in the bed till daybreak, complaining and waiting for Eddie to come back from the bathroom and explain himself. For his part, he had grabbed his smoking jacket and scrabbled down the fire escape about 1:30. Luckily, Paul Flinkenberg was alone when Eddie showed up at his place. Eddie reasoned that since Paul had loaned him the money, he got first dibs on hearing the story.

Bear with me for a second here. I want to talk about air-conditioning. It had just started to show up in the 1920s in places like movie theatres, but sure as hell not in your house or car. In the summer time, there was no escaping the heat. And here's the thing you probably don't think about – folks spent a good measure of their time in their underwear to keep cool. You might not think much about your skivvies today, but you did in the 1920s and 30s.

We had ended up with a day off in St. Louis in late July of 1929. St. Louis was as far as we traveled, remember, so we'd leave on the sleeper and arrive there of a morning with better than 24 hours ahead of you. That's why so many of the fellows had a squeeze in St. Louis. It was every ballplayer's second favorite town.

Now, it might not be Phoenix or Houston, but St. Louis in July or August has the possibility to be toastier than the devil's piles, and that's the type of weather we drew for our day off at the end of July.

We had a third baseman for a couple of years name of Gene Robertson. Thing was that Gene had been born in St. Louis, grew up in St. Louis, went to St. Louis University, and then played for the Browns. He was so at home in that town, I reckoned he could sit on the bench wearing a bathrobe and scratching his ass.

I don't recollect why he needed to impress somebody. He was already one of the town's favorite sons, but Gene asked me to pretend I worked for him and drive him out to Lafayette Square. He had use of a brand new Buick Master 6 with the 47 body style. That's four doors and seven windows. Apple red with a black top. Three speeds and mohair seats. It was a beauty.

For my part, I was not really trained to drive a car. By that I mean, I hadn't the slightest idea how. I know you're thinking: how the hell hard can it be to hold a steering wheel steady. That may be true today, but in 1929 you still had a choke and a clutch and gear shift and carburetor control and a couple of other levers thrown in for no reason whatsoever. Gene figured out right off that I was not his man for this job, but I was all he had.

Sweat was dripping off us, so Gene stripped to his underwear. Then he shimmied in behind the wheel and drove us to within half a block of our destination. Now that I think back, he may have been meeting some gal's parents for the first time. Anyhoo, he pulled us to a stop, double parked down the block, and we switched spots. He got dressed then slid over close so he could operate the pedals and levers. With us never leaving first gear, and him damn near in my lap, we drove up in front of this gal's bungalow.

Gene went on up to the door looking slightly less wilted than the general populace, and I wandered to a Rexall soda fountain a few streets over. My instructions were to kill an hour then be back in the driver's seat.

It went swimmingly from what I could tell, Gene and the girl and her family all come out on the stoop, shaking hands and nodding and laughing. Then the whole scheme fell apart like wet papier-mache. I don't know what he was thinking, but Gene climbed into the back seat of that pretty new Buick and shut the door. He and the family waved at each other. Then they waved some more. I stared directly out the wind screen and kept my trap shut. I could no more start the car and make it go than I could fly to the Moon and bring back dandelions. Gene and the family, located about 14 feet from each other, each kept smiling and waving, though after eight or ten minutes, it was getting more difficult.

Gene didn't want to ruin the illusion of him having a driver so he stayed in the back seat. The gal and her family thought it would be rude to go back inside before the car had pulled away from the house. Around about dark, I reckon they got hungry, and we were finally able to make our get away. By that time, the two of us had probably lost a dozen pounds each and ruined those mohair seats with the buckets of sweat coming off us. Certain patches of them were flat ass squishy. Seven windows don't pull much breeze when you're sitting at the curb.

When Gene drove the car back to his buddy's dealership, they were thankfully closed. So, he parked it two blocks east and had the bell hop from the team hotel return the keys, but not until three days later, after the Yankees had already decamped for Chicago. I recollect one benefit of our unexpected weight loss program. Pearl told me that I looked scrawny and kept feeding me extra slices of pie.

I ought to tell you that the ball club had been trading off a bunch of the fellows starting about halfway through the season in '28. Folks'll tell you all about Murderer's Row, but Colonel Rupert sure must've thought different cause guys started being sent away like they were short-stroking his secretary. Pat Collins, Joe Dugan, and Bob Meusel, all starters in '27, were all sold for cash. Some others, too. Durocher. George Burns. The hardest one for me was when they traded Waite Hoyt to the Tigers on May 30, 1930 along with Mark Koenig for three fellows our general manager wouldn't have recognized if they were sitting at the other end of his couch. They give Waite away for nothing. One of the three stiffs we got in return hadn't won a ballgame in two years, I don't think. I didn't realize it at the time, but it started the decline of the great Babe Ruth Yankees.

I met a girl in Philly at the end of July 1930. Nothing life changing, mind you, but one of those memorable stories that come to me just now. She lived on 20th Street, just over the left field wall at Shibe Park. Her folks was one of the families that had built bleachers on top of their house and charged the ball fans 25 cents each to climb up a ladder in their bathroom to get to them. I see you shaking your head, but during a good year it meant well over a thousand smackers to her daddy for letting people watch the game from the rooftop, and a nickel a pop to her little brother from his friends who wanted to help women up the ladder. Good money either way.

By 1930, it was a real industry, that whole rooftop thing at Shibe Park. City inspectors would make a little shaking down the residents for an amusement tax, and the coppers would take a taste for steering people off the sidewalks into a certain house. That's how I first run into Prissy. Prissy O'Halloran was her name, and she was trying to herd some lookie-loos into her front parlor at the same time I was hauling a wheelbarrow full of pork rinds through the outfield gate. There was a bar two blocks down Lehigh where some old fellow boiled them up and sold them in five pound bundles. Not bad either. Salty and crunchy with just the right number of bristles still stuck on.

The skins were for Yats Wuestling, this kid infielder from St. Louis. He was part of the Waite Hoyt deal. I know I held it against him the first week or two, sometimes it went like that with a trade, but I finally come to realize that he was a pretty stand up fellow who loved him some chicharrónes. He was likeable, skinny, wore number 2, I recollect. And he got in the habit of sliding me a few ducats to bring him those pork skins. He packed them into his cheeks and chewed on them like most fellows would a big chaw of Beech-Nut. That might be why he was back down in the minors by the next season. Most big leaguers were definitely more partial to chaw.

It turns out that Prissy O'Halloran liked the pork rinds just fine. I saw her eyes sparkle when I was passing her, though I admit that I thought I misheard her when she asked for a nibble on one of my skins. Then again, maybe not. It didn't take but a minute or two before I was back on my way to the clubhouse with an appointment to come calling for her at six that evening. I was thinking I might not be her first cracklin.

Sure enough, when I showed up that evening, she had ducked out the front door before I even reached the stoop. We grabbed a hamburger, then an ice cream, and strolled the neighborhood. When it got dark enough, we slipped back into her family house and did some courting on her sofa. It was a good date.

Usually, I stayed in the dugout during games, or back in the clubhouse, but it wasn't uncommon for somebody to send me on an errand. We was already eleven games back by the end of July, and the A's had taken it from us the day before. So, I wasn't too surprised when Bob Shawkey, who was managing us that year, threw a nickel at me and yelled, "Krimpet!"

Off I went to find old Shawkey a packet of TastyKakes. I was coming back to the park when it dawned on me that young Miss O'Halloran was sitting less than halfway down the block. My own fresh TastyKake, if you'll allow me the pun.

Prissy was in the parlor all by her lonesome when I knocked. The game was in the fourth, and all the paying customers were up top. She invited me in, and it wasn't a lickety split second till...well...I guess it was. We were doing what the young folks call getting busy under a blanket behind the sofa when there come the loudest crashing of glass I'd ever heard. It was like ten thousand Jewish weddings. Then something rolled under my hip, and I must admit I screamed like a little girl at a pony party. What made it worse was that before I could yank my trousers back to full staff, half the people who were watching from the bay window in the bedroom had run downstairs. At first, Prissy and I tried laying real still while everybody milled around.

What had happened was that Lou Gehrig had socked one out of the ballyard and right through the transom over the O'Halloran's front door. Glass went everyplace, and the baseball caromed off the umbrella stand, rolled under the sofa and dang near nailed me in the man tonsils. To make matters worse, everybody from upstairs started rooting around looking for the souvenir. Prissy and I managed to pull our drawers up and pop out from behind the furniture which scared the Beejesus out of all of them.

"Found it," I said. "The ball club sends me to fetch these back now that times are a mite lean."

There wasn't a closed jaw in the room as I strolled back out the front door with the horsehide in my hand and half a foot of shirttail sticking out my fly.

The last straw of that day was having to pull a flattened packet of TastyKakes out of my back pocket and try to convince Bob Shawkey that the only ones left at the store were pancake style Krimpets. He ate them, but he whined the whole time that they smelled like bad ham.

I mentioned it before, but my opinion is that the A's teams of 1929 to 31 were better than the '27 Yankees. I worked for the Yankees, knew 'em, picked up their underdrawers, and I'm here to tell you that I think those A's might have been the best. They beat the Yanks in defense and pitching, that's for sure.

There was not a spec of love lost between the Yanks and A's in them days, but they had some good fellows on their club. The Yankees had them at second base. Lazzeri beat the pants off Max Bishop. Other than that, they were formidable. Jimmie Foxx looked like a damn weightlifter, and cut off his uniform sleeves so everybody knew it. Al Simmons was batting close to .400 during those years and could line the ball wherever he damn well pleased. Mickey Cochrane still has the highest career batting average for a catcher to this day, I suspect. Did you know Foxx hit a home run against us at the Stadium, off Gomez, that went to the back of the upper deck and busted the wood on a seat? Smashed the thing to smithereens from 500 feet away. They called him the Beast because he was Godzilla with timing. And longer arms.

Lefty Grove? Hell, Grove was the best left-handed pitcher in the history of baseball, as far as I'm concerned. He was tall and lanky and sullen, and every time

I was around him, I had the feeling that he might punch somebody in the back of the head. In the windup, he did this thing where he pumped the ball up and down three times like he was bopping an elf on the head. Then he dropped his hands down almost to his knees, reared his left arm back and unleashed a fastball that just may have been the hardest that any man ever threw. Walter Johnson himself said that.

Paul Flinkenberg was with me one evening when we saw the great scarecrow of a man drinking alone. I had previously observed him tearing up a water cooler and seen a locker door he kicked in, so I was a tad hesitant to approach him. Paul, who had never expressed an interest in such things previous, wanted Lefty Grove's autograph.

"Pardon me, Mr. Grove," he said after we had advanced to the side of him. "Could I trouble you for an autograph?"

Grove sort of grunted, took the paper from Paul and scratched his name onto it. We thanked him and turned to go, but Lefty spoke, which surprised the dickens out of me.

"Where are you from, mister?"

"Indiana."

I think Paul was a tad shocked, too.

"I'm from western Maryland. Coal country. And though I sure as hell never want to work in one of those godforsaken mines, I'll take the rural or small town life over the cold of New York any day."

And with that, he turned back to his drink to signify that our short meeting was over. You never know what sort of mood you're catching somebody in, do you? I wonder what devil had taken hold of him that night.

It was around that same time... no, I take that back. It was the ass end of 1929 or start of '30 when I first got introduced to Chinese food, and boy I loved it. Did you know that for a lot of years, better than a third of Chinese folks in the whole of the USA operated laundries? It's a cliché now, of course, but it was the way things was back in the day.

I hadn't given it much thought for years. Living in the ball yard, I tossed my laundry in with the uniforms. I was usually the person doing it anyhow. Even after I moved out to my first apartment away from the Stadium, I kept hauling my dirty clothes back to the clubhouse. During November 1929, with the season over, somebody up top decided to upgrade our laundry room. Well, for the first time in my life, that left me with a need to get my clothes cleaned.

Most people didn't own nearly the number of shirts and pants back then that folks nowadays do. I'd say a fairly well stocked single man owned a suit, two pair of pants and four shirts. Myself, I reckon I had a bit less at the time. You tried to air your clothes out, brush them, and get as many wears as you could. Undershirts were important for just that reason.

I was down to my cleanest dirty shirt and trousers, so I had to make a move. There was a Chinese laundry on every block in New York City, but I selected one called the Hum Laundry because it sounded so happy. It turns out that was the folks' name. They had a son a few years younger than me, name of Gene Hum, and we got to know each other a little. He even come out adventuring with the boys a few times.

The first time I walked into Hum Laundry, I was hit by a smell that struck me as being out of place. Bleach and soap is not supposed to make a body hungry, but mingled in amongst all that was something good. Turns out it was fried rice. The whole family worked in the laundry and lived in the back room, and even cooked their meals back there on a green Chambers stove.

We had Chinese restaurants, of course, but mostly it was Americanized. Chop Suey, Chow Mein. Peking Duck, which is a sickly sweet waste of a fine piece of meat. These laundry folks was doing something altogether different, though. The main meat the Hum family used was pork, but they added some little cabbages and greens that appealed to me and some damn tasty crunchy bits. There was a charred pork with honey and fennel and pepper that blew my doors off. It was all new to me.

I'll tell you who loved that food the most, Eddie Ardoin. He became a fiend for the taste of ginger and hot peppers. It got to be that once a week, I'd go by there of an evening and slip old Mrs. Hum, that being the grandmother, a few pooled dollars to fix us something for the next day. Even with Gene as a translator, the contents of our order would be a surprise. But 24 hours later, I'd bring a little bucket, and she'd fill it up. Then Eddie, Paul, Izzy, and me, or a combination thereof, would meet at my place around the corner and chow down like starving urchins.

You know, Gene Hum spoke better English than I did, having never had the handicaps provided by the one room schoolhouses of Lee County, Arkansas. Still, whenever he went out with us, folks would always talk louder to him and with a cartoonish accent, as if that would help transcend the language barrier. The two of us walked past an old, faded hooker on Eighth Avenue one time, and she looked at Gene and shouted, "Why no lookee?" We laughed about that one every other time I come into the laundry.

Chapter Seventeen

Things sailed along for me those first two years of the 1930s. The ball club was doing a little better, and we finally beat the A's again in '32. We were headed back to the World Series, and Ed Barrow even said I could come along to the road games in Chicago since they needed an extra hand to help floss Colonel Ruppert.

At the same time, though, part of it was a rough spell for me. I got word from home that my mom was down in the quilts, as they said down South. That means feeling poorly.

Let me tell you something interesting about Babe Ruth. He couldn't remember anybody's name to save his own bottom, and more than occasionally the only thing on his mind was how to find a willing chippie in the next five minutes, but often times the big man took great joy in making people happy any way he could. If he knew you even a little bit, and if he felt like it, he was a generous soul, and I suppose he had a little soft spot for yours truly that went back to me keeping an eye on him back when.

Once he learned that I was fretting about my mother, he made a point of telling me she would be fine, and before long she'd even be spry enough to come visit. So that whole series, Babe would be bulling through the crowd when he'd pass by me, jerk his head to one side and say, "Hey, brother, ain't that your mom come to see you?" It become a running joke, and I must admit it made me smile, too. He'd point out my mom at the hotel lobby, in the back room of the bar, in the train station john, most anyplace he happened to spot me.

Now a casual acquaintance might think I wasn't all that close with my folks back in Lee County, having been away so long, and maybe that's what made me feel all the more guilty. I'd gone on to the big time in New York City, assistant club house and equipment man of a big league ball club, and sort of left my people in Arkansas behind, though truth was not a day went by that I didn't think of them somehow. There was things I missed a powerful lot about Arkansas.

It didn't come as a surprise when the Babe tried to keep things loose in that third game at Wrigley. Old Charlie Root was on the mound, and he and Babe didn't like each other one whit. The Cubs dugout was busy giving him a rasher of shit, too. There was bad blood the whole Series, mostly over what the Yanks saw as shabby treatment of Mark Koenig who was now with the Chicagos. For two outfits that never played one another, they fussed and cussed more than a Russian president.

In the first inning, Combs and Sewell got on, and the Babe popped the next one out into the centerfield bleachers. We were already up two games to none, so the fellows turned up the heat, really started giving the business to some of the Cubbies in the other dugout. They were especially noisy toward Kiki Cuyler, their best hitter, on account of him having a dumbass name and whatnot.

Wouldn't you know it, but the Cubs come back and tied the ball game. When that happened, those enemy fans grew into as rowdy a bunch of hooligans as you ever seen. They were on their feet yelling words that would've confused an orphan Colombian sailor, and a good bit of it had to do with the Babe's belly.

From there it got plumb ugly, and by the time Ruth come up in the top of the fifth, Guy Bush and Burleigh Grimes was having a flicking contest to see who could land a live scorpion closest to Babe's shoes. And Lon Warneke, who was from the other side of Arkansas from Lee County, was polka dancing through the dugout and snorting, "Wooo! Pig! Sooey!" to beat the band. Root got two quick strikes on the Babe.

I'm not sure I saw the Babe in what I'd call a stressed out frame of mind more than half a dozen times, but when he did, he'd try to make a joke out of it. So, when Woody English yells down from third that he's got a Chicago hot dog in his pants with hot relish, the Babe just ignores him, which was tough given how much that man loved hot dogs.

Instead, he points out to center field, turns toward where I was standing in the dugout tunnel and hollers "Hey, brother, ain't that Arkansas mom of yours sitting out in the bleachers?"

The whole passel of Yankees around me started laughing, though it really wasn't that funny. But it sure made Charlie Root madder than a monk with Tourette's.

Now, when a pitcher lets emotion get the best of him, he's liable to make a mistake, and that's just what Charlie Root did. He grooved a slider that didn't slud, and the Bambino deposited it in the outfield seats right where my imaginary mother was sitting among all those white shirted Cubs fans. The Babe starting laughing and squawking and hoorahing all the way around the bases. At one point, he fell down near third and guffawed until a little squirt of pee come out. The newsreels didn't show that. And that was the famous called shot.

On the Saturday of that 1932 Series, right after that Game Three in Chicago, I got a telegram that my mother, the real one, had taken a turn for the worse. So, on Tuesday, after we'd swept them and taken a day to sober up, I headed back down to Lee County.

Now, I know you've heard all about the Great Depression, but you didn't live it. For most of the people times was tough, but life went on. They might have to move around a little, take in some laundry or sell some of their cow's milk up to town. For about a quarter of folks, though, it was like the world as they knew it plumb come to an end. They'd lost their job, then their house, and then they wore out their welcome with whatever distant kinfolks they had, if they ever had any.

They'd roam the land. They figured that no matter how low they might be right then, something better was in the next town, or the one after that. On their journey, they'd often knock at your back door and ask if you had any work or if you could just spare a half of a cheese sandwich or a tin of beans. They reminded you of a dog that'd been out on the streets for a long time. They were rained on and dirty, run off a thousand times till they was spooked by a loud clap of thunder, but the gnawing in their gut was so bad that they'd risk getting close enough for a biscuit. The look in their eye, well, brother, it was desperation that was barely hidden behind a glimmer of false hope. Folks would start helping them out of human kindness till you just had to ask yourself why you were forking over the last crust of bread in your cupboard to some total stranger. If you didn't throw something into your own belly, you were likely to wake up someday soon and find that it was you yourself knocking on someone's back door with your hat in hand.

I hadn't been back to Arkansas for about four years, I don't reckon, and a person can sure change a lot if you don't see them for that time. When I walked across the corn patch and through the back door, the first thing that greeted me, after a minute of silence, was the front end of an eight-gauge shotgun. My own mother thought I was just some bum come a-begging with the brass to waltz right into the kitchen. It's discouraging when your own ma don't know you, and it made me feel a mite mournful about the twelve dollars I spent on that suit, too.

For her part, Ma looked to be only a shadow of what I remembered. She sure didn't look like the feisty woman who could corner my daddy with only a pickle fork. She was wrapped up in a faded flannel night shirt and a horse blanket, in spite of there not being much of a chill at all. She'd been spending most of her time in bed or in her little rocking chair except when the pigs needed slopping, though she allowed there wasn't much to throw at them lately.

I tossed my kit in the back room, and tried my best to nurse her back to a state of chipperness, if that's a word. I know she was thankful to have me there, and I had a few dollars to put in the kitty for food, so I suspect she ate better with me around, but overall, Ma didn't get any better. I told myself I was seeing signs of improvement, but it likely weren't so.

One night, I awoke from a sound sleep when my mama come into my room and straightened my blankets, maybe fluffed my pillow a little bit. It was country dark in that house on a moonless night, so I can't say I saw her, but I felt her. At daybreak the next morning, I found the stove like ice and no noise but the leaves rustling against the back steps. Ma was laying all still in her room, covers pulled up to her chin, her eyes closed. The corners of her mouth were turned down like she caught me swiping a piece of pie crust before dinner. It was clear she'd been gone for some hours. I reckoned then that it was her spirit what had come to make sure I was tucked in the night before, maybe on her way off to wherever folks go. She was dead at 54 years old, plumb used up by poor dirt farming and the Great Depression.

Uncle Stump accompanied me to the bank to help me sell the old farm which they had saved and saved to buy, but with demand low and a mortgage owing, being sole heir didn't amount to nothing. By the time I paid my way back to New York, I seem to recollect having maybe twenty or thirty dollars. It marked the beginning of the end of thinking of Lee County as home. Like it or not, it was my last shove out into the world.

America got her a new president at the start of March 1933, and though it is long forgotten, one of the first things he did in the midst of all his Great Depression fighting and bank holidaying was to invite his home state Yankees to stop by the White House for a dinner and drinks. It was what they called a smoker back in the day. A bunch of men would sit around and eat, drink, and smoke cigars. Maybe belch and play cards, too.

Bill Dickey and I had rigged up a little still in a boiler room down under the offices at Yankee Stadium, and we used it to make whiskey from fruit like they done in places like east Arkansas. Peach whiskey was always a favorite of mine, and I reckoned that the new president might like a taste of that stuff, too. So, before we lit out south on the Pullman, I squirreled a quart of that nectar away in my duffel.

Now, being at the White House was intimidating, don't get me wrong, but in those first few days, Franklin Roosevelt was just another president, if you follow.

He had yet to become the legendary figure that was a member of every poor family in America. So, the longer we mingled and cut up, the more it was just another night with the boys.

I took the bottle out of my coat pocket and held it out to Dickey who was standing next to me in a circle around the Big Man. Bill took a slug and passed it to the Babe who was relating some off-color tale. He took a slug mid-sentence and held it out in his big left hand.

"Here you go, Prez. The kid here makes this swill, and it's pretty damned good. It'll get your panties in a twist, too."

I suspect that it's possible that a high-born fellow like President Roosevelt had never shared pulls from a bottle before, but if was new to him, he didn't let on. He gulped down a slug and gave a big chin-up grin. That was followed by a curious run of expressions that I'd describe as taken aback, mildly surprised in spite of himself, puckering, head shaking, then lip smacking. That was followed by another tug at the bottle afore he handed on back to Dickey. All in all, it took maybe 15 minutes till FDR was semi-sozzled.

I took that opportunity to button-hole him with a few suggestions about how he might save the country. Get on the radio, I told him, and explain to the little folks what you're planning to do. Plain talk, that's what people need to hear.

"Mr. Wingo, that is a stroke of mastery," he said. Or something like that.

I'll be damned if he didn't take that advice and put it into play just a few days later, though he wasted the opportunity talking about the banking crisis. I still think my idea was better. Common folks would have been much more interested in hearing why he used that cigarette holder.

I don't hold it against him none. He also passed on Babe's request that he use the fireside chat to ask if that "great piece of ass in Cleveland with the mole on her shoulder" would leave her number with the stadium switchboard.

One thing I'd wager all the boys was grateful for is that there were no metal detectors at the White House in those days. The Yankees probably liberated two and a half sets of presidential silverware when we staggered out of the joint.

Let me tell you about another of my proudest achievements in baseball. Damn big contribution, if you ask me. I was the one who invented the phrase "Swing, batter". Now I know that you find that hard to believe cause every Little League team yells that sort of thing nowadays. To the point that it can get downright annoying, but like everything else, somebody had to think of it first, and that was me.

You're looking at me all skeptical, and I know just what you're about to ask. How could a big leaguer fall for something like that? Well sir, you need to put yourself back into that time. This was the 1930s, and back then, young folks respected their elders. When an old person asked you to do something, you did it. Even if you thought it was the screwiest thing you'd ever heard.

My Uncle Stump Dibrell, you remember him, well, when he got up there in years, he used to ask people to do the oddest things you can imagine. But they'd do 'em, on account of they figured he'd earned it. Seniority, sort of.

One time I had gone back home for a visit. Not too long after my mother had passed. I guess that had to be the end of 1934. It was still in the heart of the Depression, I recall, because I remember seeing folks eating worm casserole. And I'm talking about mealy grubs no bigger than the first joint of your little pinky, not those big nightcrawlers that go so well with brie.

Anyhoo, I had stopped by to say Heidi to Uncle Stump. Aunt Sacagawea was gone by then, and Uncle Stump would get mighty lonely. He liked to have folks poke their head in the front door and yell out women's names. The previous visit I had stopped by to say Penelope, but Heidi seemed to be one of his favorites. Kept him worked up for hours.

When I get there, he says to me, "Son, would you see if there's jelly on the radio?"

"Pardon me?"

"That blasted radio cain't pick up a dang thing unless you got about half a jar of preserves spread out across the top of it."

"Uncle Stump," I said. "Doesn't that attract bugs?"

"Well, it may be the durn bugs that helps bring in the signal. How the hell do I know, I ain't some kind of electric genius. Just smear some more jelly acrosst the top of the radio box, will you?"

He could get awful cantankerous, so I got a jelly jar from the cupboard and coated the top of that radio with mayhaw. Right about the time I was done, I noticed that it wasn't even plugged in. So, I reached down to take care of it when Uncle Stump stopped me.

"Don't do that, son. If you plug it in, it'll shock you when you try to lick the jelly off the top."

You see my point. People would fulfill a request from an old person just to be nice or to make them quit talking, and that's when I come up with the idea for "Swing, Batter." If I could make myself sound old, somebody was bound to fall for it.

As luck would have it, we were playing the Browns in St. Louis that week, and it was a trip where I'd tagged along. They were a bunch of nice folks out there in the Midwest. Real polite and friendly compared to the East Coast, and that included the ballplayers. Real accommodating fellows. I always suspected they did so poorly because they didn't want to be rude and make their visitors go home disappointed. You notice they started winning when they moved to Baltimore.

I worked on my plan and fine-tuned it. I don't think I slept a wink that night. The next morning, I left the hotel and was the first one out at the ballpark.

Gomez was throwing that day, and he was having an off year, so, this would be the perfect time to break out my secret weapon. Everything was falling into place.

The Browns had them a utility infielder that was playing that day, fine sort of little fellow from South Bend, Indiana named Ollie Bejma. He strolls to the plate just hoping to get a hit and get things started.

Gomez rocks back into his windup and before the ball had really left his hand good, I scream out in my best old man voice, "Swing, batter!"

And lo and behold, Bejma swings from the heels. About a mile or two out in front of it.

"Dang it," he mumbles to himself and kicks the dirt.

Gomez rocks back again.

"Swiiing, batter!" I holler.

Man, you could feel the breeze all the way over to where I was sitting. Little Ollie Bejma almost fell down swinging in front of that second one.

Well, he talks to himself a little more and steals a glance into the stands, looking for the old man who'd been telling him to swing. I guess he's wanting to see if the old man looks like he knows about baseball or just looks plain crazy.

Well, I was just getting warmed up. The guys on our bench are egging me on. Some of them are even pretending to look into the stands and then look at Bejma and shrug. Like they really felt for him.

Lefty out there on the mound has caught on to what I'm doing by then, and he just stares in at the plate really hard and mean-like. What he was really trying to do was keep from laughing out loud. Finally, he thinks he has it under control. He kicks way back and, right at the top of his windup, he couldn't hold back anymore. He started to fall right off the back of the mound, screaming with laughter, and the ball just squirted straight up in the air like a melon seed.

"Heeeey. Swing, batter!" I manage to blurt out.

Try as he might to hold up, Bejma swung away just as the ball came down on the front of the mound. Completely involuntary. He was mighty steamed, but he had struck out nonetheless. And that's what started the big "Swing, batter" craze.

It sort of slacked off after too many innocent old men were getting the snot beat out of them under the stands.

You know, not to brag, but I also came up with "we want a pitcher, not a belly itcher" after Wes Ferrell got shingles.

My great friend Eddie Ardoin got married in December of 1934. I had always been skeptical about his claims of French royalty, but if there was anything hinky about it, he sure fooled some of the people. Eddie's lineage proved very important to his new betrothed.

Now, I've already told you that me and my running buddies had an economic status that included a great reliance on coupons, sales, and free buffets, and it was one of the latter that led to Eddie meeting Mary Lynn Coletharp Bethune.

I don't reckon I've mentioned it yet, but the wanderings of our little group was not just to illegal liquor establishments. We also haunted Book Row, for next to baseball stadiums, that was the most magical spot in all of Manhattan. It was a stretch of 4th Avenue way downtown, and over the years it had turned into one secondhand book store after another, butted spine to spine, if you like. They all had different stuff, you see, so if nothing grabbed you by the shorties in one store, you meandered next door. They had sections for the subjects, of course, but you knew that some specialized in history, some in cookbooks, some in spooky witches and voodoo. Carts and tables lined the sidewalk. It was a breathtaking parade of imagination.

Aberdeen Books, a little walkup place, used to carry a good selection of used dime novels, so that became our first stop when we needed something to read. After we'd finished our finds, we traded them amongst ourselves and eventually sold them back at a third of what we paid for them so Harry Gold could share the world with the next customers.

Harry owned the shop, and he would sit up there swiveling his gaze, looking for shoplifters. In Eddie, I believe he met his match at curmudgeonry. The tale I heard was that Eddie was at Aberdeen one afternoon, browsing and dreaming, when he spied a fellow slip a volume into his overcoat pocket. Eddie carefully set down the book he was perusing, slipped one hand around the thief's collar, and removed the purloined volume with the other. The old boy was squawking enough that Harry Gold walked over just in time for Eddie to toss him the hot book. Without missing a beat, Eddie frog marched the rascal to the front door and give him a hard kick in the ass as he tossed him out into the slush.

"I hate a thief," he said to Harry.

Most of those book dealers acted like you were breaking into their house even when you were handing them money. They loved the books, and it was just a nuisance they needed to sell some of them. After that, though, Harry would let Eddie enjoy a cup of tea from the pot in the sorting room. He was a made man.

None of us was there the day they met. I'm sure I was at the Stadium. But Eddie, who was there for the free Pekoe, got into a conversation about the pros and cons of Artemus Ward with this freckled pixie with jade earrings and an upturned nose. She found some of Ward's musings to be titter-worthy, while Eddie believed him to be a shopworn old hack. To hear them tell it later, they rambled and expostulated for better than 90 minutes. Armed with the knowledge subtly dropped by Eddie that he was a long lost descendant of the Bourbons, Mary Lynn found herself back at the book shop a few more times over the next weeks.

Eddie was nothing if not entertaining, and afore he knew it, she was inviting him to society dos. See, Mary Lynn was from one of those old money families that belonged to clubs and had summer houses and maybe even shaved under their arms. Whereas Eddie paid eight cents for a used copy of the newest novel, Mary Lynn's folks invited the author over for finger sandwiches.

While they were dating, we saw them every once in a while. Rumors were that some of her family took a shine to Eddie, others amongst them were scandalized. Now I won't say that Mary Lynn put the absolute kibosh on Eddie hanging out with his old drinking pals, but after they got hitched, we sure as shit saw less of him. He loved the water, and eventually the two of them moved to the family cottage in Newport, Rhode Island. Eddie, still wearing the smoking jacket, ended up on the America's Cup yachting committee, and otherwise fishing and listening to jazz records. I was slightly jealous of some of it.

Good friends come and go, of course, but even if you don't see them for decades, they are still a light for you on a dark night, aren't they? And when you do see them again, it's like yesterday.

Chapter Eighteen

After not traveling with the club much for the twenties, I would go with them about half the time in the mid-thirties when the senior equipment men felt like they needed help. It's not like I had much of a life to hold me close to home. I'd be lying to myself if I didn't admit that Eddie getting married did make wonder about my own self. Probably the first time the thought of settling down really took hold. I dated a few women here and there. I recollect one named Alice who lived in a 23rd floor walkup. Skinniest girl I ever knew. Then there was this shapely Lithuanian gal that might have grown on me, but her moustache irritated my upper lip. Nothing stuck, though my head did still turn when I caught a waft of warm yams.

As far as the ball club, folks recollect those famous teams and like to imagine the whole roster was chock full of titans, baseball gods that lounge around the Hall of Fame, but most of the fellows was run of the mill joes. The Yankees were trying to find the next good one or wring the last drop out of the old one, just like the other 15 outfits. A bare few of the stories were inspiring, I reckon, but most were just men trying to avoid getting on with life as a farmer or insurance salesman.

A couple were just sad, too. I saw that up close on one road trip in particular. It was early in '35, and we were in a three city swing out west. We were coming off a big win in Cleveland. Lazzeri had knocked the dog shit out of the ball, and we had us a day off in Detroit. Guys enjoyed it different ways. A couple may have had girlfriends there. I know a big bunch went over to Canada for gambling and hijinks. Dixie Walker headed for Baboon Rock at the Detroit Zoo, looking to chat up the inmates.

We had us a right fielder that year name of Eustis Esterbrook. He was old for a rookie. I know he'd bounced around with a bunch of clubs. I remember one being the Decatur Commodores out in the Three-I League because it made me sad to discover that the players didn't get to wear yachting caps. Anyhoo, he had finally got it together out at Oakland, so he was getting his chance. Trouble was, Eustis had picked up some bad habits in the minors. Namely, he had a tough time staying sober.

McCarthy had told him he would be getting the start in right on Monday, spelling George Selkirk. The boy wasn't getting much playing time. Whatever was going on in his noggin', worry, stress, or premature celebration, he somehow managed to find a place to drink on Sunday. Now, Michigan was famous for the blue laws, some stick up the ass invention to stop people from accomplishing anything on the day of the Lord. Eustis, however, had developed some kind of hooch sensor, and he managed to fall in with a passel of union men from the Packard plant, and they took him to some hole in the wall drinkery.

Where he slept is anybody's surmise, but when it come time for the boys to get to Navin Field on Monday, Eustis Esterbrook, that day's starting right fielder, was a no show. McCarthy yelled for Selkirk to grab his glove and get loose, and I wager you already know who our prickly, big chinned manager set loose into the Motor City to find Esterbook and bring him back.

I didn't have the first inkling of where to start looking, nor did I know a great deal about the City of Detroit. Needless to say, I was not aware of his bender at that moment, but it was a solid guess he was liquored up someplace. We all knew he had a tough time avoiding the sauce.

You know, there were a lot of ballplayers who drank too much in those days. Not much else to do of an evening when you're stuck in another city with a bunch of ball-playing scofflaws. There was no TV to watch back in the room. You likely read the papers of a morning. Nope. Drinking it was. The difference was that, on a normal day, the fellows come to the ball yard mostly sober, and they damn sure always showed up. The stories where they didn't all ended pretty much the same way.

Where do you start to hunt for a lone man in a giant, unfamiliar city? First, I hit the bar at the Book Cadillac Hotel where we were staying, but the haughty fellow slinging cocktails reminded me that they were closed on Sundays, just like every other watering hole in the state. Then I popped round the big hospitals, just in case somebody might have waylaid the boy. After that's when I had to get creative. I talked to taxi drivers and a bunch of little, grey men who worked cooped up in a news stand all day. It was one of them who thought that he heard about a Yankee hooking up with some Packard workers. By the time they were changing shifts for the afternoon, I was up at Concord and Grand Boulevard stopping lunch bucket boys and asking if any of them had seen a big league ballplayer. I'd turned down warm invitations to two Communist meetings, four billiard tournaments, and one sleepover at a Polish guy's step-sister's house before I got a solid lead.

I found Esterbrook at a tavern set between warehouses down in Rivertown. It was not the most odiferous of locales. The one positive was that the smell of old beer and old men inside almost overpowered the truck fumes and river rot outside. E.E., as we had tried to call him, was staring at four full glasses lined up in front of him like tiny cheerleaders. One of those involuntary chills run up my spine just thinking about the work I had cut out for me.

My efforts to take the drink from E.E.'s mitts and direct him toward the ball yard proved as insufficient as booking a one-holer for a colitis convention. I'd slide one aside, and the bartender, who Eustis had already greased with a twenty, would place another in its wake. Since he was buying for the house, none of the Packard boys was ready to see the back of him, neither. For a while, I reckoned that I would just slug back his drinks myself and act like the evening was ended, but Eustis was that tavern's cash cow. Not to mention that it was still plenty light outside.

I briefly considered just using force. I could take E.E., but those union boys had done lots of front line fighting in those years, and though they might not be carrying barrel staves and blackjacks, I was more than hesitant to tangle with them. So, I took the complete opposite tack. I gave them a mixture of charm and bold faced lies.

"I sure do appreciate you fellows taking care of Eustis, here," I told the biggest of the auto men as I put my arm around his shoulders. "The ball club was getting awful worried, and the other players will sleep a lot better knowing it was some good, solid labor boys that had him in their care."

The big fellow cocked his head and give me the squint eye.

"In fact, the last thing that Lou Gehrig told me as they were sending me down here was to make sure I got a proper count of the fine men who had been watching out for E.E. so we can leave them all tickets for tomorrow's game."

I made a show of counting to eighteen, which was three more than the real number. There were a few murmurs starting to circulate, most of them positive. I was on a roll.

"Eustis here has to start tomorrow's game in the outfield, so they wanted to make sure he was on the trainer's table before the end of the game this afternoon. But after the contest tomorrow, some of the boys, Ruffing, Rolfe, Lazzeri, want to come back here to drink with you fellows. We know we'll never catch the Tigers this year, and they want to show the fans there's no hard feelings. I think you're in luck if Ruffing makes it since he never let anybody else buy a round in his life."

Now the mood was positively ebullient. Free tickets and free drinks. A couple of the Packard workers were slapping Eustis on the back.

"If a couple of you gents could just help me get him into the cab, we will see the lot of you tomorrow. Don't forget, the game is at 3."

Even E.E. had somehow got the notion that this was a good thing, and me whispering to him that we needed to grab a taxi before they all got nabbed at last call didn't hurt. He was way too foggy to notice that it wasn't even supper time yet. Three of those Detroit men walked us out the door, and one of them even hailed a cab. There was handshakes, smiles, and promises all around.

We were back at the ball yard by the 6th inning. Of course, McCarthy called poor Esterbook into his office and very loudly gave him his release as soon as that day's game was over. I suspect that he took another taxi cab right back to

Rivertown, though if he did, it would have been some costly buying to get all those assembly line boys over the disappointment.

As for the long term, I don't know if he ever got over his drinking or not, but I do know that Eustis become a two-term mayor in La Crosse, Wisconsin. Go figure.

That particular road trip had started out splendiferous. We played the White Sox first, and that meant that I got a chance to visit Pearl. She may not have always been at the forefront of my brain, but I must admit that it made my blood stir when I knew I had a chance to go to Chicago. I had long since forgotten any hurt from before.

Right from the start, though, things was different on that visit. When I rang her up on the phone, we had a longer chat than usual, but she suggested meeting me out someplace. Even after a night of laughing and drinking and a spot of dancing, Pearl said she was tired. She was tired the next night, too. It finally dawned on me that there was another man. She wasn't sporting no wedding band, but she wasn't asking me back to her place like normal, either.

On the final evening, I almost got up the courage to ask her why, or at least inquire as to what story she was giving him that allowed us to trip the light fantastic for three nights running. During the little dialogue in my head, I finally broached the subject of me taking Pearl back to New York to live with me. Social conventions be damned. If men ever had a biological clock, which I sincerely doubt, then mine was ticking. By then in my mid-thirties, I may have subconsciously realized that there was only so much lasting satisfaction you could draw from rutting with a liquored up good time gal on a cold linoleum floor. In the end, my manners and fears got the best of me, though, and I let things be. However sharp the sting might feel if her other man found out, I knew he was a lucky fellow in the long run. The whole thing left me feeling pretty down when we finally left town.

Around August of 1935, I had been pressuring Joe McCarthy to let me move up to being a scout. After almost two decades of watching chump ballplayers stumble their way onto professional rosters, I was certain that I could do better. Joe kept saying I couldn't carry our scout's jock, which, sounding mighty unpleasant, was never my goal in the first place. But, when Bill Essick left a meeting in St. Louis to head back to his home on the West Coast, the club finally allowed that they could spare me for a week or ten days, and let me go. Probably just to shut me up, but nonetheless, I was determined to prove McCarthy wrong. I ciphered that I had four or five days of scouting before I had to meet the club back in New York by the time they returned from their big road swing.

Essick's nickname was Vinegar, and I always took that to come from his sour disposition. He was in his mid-50s, had been through a game-fixing scandal as a manager, and generally treated me like dirt. Though his home was in Los Angeles, we were headed to the Bay Area, and I don't reckon he threw more than half a dozen words at me the entire train trip.

"Go away. Quit following me." Bill used to say.

I had brought a sack full of dime novels from Aberdeen's, so I whiled away reading, watching the country go past, and listening to various traveling salesman pitches to pass the time. When we finally arrived, I saved what little expense money I had by finding a cheap room. Essick had him a regular hotel, but being my first time ever in San Francisco, I wanted something familiar. A little Italian red cap at the station told me to try North Beach, and give me the name of a rooming house at Francisco and Grant that belonged to his Great Aunt Josefina. It turned out to be a fine place, which I could tell right off by the high quality of the laundry hanging from the second floor railing and the robust fig trees in the tiny side garden.

At the end of the block there was a stairway that would get you to an alley and then onto Bay Street, and from there it was just two short blocks to the water. I know Mark Twain wrote about it, but I had not brought a coat with me, it being the middle of summer for the rest of America, and I like to froze my chitlins off. I borrowed an overcoat some short, fat man had left behind at the rooming house, and it saved my bacon. Sleeves ended just below the elbows, but it got me through.

It was during that week that I witnessed one of the most amazing sights known to man, at least up to then. The Golden Gate Bridge was right smack in the midst of rising, and so was the Bay Bridge. That was some feat, both of those things together. From my perch, you could watch the Golden Gate, and it all made you dream of what was soon to be. That first evening, I spent a solid two hours just staring at it, watching the sun sink aft. The two towers were there, 750 feet above the water, and the fellows swarmed like ants working on making that roadway. Supporting something that colossal had never been done, with the possible exception of a story I once heard about Bid McPhee poking a circus lady.

Now, few things on this Earth can beat a good neighborhood tavern, and around North Beach was a little spot called DeMaria's Bar at 1232 Grant. I'd been to places just like it in the Bronx and Cleveland and St. Louis. Nice and dark with lots of old wood and the kind of comfort smells that make a bar worthwhile.

The owner of the joint was named Stefano, a short Italian gent in his 60s. He sported a big gray moustache that I suspect could retain traces of Sunday dinner till Tuesday. Taciturn fellow, but I managed to get out of him that he'd bought the place as soon as they rebuilt it after the great earthquake and fire back in ought six, and had been running it ever since. His wife was named Margherita, and she kept a pot of pasta on an old stove in the back. You already know that even one whiff of that grub was irresistible. Add that to his dark slip of a daughter who flitted in and out of there, and I knew I'd found my temporary home.

I don't reckon I'd been holding up the bar for more than 40 minutes when I got to chatting with a muscled up fellow called Elmer Nichols. Like most things, baseball was the entrée to conversation, but once we got around to what he done for a living, I reckoned I never wanted to mention sports again.

Nichols was a man with the Otis Elevator Company, which was mesmerizing enough on its own, but his bailiwick at that moment was installing service lifts inside those Golden Gate towers, and that in turn would allow men to build the cables to hold that bridge up. Cables as big around as Sydney Greenstreet after a nice steak.

I've always been a good listener, and over the next three hours, I heard a book full of details about the construction and the machinery that made it happen. I'd never give much thought to a bridge before, just rode over them. It was an eye-opener, but my heart skipped a beat or two when Elmer got this light bulb smile and slapped me on the forearm.

"Hey, what do say I take you out on the job site tomorrow. Let you have a proper look around. You want to do that?"

"Is a pig's ass pork?"

It was set. The next morning, I met my new pal at the appointed spot, and we boarded a boat out to the tower. It was a high class operation. They even had a big cooler of sauerkraut juice and a stack of Dixie Cups to smooth your hangover.

I'd gathered my mind's image after watching things from the hill the evening prior, but it was even busier up close. Men squirreling every which way. Elmer loaned me a hard hat and a clip board and said stick with him and try not to let my jaw hang slack to the point of drool. The inside of those towers was like being in the bowels of a battleship, all steel and rivets and echoes, and for a big man like me, that little elevator felt tighter than a mantis birth canal. Three of us did it, though. Squeezed in and rode up to a dizzying height with that cold wind whipping at you till you durn near begged to be lashed to something solid.

The view from up there spun you round. I'd been atop a skyscraper, but this felt like I was on the head of a pin. We savored it, then come back down to where workers had the beginnings of the roadway platform going. After we'd peered at the swirls and eddies and sniffed the salt breezes for a time, Elmer led me over to a pair of gents hard at work with some eardrum busting machinery.

"Scuse me, fellows," he asked them. "This here is a supervisor from the home office, and I wanted to let him see how that new model hammer feels."

It was not a hammer at all, but a Chicago Rivet & Machine Company pneumatic gun. Heavy little dickens all fastened onto a big air hose, and the bloke operating it handed her over bigger than you please with nary a question.

"She's set where you want her. Just point her to the hole and give it a gentle squeeze," he told me.

I wished I'd had those instructions back with Jeannie Grace.

But I did as I was told. There was a loud pop, and the fellow bucking on the other side of the steel plate give me a nod and a smile. Yes, sir. There are over 600,000 rivets in each tower of that bridge and Lord knows how many more along the road bed, but one of them is mine. I spent the next three months thinking of it as my big contribution to America.

Of course, I didn't forget the reason I was out there. I caught as much baseball as I could find. Coast League, mostly, which was over in Oakland that week, but also some Legion ball, semi-pro. A little ways into the experiment, I was having trouble seeing the long arc. All players had good days and bad, niggling little injuries that slowed them down. I also realized that even a blind hooker can find a man's acorns. Watching a guy for a whole season, it was easy to tell, but much less so if you only had two games. I spotted nary a prospect, but Essick inked a contract with Joe DiMaggio. Scouting might be harder than it looked.

Getting home to New York was an adventure in itself. That little watering hole that I'd made my own was not a busy place, but to my working class eye, some mighty important and modern people patronized that bar. I mean, an elevator engineer was big doings. Somehow, a newly minted scout for the New York Yankees caught their fancy in return, though I didn't put much stock in it.

Being an Italian-owned saloon in an Italian neighborhood, I guess it's not surprising there were lots of folks from Italy that come in there, too. About the second night, I got to know Faustino Pizzano.

"People call me Fatso. It's okay," he told me within the first minute. He was as friendly as they come.

Fatso Pizzano was born in San Francisco, and had grown up right there in North Beach. His father, named Salvatore he told me, was the butcher around the corner who supplied the very meat that went into Mrs. DeMaria's pasta sauce. Fatso, though, was not so old country. He had wrangled himself a job as a ticket clerk for United Airlines down on Geary. He was also a practical joker.

Over the course of three days, we swapped tales of things we had pulled. He said that he felt like he could picture Paul, Eddie, and Izzy just from the stunts they had propagated. I was particularly inspired by one that he recounted about getting his cousin all gangled one night then putting him to sleep in freshly painted sheets. When the poor sod woke up the next morning, he had to peel the bed linens off. I reckon he didn't think much of it his hungover state, until he stumbled to the bathroom and caught a glimpse of himself damn near completely apple green. Trouble was that Fatso had used the wrong kind of paint. He said it took the better part of five weeks for it to wear off.

On the evening before what I figured was my final day in Frisco, about an hour or two after Essick had inked DiMaggio, I had just wolfed down a bowl of Mrs. D's rigatoni and red sauce and was enjoying a conversation with Elmer and Fatso and two of Stefano's other regulars. Specifically, I was telling them how much I appreciated what they had done to make me feel at home. That was when this old man named Louis, who had already told me three times about his four weeks in the United States Navy, sat down his anisette so he could use his hands to talk.

"Fatso, you should get the boy a ticket on that big airplane of yours. That way he can stay and drink another day."

I took it as bar time funning, but poor Fatso, having been put on the spot, started sputtering his excuses. I told him to not be silly. Yet, he must have kept on mulling it over. As the drinks kept flowing, his mind was turning, until finally the balance of common sense was tipped plumb over by the alcohol, as often happens.

"You know, what? These flights will not be filled. Why not? I will get you on the airplane!"

I tried to get him off it, but about 11 o'clock that night, he went back to his office, and, a half hour later, he was back and handing me a ticket on United Airlines from San Francisco to New York. Truth be told, it was Oakland to Newark, New Jersey, but who's counting? I kept telling him that I couldn't afford such a thing. That ticket was over $220, but he wouldn't hear of anything else.

"You are my friend now," he kept saying.

Well, sir, the next day, once he sobered up a little, that cocksure look on his face had turned to one of worry, but he was stalwart to the end and held to whatever code was rattling around in his head. After another night of goodbyes, he even rode the ferry with me and saw to it that I got aboard. Not once did he express any regret for his wild drunken gesture of good will.

This here was to be my first time aloft, other than jumping out of a barn window or two. I wasn't scared, but I was definitely excited. Had been for a day and a half since Fatso come back to Stefano's bar with that ticket.

It was half an hour before 10 o'clock. The airplane was sitting out there on the concrete all clean and shiny. Bright white with a bold blue stripe down the side. It was a Boeing twin engine job, a model 247. The thing was barely 50 feet long, and its weight was not even twice that of a new Duesenberg. It only held ten passengers, which was why it didn't stick around too long, I suspect. There was one line of blue cloth seats down each side, and when you walked to the back, which was where I was to be located, you had to step over the wing spar running across the floor. Like they say about getting a fish bone, that's how you know it's real.

Now, I had been up in a skyscraper, and just recently on the bridge tower, so I expected it to be like that. It was not. Even the most blasé of those fliers seemed to be somewhat atwitter. There was no such thing as sound proofing, so when they got those two engines all revved up, you thought your brains was about to start trickling out your earholes. Lordy, that was the loudest thing I'd ever heard.

The pilots, there were two of them, plus one freshly scrubbed air stewardess named Peggy, let go the brake, and we started bouncing down that runway. My heart was about to pop through my chest wall. Then all of a sudden, without an alarm bell or any noticeable shove from a green giant, I saw the ground slipping away. I felt like letting out a little whoop, and you know, I probably did. We climbed out low toward the ocean, and then, just when I was about to see Elmer Nichols and his buddies working on the Golden Gate, the whole world disappeared into the clouds. It was rather startling. I could only feel when we swung a great big U-turn.

Almost before we leveled off, three of the other six folks on board was sleeping. One of the others, a grim-faced, grey headed fellow clutching his hat within an inch of its life, was clearly having some trouble getting at ease with the loud thrum of the propellers and the undeniable fact that we were several thousand feet in the air. Me, I had pulled back the window curtains and was plumb mesmerized by the view out into the clouds. Mostly it was just an unending sea of fluff beneath and snatches of blue above, like riding on top of an umbrella. Once we were up there a few minutes, you began to make out the outline of mountains, and then 20 minutes after that, we busted through to a clear sky, and I could I damn near touch the tops. I imagined that a body would be able to just step out the door and drop into the snow caps.

The most interesting part for me, though, was after it got dusky. Every so often I could spy a tiny little spot of yellow way down there. Like a firefly shimmering below us. I pictured a farmhouse, not too different than the ones back in Lee County. Rarely, there was the glow from some flyspeck of a burg where the mother had washed the dinner plates and the family was settled onto a worn chintz sofa listening to Major Bowes or Fred Allen. I found it real comforting.

Flying in those early days was patterned after riding the train. You was liable for more than a dozen stops on a cross country jaunt, dropping the mail and letting folks grab a bite and take a squirt. I come to realize that stretching your legs was much appreciated, too. All told, the trip was going to take 28 hours, so your bones took what they could get. We put down at Sacramento, Reno, and Elko, Nevada before we got to the next big terminal at Salt Lake. That stop in Elko was to pick up a fellow who carried himself like a cattleman, and be damned if he didn't sit across from me and back that up. He was going as far as Chicago where he had business at the big stock yards. He give me a knowing nod when I told him I once had that smell stuck in my nostrils for damn near three days. Everybody on that plane had an interesting story, I reckon.

Salt Lake was sort of like a hub, if you will. We had us about an hour and a half to take care of our business before we were off again. Nobody had so much as give me a sideways glance about that ticket of mine, so I saddled back up, fortified by two ham sandwiches, a Coca Cola and a Payday bar. It got dark just after we took off. Everything was hunky dory through Cheyenne, but just about the time I was finally accepting my blessings as one of the luckiest fellows on the planet, not only flying in a fancy airplane, but doing it for free, well, let's say I should've knocked wood.

We squared up on a little field at North Platte, Nebraska. Nobody was getting off there, so we reckoned one of the last two remaining seats was about to be filled up. Didn't think nothing of it. Coming down into those fields at night was like a pebble dropping into a barrel of ink. As we taxied in, I spotted a round topped tin hangar and a low wood tower that looked like the place that Yogi Bear would watch for forest fires. Being in the back, I was the last one to unfold myself and sidestep down the little stair, right behind my new rancher acquaintance. As soon as I was on solid ground, some little fellow in a light gray double breasted and a Barrymore moustache come huffing up to me all red around the ears.

"Mr. Wingo, there seems to be some mistake as to how you got aboard this craft as a guest of the airline, but I am afraid that we must rectify it forthwith."

He was a solid foot shorter than me, and appeared to be bracing for a punch in the chops.

"Mr. Galworthy in Oakland denies knowing you at all, sir. Though, I'm certain it was a misunderstanding."

He was still looking up at me with a slight whiff of trepidation.

My first thought was, "Who the holy hell is Mr. Galworthy?" For once in my life, though, I kept my big trap shut. It finally occurred to me that my good buddy and all-around rascal Fatso Pizzano, even drunk on his ass, had the good snap to sign somebody's else's name to my free ticket. I couldn't help myself. I'll be damned if I didn't start laughing, and that confused all dog shit out of the little man in the gray suit.

"I'm not casting aspersions, Mr. Wingo. It's just that another gentleman boards at Omaha, then after Chicago, we will be full."

I was still shaking my head and grinning which he took to mean a right cross was imminent. He took a step and a half back to deliver his next line.

"I'm afraid that we're going to have to leave you here in North Platte. If you'd be so kind to retrieve your bag…"

He kind of trailed off, and that's when I stopped mirthing it up. It dawned on me that here it was past midnight, and I was now stranded in the muggy asshole of Nebraska. Thinking my plane flight would get me home, I had also spent more than I should at the bar on Grant Street the previous night, plus bought two dime's worth of peaches to leave as a thank you for Mrs. DeMaria's cooking. The financing would be a close run thing. On top of it all, I now faced the prospect of being late for work.

After doing some cogitating, I gathered a handful of change and dropped it into a pay phone next to the unmanned counter with the stale sandwiches. Dialing long distance was sort of an event in those days, but the only thing I could think of was to see if Paul Flinkenberg could come up with a scheme to help me out of a jam. By delaying a day, then transferring to the train, I was not going to be back to the stadium in time for Monday's game. I needed some cover, and I was hoping that Paul was at home.

He was not. I left a wordy message with the normally sweet little lady who lived by the hall telephone in his building. I say normally because by the time she answered after 29 rings and two "give it a little longer, operators," she was mightily pissed off. I did not have high hopes about Paul ever hearing of my call.

As far as moving along, I was in great luck. I begged a ride to the train depot with the combination fuel and baggage man who had been called out to the air field in case he was needed. In an amazing stroke of fortune, an eastbound U.P. streamliner was rolling through at 1:46. You have no idea what sort of kismet that was. Trust me when I say I was the only person standing on the platform. Once in a seat, I stretched out and reflected how much more comfortable I was anyway.

The punchline of the whole trip came after I walked into the clubhouse on Tuesday morning. As the players started trickling in, they began to nudge me and offer a whole coterie of off color commentary. It turns out Paul did get my message, and he rode up to the stadium during his Monday lunch hour on my behalf. He cornered Joe Sewell, who was coaching with us that year, and explained that I was going to be a day late getting back from California because I had hooked up with Mormon twins and just could not bear to break away. He had even clipped a photo from a Doublemint ad and slipped it into a celluloid sleeve in his billfold. He showed that to Joe and regaled him with a brief technical description of the three of us in a hammock, collectively doing the nasty and further flaunting our ungodliness by swilling caffeine. Any tardiness on my part was forgiven.

It was along about this time that Gehrig's games played streak started getting real interesting. Now, let me back up and tell you a little bit about that. Deacon, that's Everett Scott, had been the shortstop for the Yankees when I first got to New York, and he was the holder of the streak that Lou had passed.

I recall Deacon getting a gold medal in Washington from the Secretary of the Navy during my first full season in the big leagues. That was for playing one thousand games in a row, and I must say it was just about the strangest ceremony I ever did see. The Secretary of the Navy might seem an odd choice to hand out a baseball medal, but this old boy was a big sports fan. And a giant of a man to boot.

He had played football for the Michigan Wolverines back when it was perfectly legal to actually kill people on the opposing team. Yep. Teddy Roosevelt changed that rule. Little known fact. After that, the Secretary joined the Marines when he was almost fifty years old. He was what folks back then referred to as a man's man, and by that I don't mean bath houses and Greek ointment.

This old boy was bigger than two houses and always out to prove how tough he was. So that day in 1923, in front of over 10,000 people at old Griffith Stadium, this government official handed a medal to Ev Scott then punched him right in the mouth. The Deacon hit the deck knocked out colder than Vermont ice cream. Lucky for us, we managed to wake his ass up and run him out to shortstop, or his streak might have ended right then and there. As it was, Walter Johnson shut out the Yankees that day, 3 - 0.

Lou's streak started the same year the Deacon's ended, and he finally passed him up in 1933. The ball club brought Deacon in from Ft. Wayne, Indiana just so he could watch his record get broken. I always thought that was a mean thing to do to a fellow. It's like some old boy's ex-wife calling him over to see her make sexy no pants with the milkman. It ain't natural.

Now playing in over 1,300 ball games without ever missing one is no easy feat, let me tell you. Folks get sick. A man gets run over on the base paths, takes a bad hop to the kisser, or just gets stuck deep in a slump and needs a day off. So, you shouldn't make light of what Ev Scott done. Hell, did you know he's still number three on the list of consecutive games played to this very day?

I say that to point out that it's all the more amazing that when Lou moved into first place in the record books, he still had another six years to go on his streak. If you don't think that included a good number of close calls, then I got a one-legged horse to sell you. The stories of Lou Gehrig almost missing games is pretty interesting.

Everybody knows about that time he got an attack of the lumbago and Mc-Carthy run him in there in the leadoff spot then pulled him for a pinch hitter. He got knocked unconscious twice when a pitch hit him in the noggin. Remember, they didn't wear batting helmets back in those days. Another time Lou got him a flu bug that was meaner than an Iraqi alley cat. He was back in the clubhouse throwing up breakfast that might have been from two weeks prior. Leastwise it seemed that way when I was cleaning it up. Ed Barrow got that game postponed on account of rain even though the closest cloud was probably in New Hampshire.

But those are just the normal ones.

The longer the thing went on, the more it seemed like everybody with the organization built up their own personal stake in the thing. One time he had a wicked hamstring pull, and the doc and me wrapped his thigh so tight and thick that he looked like Long John Silver with a full peg leg. For three days, McCarthy watched grounders roll past him like freight trains cause Lou couldn't bend his leg to field them. After each one of those games, I accidentally took a little nick out of his thigh trying to cut the tape off, but the next day, there he was, groaning as he climbed on the table to tape him again.

The Gehrig story I recollect the best took place in September of 1935. The ball club had dropped into second place when we lost a series to Detroit in late July. Later that year, the Yanks had a 24-game road trip. The schedule used to work that way when you traveled by train. I had not been with them, but I got advance word as they headed home that tempers were a mite frayed.

The first games at the stadium were a Saturday double header against the White Sox after damn near a whole week off. It was a strange thing, too, cause they just had that match up for one day. On the Sunday, we had another twin bill, but against Cleveland. Sure, there'd been a whole raft of rainouts in a row, but I still suspected that American League schedule maker must have been a hellacious drinker.

Now, Chicago was about a .500 team, but they had plenty of good talent. Al Simmons, Luke Appling, Zeke Bonura, and they had Ted Lyons throwing for them in the opener against Johnny Allen for us. Well, it just so happened that Gehrig had come to the ballpark that morning with a .336 batting average and a neck that was stiffer than the front row at a Sally Rand concert. Always the first one at the stadium, he headed right to the trainer's room. Lou figured that he had slept funny, and that a good hard massage would have him right as rain.

Doc Painter hollered out, "Wingo, get me some horse liniment."

See the liniment they make for a horse is good and strong, and most trainers in baseball used the stuff to loosen up a sore muscle. Nothing out of the ordinary in that. As I grabbed the big jar of the stuff off the shelf, though, a tiny little gnat flew into my right eye. I swiped at it out of reflex, and when I did, I transferred some of that menthol smelling horse liniment from the side of the jar right onto my cornea. It was like placing your eyeball on the surface of the sun.

I took to dancing and hooting and hallooing, trying to find a sink to splash water in my eye, and doing my best to rub it without using my hand. I must have looked like a scalded cat with a sock over its head, twisting and turning, banging into things, but it hurt like a son of a bitch, I tell you.

The first thing that cut through the pain was Doc Painter screaming my name.

"God damn it, Wingo. I need that liniment. This is Lou on the table here. We got to get him loose."

He had a good point. Gehrig was our biggest star by a long shot, and making $23,000 that season. A lofty number. If he had a sore neck, it needed fixing straight away.

Even though I was blinded by the tears streaming down my face, I scooped the jar off the shelf and handed it to the Doc. Then I went off to do some more rinsing. When I come back, he had Lou slathered down with the stuff to beat the band. He looked like Gertrude Ederle fixing to swim the Channel, but neither of them appeared satisfied.

"Wingo, I think this jar has turned," the Doc told me. "It's got no bite and no smell. Grab me a new one, will you?"

Now, I sure as shit knew that the liniment had plenty of bite. It had done took a huge chomp out of my eyeball. I begun to have a queasy feeling, and not without cause.

Well, son, it turned out that what I had snatched off the shelf in my blindness and pain was a jar of hemorrhoid cream. It had been there for a few years, I'm sure. The Babe used to sneak it into guys' jocks as a practical joke. He was convinced it would make their dicks shrink to the size of a pea and scare the beejesus out of them.

The trouble was that's kind of what it did to Lou Gehrig's neck. It tightened that skin up like nobody's business. He couldn't even look at his own shoulder, but there was still not a speck of a thought of sitting him down. The streak meant everything by that time, not to mention that we was desperate for some wins.

I tell you, when McCarthy found out what had happened, he come completely unglued, and once the game started, it got worse with each at bat. Lou struck out then grounded out to first twice. In his last AB, he finally got it out of the infield but straight into a White Sox glove.

We lost the first game three to two, and in between contests old big chin Joe ripped me four or five new assholes. Lots of times, McCarthy was more of the humorless, sour stomached type, an attitude that fit most of the ball club, to be honest, but he was sure a yeller that afternoon.

"I might take a mistake from a ballplayer because they can come back with a winning hit tomorrow, but you've got little to offer around here, you dumb bastard. You're hanging by a thread, and I've not yet decided what to do to you."

We had lost ground to Detroit while we were sitting on our butts during the rain outs, and after we dropped that game to Lyons and the Sox, we fell ten games back of the Tigers. It was a very un-Yankee position to be in, according to the folks who worked at the stadium, and you just felt the storm coming.

It took right at an hour to get there. When Gehrig come to the plate in the bottom of the first with two on and one out against a new kid named Monty Stratton, it was exactly the situation where Big Lou normally shined. He popped up to Bonura at first. Selkirk grounded to short right behind him, and without taking even a deep breath, McCarthy turned to me standing by the bat rack and said, "Pack up your shit and hit the bricks. Now! You're fired."

My time with the New York Yankees was over. It ended between the first and second innings of Game Two on September 7, 1935 on account of a goddamned gnat.

The boys ended up winning that second one plus the next four after that, but I wasn't around to see it. You know, I mentioned the ballplayers' attitudes on those 1930s Yankee teams. They wasn't like the boys from the 20's that I remembered, loose and fun. It was Gehrig's team and McCarthy's by 1935. Frank Crosetti and most of rest of them was more like a passel of dyspeptic stock brokers than the bunch of baseball players I was used to.

You go through life and there are lots of forks in the road, of course. As it turns out, taking the path presented to me that day was one I never regretted.

Chapter Nineteen

There not was the slightest debate in my head as to my next move. The following morning I was over to the Polo Grounds, and within about two minutes I had secured a clubhouse position.

It's funny for me to say this, coming from the famous New York Yankees, but the very week after I was given the heave ho I had one of my best baseball experiences, though part of the reason I say that is no doubt the camaraderie.

The Giants were on a western trip when I got hired, so though I had a job, I didn't have much to do for several days. And the weekend they were in St. Louis happened to be the same days as the first three games of the Negro National League Championship Series. Middle of September 1935. Boy howdy, that helped take the sting out of things and remind me of how much I loved baseball, especially once you took the personalities out of the thing. It was restorative.

The New York team was the Cubans, and they were owned by a flashy gambler and numbers runner name of Alex Pompez. They called him a gangster, but the folks up in Harlem loved that man. His lottery was always honest, and he paid for little things around the neighborhood. Dutch Schulz horned in on him for a few years, but getting himself shot put an end to that foolishness. Pompez had his numbers going again quicker than a crack addled pronghorn.

They were playing the Pittsburgh Crawfords, who are the betting favorites for being the best Negro League team of all time. They were assembled by Gus Greenlee, another numbers man and old bootlegger from the Hill neighborhood out in Pittsburgh. Greenlee had his fingers in a whole passel of things. He had a stable of prize fighters, taxi cabs, and a couple of posh cafes. When it come to putting together a ball club, he pulled out all the stops.

Paul Flinkenberg, ever ready to take my mind off my troubles, went with me to all three of those games, and we had a time. You know some of the Negro League teams rented ballparks from the white big league clubs, but Pompez had him the nicest yard in Black baseball. It was called the Dyckman Oval, and it was way up at 204th Street, a good ways past where the Giants and Yankees played. It was built as an ice skating rink, but Pompez sunk a big wad of money into the place. It had lights 10 years before the Giants did. The fare was 55 cents to get into the grandstand and twice that for box seats. We went the cheap route to save our money for beer and dogs.

The games were fine, I reckon. The first one, on Friday night, was all Cubans. Frank Blake shut down the Crawfords pretty good. Saturday they played down in Philadelphia, and Paul and I rode the train down and saw Neck Stanley blank the Crawfords four to zip. As the game was letting out, an amazing thing happened. I smack dab run into my old pal Sam Estill out in front of the Philly ballpark. He still had his job with the American Giants out in Chicago, but he had come to that game as a scout and spectator. Sam was fixing to head back west since he said he had no place to stay in New York. After a little cajoling, he fessed up that he was there on his own dime, and suspected that his ball club might be headed for a spot of financial trouble. Well, you don't leave a buddy hanging, so Paul and me got Sam onto the train with us, and I told him that I had the best blanket and floor in all the Big Apple.

Not that I needed anything in return, but mercy me, I got the favor returned almost before we even left the station on 30th Street. Heading through the big lobby, Sam stopped to say hello to Jimmie Crutchfield who shook all our hands. He was a little man, but a solid outfielder. Even though the Pittsburghs was down in a two game hole, Jimmie had a big old smile on his face, and you could feel the confidence.

It was like that with most of the players, and that was not a mood I had been used to lately with the Yankees. Once we got settled in the car, Sam introduced

Paul and me to damn near the whole lot of the Crawfords who was seated around us. Looking at those fellows, you'd figure they had not a care among them. I didn't see too awful many of the Cubans players since they were in the next car along, but their pitcher Luis Tiant nodded a hello as he passed through to the diner. Just like his boy who come up later, he had that herky stop and go windup. Of course, you couldn't tell that with him walking on the train.

It didn't take much in the way of soft soaping before those ballplayers was on my side, neither.

"This here's my friend, Rube Wingo," Sam told them. "We grew up together down in Arkansas. He works for the New York Giants now since the Yankees just canned his ass last week."

You should have heard the hooting chorus that started up. Every one of them was telling me I was better off.

"Shit, since Ruth left, the Yankees are a bunch of stick up their ass mules."

"There are some no good crackers on those Yankees. You ever talk to Chapman?"

"Oh, he is sorry, and some kind of butcher in the outfield, ain't he?"

"Some of them Giants is all right. Bunch of southern boys in that dugout."

"Hell, brother, I been fired so much my backside is permanently singed."

It didn't matter who I was, see. I was baseball people. That was the stamp of approval.

Gradually most everybody went back to their card games or magazine or what have you, but there was a little circle that stayed around. One of them was Pat Patterson, a spry little second baseman who had led the team in batting average that year. Popeye Harris was another one, a utility infielder from Texas, and Spoon Carter. They were happy to welcome us into their world for as long as we needed, happy to be ballplayers, it seemed.

It was all heady stuff. Finally, Paul said he wanted some air, so we headed toward the back platform. There was a fellow standing by the door, a tough I guess we'd have called him in those days. I recollect thinking at the time that he probably worked for either Pompez or Greenlee. We hitched up for a step, but he just moved aside and opened the door for us. Baseball people.

It was one of those Tennessee Williams nights. Wet air that smooths your skin and curls your hair. It was dark, and there was someone standing to our right, watching the rails clackety through the gap and smoking a cigarette.

"How are you gents this fine evening?"

I knew that raspy voice right off.

"Take a drag of this. It'll make you forget your troubles."

With that Louis Armstrong passed me a reefer.

Now I love a tasty drink, but I just never got into the adventure of marijuana. I'd tried it once or twice back in Memphis, but it never done a dang thing for me. I don't know if whatever Satchmo was smoking was better or if I just accidentally stumbled on the proper way to inhale. I do know, from what Paul has told me eighteen dozen times over the years, that after two hits, I stared at the lamp on the next car behind us for a solid ten minutes. Never said a word.

Next thing I remember was when our new friend said goodnight and went back into the car. The one time in my life I got high off the Mary Jane, and it was with the great Louis Armstrong.

Game Three was Sunday back in Harlem, and Sam Estill got the tickets from Gus Greenlee's secretary. No grandstands for us that day. From down in the box seats, you could see all the stars. Cab Calloway was one section over from ours. Count Basie was there. I bet I watched those two for a good half inning. Next to us in those seats was a young boxer who I'll admit I'd never heard of. His name was John Henry Lewis, and Greenlee owned his contract. He become the light heavyweight champ about six weeks later.

Maybe it was my outlook, but the baseball seemed brighter. Let me tell you the names of the hitting heroes. Josh Gibson knocked in a run in the first. Cool Papa Bell tripled and scored on an error, and my old acquaintance Oscar Charleston knocked a dinger out of the yard in the sixth. How's that? Three A-list Hall of Famers.

To show you how things worked in those days, especially for the Black ballplayers who were surviving on less of a margin, Charleston had the Crawfords booked to play an off day exhibition in Altoona against old Pete Alexander who was touring with the House of David. In the middle of their World Series, they stopped for a payday and a pickup game. Things moved back to Pittsburgh after that, and the series went seven with the Crawfords coming from behind in the final game. I wasn't there, of course, but the whole thing sort of renewed my faith in baseball and friendship.

I had a few days of baseball left when the Giants got home, but we was done out of the race. The 1936 season was my first time really getting used to the club again. It had been 13 years since I'd worked for the Giants, so things had changed considerable. The primary difference being that rambunctious little martinet John McGraw having gone on to his great reward. Though by name he was only the manager, McGraw had his stubby little fingers in every part of that operation. The owners, the Stoneham family, loved the man. He and old man Stoneham even bought a horse track down in Cuba together before old Buttocks Landis made them give it back.

By '36, Bill Terry was managing the club and spending his last season as a player, though Sam Leslie was our primary first sacker. Terry was an okay guy, I reckon. If I was a psychologist, I'd tell you that his personality come from him fending for himself as a teenager on the streets of Atlanta, but that might be total horse dookey. I do know that he had little sentimentality and would wring a buck like a dishrag hoping that another two pennies might fall out.

Among the players I hit it off with almost from day one was Gus Mancuso, one of the best defensive catchers in the league. We yukked it up about his semi-pro days, prior to him getting called up to St. Louis. Branch Rickey had him bouncing among every level of the Cardinals farm teams, from Syracuse all the way down to a couple of East Texas League towns so small that the tow truck driver doubled as the proctologist. But where he earned his real money was playing for the First National Bank down in Houston.

A company baseball team was top bragging rights when the fat cats gathered at the country club card room, but there was a veneer you was supposed to keep up. Everybody knew there were ringers, but you acted like they were employees. They put Gus on the books as a bank teller. Trouble come one day when a bloodhound of a bank examiner started sniffing around enough that some paper collared manager thought they should bring Gus in to make a show of it. They stuck him behind a window and left the closed sign up for half an hour. When the examiner didn't leave, it left no choice but to throw caution to the wind. As it happened, the first customer to step up was an alleged roughneck who had been the right fielder for the Shell Refinery the previous season. He and Gus proceeded to shoot the shit through the teller window for about 22 minutes. As the other employees breezed through one account holder after another, Gus saw three people in over an hour until the examiner finally asked why that one teller was so slow.

The bank manager looked him square in the eye and said, "He only handles our most complicated deposits."

The Giants hitting star was Mel Ott, an unlikely looking little fellow, but a wizard with that bat. It was especially true at the Polo Grounds. He used that short right field line, and dropped homers over that fence like he was using a nine iron. He come up at age 17, which is well known, of course, but ten years later, he was still that soft spoken kid.

The other guys called Carl Hubbell the meal ticket, and he was a good one to watch. Buckle your knees with that screwball of his. Won the MVP that year, he did, but the pitcher that year that interested me most was Firpo Marberry. The Yanks had faced him regular when he was with Washington, and he and I had visited on occasion. Nothing but fastballs, which was why he become one of the first relief specialists. He had ended up 1935 with a sore arm, and the Senators cut him loose. In 1936, he got a tryout with the Giants, and we signed him. Here's the weird part. Someone had convinced him that the cause of his arm woes was bad choppers, and he had 14 abscessed teeth yanked out. Marberry pitched a third of an inning for the Giants, give up one hit and an out and an unearned run, but the club released him. He went back to the Texas League and threw another five or six years. A few years after he retired, he was in a car wreck and lost an arm. Between that and his teeth, it always reminded me of the old joke about the pig: "We like him so much; we're only eating him a little bit at a time."

After a good year, facing the Yankees in the 1936 World Series was a bit of a blur. I had steered clear of them since getting the heave ho. I shouldn't have been surprised that the majority of them failed to give me the time of day during the Series. On the other hand, Dickey, especially, made a point of shaking my hand and asking after things. I told myself I didn't care, but it stung a little. The games were close, but we lost to them in six. Hubbell started things off with a masterful job at home, giving up just a solo shot to Selkirk, but Lordy, we got hammered in a couple of those other games. After that bad taste, I was ready for the off season.

Just before Halloween in 1936, Izzy Levy called me and asked me to meet him for a drink. He was going to be in Manhattan and had something to tell me. His news was that he had joined up with the Abraham Lincoln Battalion to go fight in the Spanish Civil War.

He sent me a letter from Barcelona right after he arrived. Had a row of grey stamps that said República Espanola. That always set my mind racing, foreign stamps that brung a letter clean across the ocean. There is something about stamps and currency that is almost like visiting a place yourself.

My friend Izzy was fired up. You could tell that from reading his words. It made an impression because I think it was the first time I got any notion that politics mattered. I mean, I knew they did to some folks, but hearing Izzy's voice about the fellows he'd met on the ship ride over, Whites and Negroes standing side by side. Canadians and Americans, then they'd met up with Frenchies and Brazilians and Englishmen and God knows who else. They were doing something right for the world, Izzy said. They were stopping the bullies and protecting the little man.

They aimed to see that folks got a fair shake to move up in the world. It made my hair stand on end, it did.

He was starting his training the next morning, though from jawing with the other men, he had already learned that there was not much to it other than them handing you a rifle and a box of bullets. Some of the more experienced volunteers was being put into a machine gun company, but since Izzy had never hunted anything bigger than a sewer rat with a mop handle, he figured he'd be starting on the ground floor. On the plus side of things, the women in Spain were first rate and the wine was cheap.

My buddy Paul got sent on a business trip to Los Angeles in late January of 1937, and asked if I wanted to go along. He had got a couple of nice promotions over the years. Whatever his job title, it now had the word manager appended to the end of it, so the company was footing the bill. He said he could talk the hotel into a room with two beds as easy as a single, and that with a little bit of fudging on the expense account, all I'd be liable for was my train ticket. You'd better believe I jumped at it.

Visions of movie stars danced in my head. I was prepared to drop as many ballplayer names as I could muster. By the time that Pullman was crossing the Great Plains, I had worked up a scenario where I knocked back whiskey with Wallace Beery himself and ended up with a bit part in a blockbuster.

The one old cohort I did see was Bob Meusel. He was from Los Angeles, and since he retired, he had been working as a security guard out in Long Beach. Paul and I took the Red Car down to San Pedro and met Bob at a bar called the Alhambra. It was a smoky joint filled to the gills with dock workers and Navy men. San Pedro in general was a hopping spot, but the regulars treated Bob as their local celebrity, and we had no trouble getting ourselves a prime standing spot by the bar.

Silent Bob might have loosened up a touch, but there were definitely a few stretches where we sipped our drinks and stared at the bar mirror. Mostly, though, we recounted old tales. Occasionally a new detail might even get added.

I think we laughed the most listing the hundreds of times that Huggins managed to make Babe stretch out his cussing vocabulary. You know, he was pretty spoiled when you got down to cases. He was the most famous person in America for a time, and he expected to always get his way because of it. Bob said that he reckoned Huggins sometimes deliberately baited Babe just to watch him get cheesed. Once or twice, when the rest of the boys sensed him torquing up, Hoyt would start taking wagers on the number of swear words that would come out of the Bambino.

It was nice seeing old Bob.

Of an evening, Paul and I took in the sights. Thanks to the expense account, we caught dinner and a swing band at the Palomar Ballroom downtown, and I got to say that was a view to put your eye out. There were plenty of pretty people, but we was still lacking our movie star moment. I swear to this day I followed Joe E. Brown into the men's room, but when the stall finally opened, it was just some nervous pharmacist from Toluca Lake. It still galls me that I wasted ten good minutes telling that closed toilet door how much the ball club enjoyed Alibi Ike, not to mention begging him to hook me up with Olivia de Havilland.

Paul was being paid to be there, but getting the whole Hollywood experience was one of my main reasons for coming, though it was admittedly difficult on our budget. For several nights we ventured west from where we were staying downtown. We strolled through the lobbies at the Hollywood Hotel and the Roosevelt. We stood outside fancy restaurants, trying to get a peep into the window. The Brown Derby was fascinating, shaped like a hat and whatnot, but there was nary a celebrity to be had.

One night we caught some new prison picture at the Chinese Theatre. The ticket taker said that we'd missed Clark Gable putting his mitts in cement by about 22 hours. We each tried to match our hands and feet to the prints, of course. I think I come closest to Tony the Wonder Horse.

Eventually we found this spanking new bar called the Frolic Room which not only had a fun name, but sporty neon, too. By our way of thinking, movie stars like shiny things as much as the next guy. We couldn't miss.

About midway down the wall, there were two young things who may well have been quite beautiful. It was dark in there, and we had a handful of cocktails under our belt, but they appeared to be symmetrical, and their makeup seemed to be that day's. We eyeballed them from the bar for a spell. They shook off a couple of other fly bys, but Paul and me had built up a good head of confidence. We asked the bartender for another round of what the ladies were having.

"I'm not trying to bother you," Paul told them as he set two hi-balls on their table. "But you two looked parched."

They didn't shoot us, so we kept going.

"We're out from New York."

That was my addition.

Paul tagged that with, "We're on assignment."

I had no idea what the hell that was supposed to mean, but evidently it dumbfounded the two women, as well. The red head suggested we pull up a couple of chairs.

Their names were Bebe Rudolph and Myra Sloan. We figured them to be movie starlets, by which I mean dishy actresses who are just shy of getting their big break. After visiting a spell, it turned out they were sort of waiting on the lucky chance to be notified about the street address of the right place to get their big break, but that was close enough for us. We were from out of town.

They were quite talkative, those two. They had moved to Hollywood together from Columbia, Kentucky about four months hence. Back home, they had been quite the stars. They had trod the high school auditorium boards together in *Tilly of Bloomsbury* with Bebe playing Lady Mainwaring and Myra being Diana, who didn't warrant a last name. On the other hand, Myra had been third runner up in the Miss Adair County pageant. They were bullish on their chances at the big time.

"We both had an audition over at Republic just this past week," Bebe told us.

"We're still waiting to hear back." That was Myra. Next thing, they were both talking at once, all on top of the other, sharing the load of the story.

"It was a Three Mesquiteers picture. That's their top franchise, you know."

"Oh, yes, this one was called Range Defenders."

"You know there aren't a lot of girl parts in these serials, but the character I read for throws eyes at Lullaby Joslin."

"Do they still call it "reading' if you don't have lines?"

"No idea. But it sure was aces going onto the studio lot."

"This wasn't our first time, you understand. We met a guy last week who we think might be an agent, though he didn't admit that. Still…"

"He's from New York and circumcised."

Eventually, we brought our two comely starlets back to our shared hotel room, and that presented a bit of a problem. These were high class gals, and we couldn't very well do the old Gable and Colbert thing. We might have tried it if we'd had a length of rope. As it was, each couple was sitting on their respective twin beds, well on our way to getting electrified, when Myra starts whispering to Paul. All of a sudden, he cleared his throat, sat up straight and looked at me as if he was peering over the top of imaginary reading glasses.

"Sorry, but you're going to have to get out of the room for about ten minutes."

Myra done a tad more whispering.

"Fifteen."

It was only fair, being Paul's room, but I'm not sure that cut much ice with Bebe. I was desperate. I needed to think of someplace where I could be alone with my soon to be movie actress. The best thing I could come up with was the bathroom about half way down the hall. I see you're squinting. In those pre-war days, most hotels had a common bathroom. All you got in your room was a little sink, or maybe just a wash bowl. It could sure spell trouble after an enchilada dinner. Some mornings you could get a line six deep wearing dressing gowns or undershirts waiting their turn. It was the middle of the night, though, so we peeled off to do our petting in the loo.

I won't get too graphic on you, but there are a few things that stand out. One is that cracking your head on a toilet tank can knock you silly. Two, even one foot is heavy enough to go plumb through a radiator grill. Top of the list, however, is that Bebe Rudolph, bless her heart, was a screamer. I'm not talking lusty growling here, son. I'm saying Marian Anderson would've asked this chippie to dial it back. Coyotes in Laurel Canyon were answering her.

Now, if you pull off some vocal shenanigans like that in the safety of your own hotel room, you can always pass it off the next morning. Just shake your head at your neighbor and act like you heard it, too. On the other hand, when you and your partner drunk stumble out of a communal water closet to find every last man, woman, boy and dog on the floor staring at you from the hallway, well, you got to own it.

I was limping ever so slightly on account of my singed trouser leg. Bebe had broken a heel, had a bright red towel rack imprint across her forehead and almost exactly half her head was dripping wet from when she inadvertently turned the shower knob. Most of the folks lined up down the corridor was just watching, silent and slack jawed. A few was still steamed by us waking them up, and three or four applauded politely like it was a golf match. Her caterwauling had proved to be hijinksus interruptus for Paul and Myra, so they weren't too thrilled to see us back, even though I swear we had been gone well over the afore stated fifteen minutes.

The worst part of the whole deal is that when the two ladies left us, maybe an hour short of daybreak, we forgot to get their phone numbers. We went back to the Frolic Room a few more times before we left town, but never could catch up with them. I spent the next thirty years scanning crowds of movie extras hoping to see Bebe Rudolph dressed up as a perfume counter girl or something. Hell, a roughneck or a gladiator. It just would've been neat.

One or two nights in L.A., I found myself on my own. That was the case when I went to the bar at the Biltmore Hotel. It sure as shootin' wasn't anyplace I could afford to stay, but I figured I could always scrape up enough for a hi-ball. That's the best way to check out expensive places like that, you know. Walk past the maitre'd and tell him you're just going to the bar. I've missed more than a few meals while I was slow sipping a Scotch and water and dipping my mitts into the cocktail peanuts, but it let me see the world.

So, there I was at the Biltmore, and I met this writer. He worked for a magazine that I liked to read called the Black Mask. Heinie Groh used to love that rag, and he got me hooked on it back in 1922. He'd let me read his old ones. Brought them up to the clubhouse, and I'd keep those things rolled up in my cubby till the covers fell off.

They don't make that magazine anymore, quit it a whole lifetime ago, but if you ever run across a copy, you need to pick it up. Nothing against the kind of writing you do, son, but this was the real thing. It was filled with detectives and mystery. There was a whole passel of private gumshoes who would smack a bad guy right in the chops. They talked about the hot wind and hot dames and cold lead. I think it was just about the finest literature ever produced in the whole United States, so I guess that means the world, don't it?

Well, this writer, he was a thin lipped, quiet fellow. Had a pipe stuck in his shirt pocket and was sucking down rye whiskey like it was beer. He must've been a regular cause he bought a drink for one of the bar maids, told her the magazine had just sent him a check that morning.

Now, as you gathered, I never have been much for keeping my mouth shut, so I sidled over to him and asked him how many subscriptions he'd sold. He looked at me for a second over the top of his glasses, and then he answered all proper like.

"Actually, sir, the check was for a story of mine. They pay me to be a writer, when it suits them." And he sort of smiled.

Well, that was all I needed. I've always loved to read. Back in those days, a good magazine or a dime novel was many a ball player's best friend, and that went just the same for assistant equipment managers. But when he allowed that the magazine in question was the Black Mask, I liked to wet my britches.

I went to pumping his hand, all carried away and telling him how pleased I was to meet him until he had to wiggle his way out of that handshake like Pepe le

Pew's girlfriend. He glanced down at his fingers like he thought I'd kept a couple of them for souvenirs.

Naturally, I wanted to know all about being a writer, but then it occurred to me that I might be able to help this old boy out. One of the things that run in my family was a way with words. I sort of inherited it from my Uncle Stump Dibrell. He was a real literary genius in his own way.

See, Uncle Stump had him a hobby. He used to make up old country sayings, and keep annoying people with them in hopes that they stick. Now you think about things like "thicker than thieves" or "stubborn as a mule". Well, they don't just happen out of thin air. No, sir. Somebody has to dream them up, and one of those folks was my Uncle Stump. Not to toot my own beans, but he passed the talent on down to yours truly.

I'm not afraid to admit that some worked better than others. They can't all be little pieces of honey. I recollect that he spent close to eight or nine weeks trying to build up a following for saying that somebody was "madder than a water-retaining ox who had suffered a serious farming accident". Don't exactly roll off the tongue, in hindsight.

On the other hand, some of the things Uncle Stump coined was nothing shy of poetry, the kind of words that would have made Billy Shakespeare pee green with envy, though you can also get that with asparagus. Not to mention the smell.

Anyway, this little writer fellow, we sure did hit it off. He was working on a novel, he told me. Had this hardnosed private eye, you see, chasing down gangsters and gamblers and conniving women. Trouble was he didn't have a name for the fellow. He wanted something no nonsense, he called it.

Well, the ideas just came pouring out of me like burps of cucumber freshness. Rock Derby. Pete Hocker. Luke Dog. Dutch Uncle. Rhett Butler. Max Harpo. All good ones. He didn't take notes on account of him having a really good memory. Most writers are like that, you know. I don't recollect saying Phillip Marlowe, but I must have because that's what he ended up using.

Chapter Twenty

I took a week to detour back to Lee County and see the few folks still left there. I was back to New York at the end of February 1937. Amongst my few items of mail were a dozen more envelopes from Spain. Those stamps were sure pretty, too. Even better than the first ones. I recollect these had Don Quixote and Sancho Panza riding a wooden horse. I recognized them from the movie that had come out a few years previous. That was really something. I was pleased that Izzy remembered me, of course. I suppose there is a lot of down time being a soldier. Kind of like a ballplayer, and letter writing is as good a way as any to pass the hours.

The Loyalists, Izzy's side, were starting to have some trouble amongst themselves from what he told me. The Russians were trying to run everything, while some other folks, like Izzy, were for the workers but not the Communists. Then there was anarchists who I always took to be akin to the Three Stooges but with rifles. It was a mess.

Izzy was keeping his head down, drinking a lot of Rioja wine out of goat skin bags and making time with a different kind of Spanish red, a fighter name of Cristina Vargas Delgado. Izzy wrote that she wasn't too bad looking. She had big brown eyes and a butt rounder than one of his old bumper cars. He also said that she'd durn near worn the skin off his johnson. For a fellow getting shot at, he sounded pretty happy.

He'd enclosed a ration coupon for me as a souvenir, as bad as he might need it to get some food, but he'd make out, he said. This little square of paper was orange and yellow and good for a few handfuls of arroz. I looked at it in great detail before I tucked it into my little box of treasures.

I don't figure it was even two weeks afore I got another letter from Europe. More pretty stamps with words I didn't know. The handwriting was different, though. I could tell that right off. It was from Cristina Vargas Delgado, it was.

There'd been a big battle at a river called Jarama. They'd pushed each other back and forth for near three weeks, and it was bloody. Izzy had got shot on the 25th of February trying to storm a fascist position up on a hill. He wasn't the only fellow killed, of course. A whole passel of the International Brigade boys had been. Thousands of them. Izzy took a couple of machine gun bullets to the gut, Cristina wrote me in her bad English. From what I could make out, he hadn't lasted too long. She figured I'd want to know about my friend. She was sorry. And she planned to fight on to save Spain and the workers.

There was a song written about the Battle at Jarama. I don't reckon it was a chart topper, but I'd hear it every now and again in a night club. It never failed to bring an ache to my heart, thinking about Coney Island and Izzy Levy, wearing his little beret and bandana and saving the world.

Oh. Something I forgot to mention: I had moved downtown after the 1937 season ended. Top floor apartment at 135 W. 13th Street. It was a combination of things, I reckon. I'd lived right around the ballyards in the Bronx ever since I come to New York. As you recall, the first several years, I lived right inside of it. By the time the Depression was in full swing, I was spending a fair amount of my free time down toward Midtown or below. The visits to Book Row had been a regular thing for years. A couple of women I saw briefly lived that direction, and so did my buddy Paul Flinkenberg. The best pizza pie in Manhattan was down that way, too, a place called John's on Bleeker Street. Lordy, it was a good one. I wasn't getting much money, mind you, but I didn't have a lot of expenses either. Between the Giants and an odd job here and yonder, I generally had enough jack to enjoy myself. On top of all that, Bingo Tavarozzi had moved to Youngstown, Ohio.

Probably the biggest thing that got me to ruminating on a move was being a lower man on the totem pole. When a body was expected to be at the Polo Grounds late at night or at the butt crack of dawn, it was usually me.

"He lives right around the corner, he won't mind," they'd say. Well, sir, I was starting to mind. Not that I had much of a life outside of the ball club and drinking with my buddies, mind you, but if things kept on that way, I never would.

It's another one of those odd stories how I ended up on W. 13th. The short of it is that I found an apartment key stuck inside a slice of rhubarb pie at the Horn & Hardart by Union Square. I'd been playing billiards upstairs at a joint called Julian's.

Come to find out later that there was a hairy Romanian fellow who worked in the automat kitchen and was carrying on with his cousin's wife. Now, this gent's brother was the super at a building a few blocks west, and he slid over the key to a flat that was currently empty for the illicit purposes of this little tryst, though he didn't know any details at the time. The secret master plan was that the hairy fellow would pass the key to this... not that I'm judging... to this harlot, by hiding it inside rhubarb pie. I mean who the hell is going to order that? Well, an assistant clubhouse man trying to focus with one eye, that's who.

Yep. Truth be told, I had been swilling a few tankards at the pool hall, and I thought I was grabbing a slice of cherry pie. That's a personal favorite. Might have saved my life, really, since I would have damn near inhaled a slice of cherry, but I was so disappointed with the rhubarb that I was just poking at it with my fork. Otherwise, I could have choked on that key right in the slap middle of the East Village.

I turned up the key, all red and sticky, and I'll be damned if the building address wasn't tied on with a tag. Thinking it was some kind of treasure hunt, I did what any other naturally curious person would do. I walked over there and commenced to trying the key in every lock I could find.

The hairy fellow, his name was Constantin, had been watching through the little food windows in abject horror as I grabbed the scarlet pie. After deliberating for a brief spell whether his boss's yelling or his cousin's shotgun was the greater of two evils, he come running after me. He caught up just as old Mrs. Spinozzo in 1B was loudly inquiring why a half-in-the-bag stranger was testing his key in her front door at 11:00 PM. Dumitru, the super, was standing there in his underwear, and things were getting a might testy when Constantin arrived.

He took to shushing and apologizing and telling Mrs. Spinozzo that I was his friend and "No worry. No worry." Between the two hairy Romanians and the slightly less hairy Mrs. Spinozzo, I couldn't make out much. I was wondering how come I didn't know this "friend" of mine.

Eventually, we ended up in the super's apartment down in the basement, and Constantin, overwhelmed by guilt, busted open like a freeze dried rubber. He spilled the beans about the hidden key and schtupping his cousin's wife to the both of us, including an undainty detail or twelve. Dumitru took to yelling in Romanian, and Constantin blubbering back at him. Just when my buzz was damn near wore off and I was plotting my way out of this overheated little basement room, both brothers turned on me in a panic. Suddenly they were both afraid that I'd tell their crazy cousin about his loose wife.

"What we do, mister? What we do you no tell Ion?"

Son, I had no idea what that sentence even meant, but after they repeated it a few times, it slowly become clear that it might be an opportunity for me.

"Well, tell me about that vacant apartment you got."

Dumitru was falling all over himself by that point.

"No problem, mister. No problem. I make you sweet deal. I square with landlord. You no tell Ion."

I ended up living there six years in a tidy one bedroom flat in a nice little building with some of the cheapest rent south of Albany. Dumitru stayed a regular fixture for me, and Constantin eventually married a woman who wasn't already married and opened him up a radio repair shop. I never heard another peep about Ion's wife.

Do you have a type, son? Blonde or brunette? Tall, short, busty, skinny? A certain looking woman who will always catch your eye? Well, I thought I did, too. And then I met Jenny, and the whole notion flew all to hell.

I suppose some folks would call her hair dishwater blonde, though that never made much sense to me on account of dishwater normally being a dull white. Or maybe I'm using too much soap. Anyhoo, I'd always been a brunette man until then, but once I got a look at Jenny's face, that dishwater shade would do me just fine.

Her smile is what I noticed first. Teeth so straight and white you'd think they must've come from Woolworth's window, but they were hers, all right. That smile would flash real quick sometimes like lightning. She was an easy laugher. Jenny always saw the humor in everything. I reckon that's part of why we hit it off so. I'd always tried to enjoy myself, as well.

Her eyes? Funny you should ask. They were elusive in color, but if you press me on it, I'd call them grey. Clear, bright grey like the sunrise when you're walking in the winter woods up north. It's a color that put me in mind of a still, cool pond with geese flying high in the sky. You'd want to dip your toe into a color like that. That's how I saw her eyes, as an invitation.

The day I met Jenny, I'd only been living downtown for six weeks. It was freezing cold. January 4, 1938. My winter job that off season was stocker and janitor at a neighborhood grocery over on Sixth Avenue right across from St. Francis Xavier Church. Mostly I worked a few hours stocking the shelves and sweeping up. Mopped the floor every other day after closing. But I also done deliveries. This wasn't a supermarket, now. It was a small grocery. Four aisles. Most people stopped every day or every other day and left with a single bag, but now and again, there'd be an order that required my carrying services.

That day, it was a Tuesday, the church rang over to fill a list of odds and ends for a supper they had planned for Epiphany a couple days later. A big box worth of dried beans, onions, leeks, what have you. Esther, the boss lady, gathered it all up and told me to schlep it across to the church office.

Now I'd never had cause to go to that big church. I'm not much of a churchy type, as you know, but I do have curiosity, so I took the scenic route through the front doors. Not that I knew exactly where the church office was anyway, mind you. There were only a handful of people inside, all bundled up tight in their winter garb and kneeling here and yonder, but lordy what a first impression. The organist was practicing, and that music was just bouncing off the arches. Statues of saints by the passel was spread around above me. Artworks on the ceiling and beams of light shining bright. I stood there with my jaw hanging down most likely. I know full well my breath was visible before me since it was colder than polar bear whiskers, and all the time I'm holding a big old box of canned goods, Crisco, and onions.

"I'll thank you to remove your hat, my son. It's God's house, it is."

The priest had sort of snuck up behind, and give me a bit of a start.

I whipped my tweed hat off and spun round.

"And if those be our groceries, you might take them through to the office. We shan't be handing them out to the pews."

The Father directed me to the proper doorway and give me just a hint of a wink.

It's impossible to tell from this distance, but I don't believe it was love at first sight. Jenny was reading a book. *Poirot Loses a Client.* It was a big seller that month, all the rage. Even though I was interrupting her, she flashed that big smile I told you about, and slipped a marker into the pages to save her place.

"Hello."

That was the first word she said to me. Not original, but it proved to be a conversation starter. Once she signed the receipt and handed it back to me, she just kept smiling. It involved her whole face, that smile did.

"Do you like to read? This book is wonderful. I picked it up from the newsstand yesterday morning, and I just have not wanted to set it down. She is a wonderful writer, and I do like the notion that a woman can write detective stories."

"Well, I do like detective stories in the magazines." Something about her just put you at ease from the git go.

"Then you should definitely try Agatha Christie."

She sized me up a little.

"*Murder in the Air.* That's where you ought to start. The detective is a pompous little Belgian, but he definitely grows on you."

She sure grew on me, not that I wasn't smitten already. At first, I did what most men would've. I made shit up. I come up with a variety of reasons, including fake deliveries, to stop by the church office. I debated myself for the best part of a month over where to ask her on a date. Normally, I'd have sought advice from some of the guys from the team, but it was the off season, and they had scattered to the four winds. That also meant I couldn't just give her tickets to a game to break the ice. My first instinct had been a movie, but I finally decided that since our first conversation had been about reading, that must be a sign.

I called for her one afternoon, and we strolled over to Book Row. Would you believe that we browsed the shelves and tables for close to four hours, stopping frequently to chat and laugh. Normally, some of those bookmen would run out customers like that, but nobody paid us a whit of attention. For all our trouble, I came away with two new reads, and she picked three. Some of the previous year's titles were starting to be available used. I recollect scooping up a slick copy of *To Have and To Have Not* which you will find on a shelf in my bedroom, and Jenny, I still know what she picked out. A used copy of *Out of Africa*, which is a bit girly for me, though I sure liked the animals like Lulu the gazelle. *The Red Box*, a Nero Wolfe story that she had not yet got around to checking out from the library, and *Burmese Days*. We had an ice cream on the way back. Rum raisin for her. I'm a chocolate man, still today.

You worry about everything at that early point in a budding relationship. Getting to know each other can be hard when a man fully realizes he's playing out of his league. I found myself tossing and turning over what stories I could tell her without her figuring I was some kind of degenerate hoodlum, but I guess I chose okay.

I was mostly on an egg salad budget, but I did save up and take her to a nice dinner at Nino and Nella one night. Like every place else in the city, it had been a speakeasy during the Prohibition, but it was a good Italian restaurant, and right there in the Village. Bing Crosby talked about it on his radio show, and though he was a total hack as a singer and had ears like open taxi doors, I thought it would be worth the splurge. That was my first taste of veal marsala, sautéed in that wine with mushrooms. It probably brought some pain to my wallet, but I recollect it being a grand evening.

It was also gratifying to find out that one of Jenny's favorite spots in New York had been special to me for then on 15 years. Even before I was mesmerized by the sea shore at Coney Island, I had come to be dazzled by Battery Park. It is right there on the tip end of Manhattan, of course. You could stare at the horizon and watch the ships billowing smoke, and it was never so easy to imagine the breadth of the world. With free entertainment options limited, there could be a healthy competition for a place on the park benches. Once I moved downtown, I come to see that old men were thicker than pigeons down there.

The place I'm thinking of, though, was the aquarium. The building itself was something else, a fort built to keep the Europeans out that became the place to welcome Europeans in. Bingo Tavarozzi told me that his great uncle entered America through that building, but they had switched it over to menagerie service not long after I was born.

My favorite residents there were the seals and walruses. They were not the most aromatic animals, but in those days, neither were most New Yorkers. There was one old sea lion named Beowulf, and we took a bit of a liking to one another. I will tell you that his breath was a cross between week old sardines and the ass end of a Bowery bum. He never let on what he thought of mine. I could stand by the edge of his tank, and we'd communicate with looks and nods. Not deep conversations, you understand, but satisfying nonetheless.

It was Jenny who brought up the aquarium to me, and we ended up there often. She and I shared a common sentiment that the biggest inmates there were getting a raw deal. They kept a Beluga Whale there for many years, and presumably not for the caviar. Made both of us sad, it did. Open water not two hundred yards away, and that poor soul barely had room to turn around. I doubt if he could look out a window, but I sure had him pegged for wistful.

Jenny and me got married on the second day of March, 1939. Even though I am not the pious, bible-toting kind, and even though it took some fast talking and more than a few winks and nods, Father Scola at St. Francis did the solemnizing. Since I wasn't Catholic, it wasn't official, you understand, but as a favor to Jenny, he pulled us into one of the side chapels and did a blessing, gulped some wine and fed my new bride a vanilla wafer. The whole thing gave us both a case of the giggles, and the good father looked askance at that, but he was a fine man.

The Giants trained in Baton Rouge again that season, and I would be packing up in a few days, but Jenny and me scraped together enough money to spend the weekend at the Indian Queen Hotel in Stroudsburg, PA.. Room Eight. There was still snow on the ground, so the place wasn't too crowded. We bundled up and strolled the town and walked out some roads toward the mountains. That Monday, she moved into what had been my apartment. It was the first time I'd lived with another human since I was 16. Unless you count hookers and ball fans.

The reason we were going to Baton Rouge was because of Bill Terry, who was still managing the Giants. People forget how big a star he was. As an investment, Bill had bought him a string of Esso service stations. He had a job with Standard Oil in Memphis back before his playing days, and someplace along the line, he become tight with a bunch of Southern politicians, including one who had become Governor of Louisiana. That's how the local government greased the skids to bring us down there.

Leaving my new bride back in New York was vexing. Either way, Baton Rouge was not an exciting town. What they say these days about Louisiana is true, everything north of I-10 ought to be Arkansas. Of course, there was no interstate highway in 1939, but the sentiment was the same. It was apples to possums compared to my adventure down in Houma with the Yankees. Don't let the French name fool you, Baton Rouge in 1939 was much more redneck than Cajun charm.

One thing about the Giants, though, there were a shit ton of Southern boys on that team. Early on, I heard from one of the groundskeepers that we needed to try Delpit's Chicken Shack, and they weren't lying. That was some tasty hot bird, right there. I'd bet there were a dozen of us eating that fried chicken three times a week. Admittedly, it might not have been the best training regimen, but since one of the fellows scarfing down all those wings, thighs, and gizzards was our manager, Bill Terry, nobody was too worried.

The facility where we played was shinier than Ben Franklin's pate. Louisiana State University had built them a brand new ball yard, a big one, and we had been the first ones to use it the previous year. It still looked spanking that spring. We were big dogs in Baton Rouge. The king down there was Ott, not only because he was our star hitter, but he was from right down the road. There sure were a passel of cousins and alleged cousins trying to get a piece of something free. For me, I was just relieved when we headed home.

Even though I might have harbored a touch of bad feelings for the Yankees, I had more than a little twinge at the end of Gehrig's streak on April 29, 1939. I had spent probably a hundred days a year around the man for over a decade, so even if we weren't besties, it still made me a mite sad. He may have been duller than a paint store puddy knife, but Lou was a good man, and his diagnosis was certainly no secret amongst the baseball world.

The very next day after Lou left the lineup was the opening of the big World's Fair of 1939. Did you know that? Yep. The World of Tomorrow, it was. The Giants had been wearing patches on our sleeves all the previous season promoting the Fair. In spite of any sadness from the baseball crowd, folks was bully on the grand opening.

You know what the 1893 Chicago Fair meant to me as a young 'un, and while this one didn't rise to those heights, it was a humdinger nevertheless. There was lots to see. Frank Buck's wild animals. Billy Rose's Aquacade where Tarzan and synchronized swimmers cavorted in the fountains. I still wonder why Jiggs the orangutan never hooked up with Tarzan for those splash shows, but it wasn't my decision, I reckon.

Jenny and I must've gone to the Fair a dozen times. She loved watching the monkeys as much as I did, or at least she put up with my desire to spend as much time as possible at Monkey Mountain every visit. Six hundred of the critters. That was a show, right there. Jenny would hug me and call me her big monkey, and I suppose it was on account of that. She gave the best hugs. Real love in them.

I got one more for you. Did you know that the original Elsie the cow was at the World's Fair in 1939? They had her and 100 other cows on a big round contraption that milked them and bathed them and fed them while it turned in a circle. They called it a Rotolactor, and it give me nightmares for several years, it did. I used to wake up in a hot sweat making sucking noises. It wasn't natural, that thing.

Not every day was a trip to the Fair, though. We settled into life together the way couples do as the new smell wears off. Roles tended to be traditional in those days, but Jenny kept her job at the church, and I scrounged up an off season gig every year. She did most of the housework, and I grew to enjoy the food shopping which I did most every other day at little stores and stands within a couple of blocks. At least one night a week, we had a date. Movies mostly, but sometimes dancing, though I was no good at it. Cutting a rug was something I might have done by accident with my big feet.

She planted geraniums in a little window box. Hopeful little plants, but they hadn't a prayer. Jenny wasn't very good at growing things, but bless her, she kept trying. She'd plant them in the spring, and by the Fourth of July, all you'd see was a couple of brown stems.

Once in a blue moon, I saved up enough for a splurge. One night we went to see Louis Armstrong front his own band at the Strand Theatre on Broadway.

Jack Teagarden was playing with him. Big Sid Catlett on drums. I caught him backstage and asked him if he remembered that night on the back of the train car, but recollection ain't necessarily part of the ganja experience.

If you've never treated yourself to vintage Louis Armstrong, you've deprived yourself of some of life's very blood. He was doing more big band stuff by then, and less of the early jazz licks where he cut his chops. But there was a new arrangement of *Perdido Street Blues* that was worth the admission all by its ownself. His horn produced a church moan on those low down blues. It was louder and clearer than anyone else ever mustered. You could close your eyes when Satchmo played and float away in some fever dream, oscillating betwixt heaven and hell. Jenny mightn't have had the passion for that music, but she tolerated it in me.

Memory is a fickle thing, and the ones I hold dear from those days are probably a thousand different times mashed up like potatoes. It's the nights at home. I can still feel the big reading chair that I sat in every night. It had wide, oak arms with a gentle curve, and the green wool of the cushions had a nap that was real popular then but that I haven't seen since before you were born. It was bristly when you rubbed your hand across it, but was comfortable all the same. Our furniture matched as well as the second hand stores allowed it to, I reckon. Jenny had done a fine job of sprucing up our little flat. She'd curl up on this little orange patterned love seat and crochet. On frisky nights, I'd move over there with her and listen to band music and breathe her perfume.

Chapter Twenty-One

Nineteen thirty-nine was a watershed year. The rumblings of a big war had been going on for over a year already. People had been hearing the news, and except for the most vile of the German immigrants, Americans shook their heads about Hitler. Few wanted to do anything about it, though. It was an awakening for lots of us that September after the Germans invaded Poland. Now they had done gone and captured a country people could pronounce. It sure didn't bode well, but the next year and a half, we were still whistling in the dark.

By the start of the season in 1941, me and Jenny were no longer newlyweds. Paul Flinkenberg had gotten married, too. A legal secretary with blonde hair and a rack bigger than the one that held our bats at the Polo Grounds. I stood up for him just like he had for me, though it was down at the courthouse, and he had to go back to his office afterward.

A real nice girl, his wife was, though a titch high strung when she drank. There were a few times that the four of us was out someplace, and Rita stormed off to the powder room and never come back. Paul would be obliged to leave early to go looking for her. It was passionate.

Once or twice, we even lured that mogul Eddie Ardoin and his diamond encrusted missus to meet up with us. They had the first of what developed into a litany of rich children, all of whom went through life dragging fancy sounding names behind them. For an heiress, Mary Lynn was a lot of laughs once she let her hair down and took the pickle out of her ass. We always toasted Izzy Levy. I know he would have enjoyed that.

Gehrig died at the start of June. Joe D was in the middle of his streak but it was not much of a news item at that time. It went on into July. Shit, even at the end, it wasn't quite like folks make it out today. Did you know that smack in the center of the streak, were two back to back games against the White Sox where Luke Appling dropped DiMaggio grounders that got scored a hit? They were the only hits he got on those days, too. So, the streak wasn't really a streak at all.

The official scorer was Dan Daniel who had changed his last name since the bosses at the *New York Telegram* thought people would be offended by a Jewish scribe. The Yankees ball club paid his expenses, so it's not like he was unbiased. Hell, if he didn't even insist on using his real name, then why couldn't an error be a base hit? Twice.

When I say the whole thing was not top of news, I'm not exaggerating. Most ballgames, even in New York, were drawing fewer than ten thousand fans. Britain was getting bombed more often than the Milwaukee town drunk, and American boys had either been drafted or were building airplanes to ship across the Atlantic. We all knew our time was coming.

There are moments in the life of a family or a town or even a country that you always remember, and every American alive that day can tell you right where they were when they heard the news. There was never a bigger kick to the innards than hearing about Pearl Harbor. It was a Joe Louis punch right to your breadbasket.

As far as my own story goes, I was sitting in our little living room listening to a football game on the radio. Jenny was cleaning up the kitchen, Sunday lunch being a special meal. We'd had roasted chicken and butternut squash. As was my general Sunday routine, I was likely trying to work up a satisfying burp at a volume low enough so's to not catch flak from Jenny when they come on with a special announcement. I gulped down whatever air I been cultivating as she stepped out of our little kitchen drying her hands on a cup towel.

The football Giants were playing the football Dodgers, and Pug Manders of Brooklyn was having the best of it when the radio man cut into the game to read no more than two sentences. It was just to the effect that they were interrupting to say the Japanese had attacked Pearl Harbor and to stay tuned after the broadcast for more details. Then Ace Parker threw another exciting pass.

Jenny and I stared at each other, not saying a word. I suppose there was an unspoken dialogue in our heads, checking the boxes together of just what this might mean. Finally, I noticed a tear come from the corner of Jenny's left eye. Then I let out a belch to rattle the windows.

The very day after Pearl Harbor, young men and raw boys lined up outside of recruiting offices from Bangor to San Diego. The United States military was woefully undermanned, and there was a passel of 16-year olds who joined the Marines that first week or two. Underage and underweight. Ninety-six pounders who were sent to the diner next door with the instruction to eat four bananas and drink all the water they could hold, then come back and take the physical again. We were a nation in need.

Among the ballplayers were some who went off to war, and some who stayed home. Just like in Hollywood where big stars like James Stewart, Henry Fonda, Clark Gable, and Jackie Coogan volunteered and served in harm's way while slackers like John Wayne scratched his ass in a studio commissary. In baseball, you had your genuine heroes. Fellows like Greenberg, Williams, and Feller, who were already stars, and others, like Spahn and Berra who were still in the minors, but them and others saw combat a plenty. Nobody wanted to be shot at, mind you, but they reckoned they were as much Americans as the next guy, and they signed on to do their part.

Though the minor leagues shut down, President Roosevelt thought people needed the distraction of the bigs, so everybody fielded a club. Some of the fellows spent the war on a roster, but working night shifts at a job that classified for defense. Some players missed a matter of months, while others were gone the whole war. For assistant equipment men, there was much less wiggle room when it come to doing your part for Uncle Sam.

I was less than a month shy of 41 years old when the sneaky bastards bombed Pearl Harbor, but I had worked the previous two off seasons at the Brooklyn

Army Terminal, so my defense job was already in place. I'd been on late shift since early October, stationed in Warehouse B, which, when it was constructed, had been the biggest building in the world. It was something else, boy. Had a railroad running through this big courtyard in the middle, double decker piers out on the water, and it stretched five blocks.

My billet was counting off pallets as they were fixing to be scooped up in a big net and swung into the hold of a troop ship. Some days, I'd get distracted and end up telling baseball tales to the boys in drab who were ticketed for a crossing. Just shy of three and a half million of them left through the terminal during the war, so my material was evergreen.

I don't know if it helped or not, but after twenty seasons in the major leagues, I had met a lot of ballplayers. If one of them boys looked nervous about saying so long to the U.S. of A. so some Geri could blast away at them with a tommy gun, then I asked the fellow where he was from, you see. Say he answered Fredonia, Ohio. I'd tell him some tales about Woody English. We had faced him during the Series back in '32. Woody played short for the Cubs then, and I would relate to this wide-eyed soldier as to how Woody had hands that looked like they'd been transplanted from a Barbary Ape, or how one of his favorite pranks was to crawl across a hotel lobby and light the bottom of some businessman's newspaper on fire. A few minutes of that, and the soldier boy, who probably took great local pride in knowing Woody English's cousin back home, had forgot all about the Nazis. At least for the moment.

I had a story like that for hundreds of ballplayers in a thousand home towns.

As for the goods we were loading, it was everything from jeeps to rifles to C-rations. One of the reprobates on the shift with me was an old Irishman name of Cormac Brophy, veteran of the Great War and Brooklyn born and reared. Not to stereotype, but Brophy stayed liquored up from lunchtime forward. He was a good natured drunk and a generous soul. Always ready to give a gift to a stranger, old Cormac was.

I recollect a time when he and a new worker from another department got to trading lies about crooners. This young fellow was a Sinatra fanatic, like most were at the time. Well, they should be, since no man ever phrased a song better before or since. Cormac Brophy, though, amid nips from his lunch bucket, was extolling the virtues of Henry Burr. He might as well have been claiming that he could eat chicken and fart eggs from the blank looks on this young fellow's phiz, but the next day, when lunch rolled around, Brophy had scoured a handful of music stores and nonchalantly presented the new man with a 78 record of *Are You Lonesome Tonight*. Henry Burr at his finest. He wasn't trying to show anyone up, mind you, and he didn't even know if he'd ever see the new guy again. Brophy was just trying to share the joy.

It was the same ardor that made him come up with an idea to lift the spirits of at least a few lucky soldiers on the ground in North Africa. Everybody in the whole country wanted to contribute somehow, and the bunch of us at the warehouse bought into that drunk Irishman's plan through and through, even if it was a bit of thin gravy.

Every man in the army had complained about C-rations. They'd trade their tins of franks and beans for a can of three year old peaches in syrup, but that was a about as good as it got. So, Brophy developed a dream of bringing in what he saw as treats and slipping them randomly into the boxes. He imagined that some homesick schmo hunkered down in the sand would open his ration package and find a froofraw that would be like a nugget of gold. Now, you couldn't buy chocolate in the drug stores. It was already going to the soldiers. Even m&ms. Most other food wouldn't keep on the five week journey that it might take to get all the way to the Sahara Desert, so Brophy set his mind to working on other ideas.

He ruled out rubbers on account of there being a dearth of places to wear them. Socks? Well, their grandmothers was likely shipping those over. I suggested paperback novels, but those were too big to slip into the box. He was committed to his scheme, but hadn't yet lit upon what the treats would be.

One day, Brophy stopped in at a newsstand to pick up the new copy of Ladies Home Journal. He claimed he was hankering for the new shrimp tomato aspic recipe. On impulse, he grabbed a box of Cracker Jack, and had his epiphany. We would take the prizes from the boxes and send them on to our boys overseas.

Well, son, I don't reckon you've ever given much thought to how you would eat, say, a thousand boxes of Cracker Jack, but we sure did. Brophy was short on teeth to begin with, so it took an extra toll on him. Like I said, there were maybe eight of us in on the venture, so each of us developed a team of suppliers, folks who would be willing to drop a nickel then cough up the prize. Not literally, though that did happen if a body was particularly hungry.

You probably don't know this, but before the war, Cracker Jack prizes were made in Japan. Those rat bastards didn't think about that when they bombed Pearl, did they? America stepped in to fill the void, though. Take that, Tojo! Depending on how old the box was, you might get a little doubloon, or a cardboard clown, or, if you were really lucky, a blue goose made out of tin. Early in the war, they started making these little spinners that said "Keep em Flying." When you blew on it, it whirled around and the little blue planes looked like they were soaring through the ether.

Brophy, with that accent of his, used to tear up at the prospects.

"Faiths above us, may our soldier boys in Tunisia, the little darlings, have a moment of glee as they pick up their carbines and say, 'Let me kill a bushel of Germans so I can get back to blowing on me airplane spinner.'"

Made a person proud.

With most fellows in the service, big league teams during the war had a collection of old timers and misfits filling out the rosters. We were just glad to have the routine and distraction, but it didn't always make for great baseball. Thankfully, it was before television, so you didn't have to watch the highlight reels.

Meat was hard to come by, but one time the old Russian fellow at our little meat market ended up with a few crates of nice roast beef. He whispered to me that he'd trade me a whole one, maybe four pounds worth, for ten tickets to a Sunday game. He wanted to take his whole family, he said. I tried to warn him that the quality of play would be lacking, but I didn't warn him too hard, just said enough to assuage any guilt.

I don't know what possessed her, but when Jenny saw that roast, she insisted I invite a few guys from the ball club. Single guys, she said. Fellows who didn't get much home cooking. Four pounds of meat would go bad well before we could eat it, so spread the wealth, she told me.

One night, after a win over the Pirates, I invited two rookie pitchers and the new man from the grounds crew, Dicky Crystal, a boy from Binghamton who was only 16 and too young to serve as of yet. Everyone got to guzzling wine and laughing at the dumbest jokes, and wouldn't you know it, but Jenny burned that free roast beef to a crispy black. She was normally a reliable cook, but cheap Muscatel can impinge on your ability to read a stove dial.

After a brief pause to say a prayer for our departed supper, one of the rookies took the carving knife and started trimming off the burned parts. By the time he was done, each us had enough meat for a very skimpy sandwich, but no complaints were heard. We all cackled the whole time, and when it was done, little Dicky Crystal announced that the roast was exactly like his mother used to make upstate. Jenny laughed herself tired hearing their tall tales. It was nice to see. There was a bunch of wonderful knuckleheads on those wartime clubs.

You've heard about some of the outliers, I reckon. The Reds signed Joe Nuxhall whose balls hadn't even dropped yet, but there was some decent ones, too. Minor leaguers getting a chance for the first time. Sid Gordon was up with the Giants for his first year in the bigs in '43. Jewish kid who grew up in Brooklyn driving his old man's coal delivery truck. On the days he played, the bleachers got rowdier than a bagpiper on meth.

Then there were the wartime characters, and you never knew where you would find them playing either. Danny Gardella come to the Giants the following season, but we'd heard tell of him that year, and he was playing in the Consolidated Shipyard League. He was another local boy who boxed welterweight and sang opera. He made a name for himself as one of the worst fielders to ever mis-tie his spikes. One time he pulled his cap down over his own eyes while waiting for a pop fly, and on another occasion, he damn near lost his pants running for a less than screaming liner. He may have been just a neighborhood lug, but he was the first guy to jump ship for Mexican baseball, and in my book that means every modern player ought to say a prayer of thanks to Danny Gardella for laying the groundwork for free agency.

Of course, some old guys stayed around when they otherwise would've been back in Iowa hoeing corn. Some of them were damn near my age, and that is not a recipe for success. We had four future Hall of Famers on the 1943 Giants squad, but we finished dead ass last in the National League. Hubbell was 40, and only made it into 12 games before he called it quits. Ducky Medwick come over from Brooklyn during the season, and should've been still in his prime. He had a decent year in '44, but his best was clearly behind him. He was a prickly son of a bitch, anyway.

Ernie Lombardi came to the Giants in 1943, too. He was an All-Star, a .300 hitter, former MVP and the slowest damn human that ever walked. Interesting fellow, the Schnozz was. He had won a batting title the year before he got traded, and as long as it took him to get to first base, you know he had to knock the ball to all corners of the yard. On the face of it, he never should've been that good, but he compensated. Like an ugly girl learning how to cook. His hands were so big that he could've been employee of the year at any car wash in America. He used a 42 ounce bat. Not near as heavy as those monsters the Babe swung, but it sure was bigger than the flyswatters some guys like Rod Carew carried.

Lom, as most of the fellows called him, was six foot three, about the same size as I was. He had grown up working his folks' grocery store in Oakland, and I liked to think that he had developed that rifle throwing arm of his by winging onions at shoplifters. He never confirmed it, but it was true to me.

I mentioned that most players served at least some time in the services. We'd see some of the guys who were playing ball on military teams. DiMaggio and Musial were the two most famous cases, but a load of the fellows donned the uniform only to end up traveling the world playing baseball to entertain the fighting men. Every base had a team, and then there were regimental teams. It become a big thing. They hadn't integrated the military yet, but the Army did have a couple of the Negro League stars mixed in with white players over in Germany.

Saying that the War was tough on the whole country would be pretty durn pointless. Everyone knows that already. I had friends everywhere that lost brothers, friends or worse yet, lost boys. They say that parents aren't supposed to bury their children. It was a painful thing to watch.

You raise those little buggers, and somewhere in between the wiping their butts and noses, the apologizing to their teachers, the getting told how much they hate you because you won't let them go off to some bad part of town at midnight with a bunch of strangers, well, you grow attached to them. You got any kids? A girl? Oh, they're the best. Good for you.

No, I couldn't imagine having to bury my boy in the prime of his life.

I looked into the eyes of those that did, and I can tell you true that every last one of them drew at least a little consolation from pride. World War II wasn't like anything since then. It was really necessary. We were defending ourselves against somebody that could have beat us and changed the world for the worst. The dying is always senseless, especially if you look at it man by man, but there was a cause that we all believed in. I think that made the grief just a hair lighter for the folks that gave one of their boys up for it, though I don't imagine that it ever stopped the tears next Christmas.

I say that so you know that I am not trying to compare my own loss during the War to those brave boys, but I lost my sweet Jenny on the 21st of February in 1944. Never married again, you know.

I don't think I showed you her picture, did I? Yeah, that's her over the fireplace. I couldn't recall if I had told you or not. She was so pretty.

She was a hard worker, my Jenny. I had it easy, just working for the ball club or the warehouse, one job at a time, and maybe helping out with some bond drives, but Jen, she kept her regular job typing and filing and putting up with occasional crapola from the big wigs at the archdiocese. On top of that, she was running an operation collecting scrap metal and war material across the whole neighborhood. Had 12 or 14 people working under her. They'd spend every Saturday out there dragging whatever they could find back for the war effort. I ain't ashamed to tell you that I should have been doing more.

I saw that look on your face when I mentioned the scrap metal drive. I ought to explain about that. I forget that folks like you are too young to remember.

All those drives started not long after Pearl Harbor. People were scared. You got to understand that things wasn't going very well for the old U.S of A. back in 1942. The Japs and Germans were beating the living shit out of us most of the time, and regular people wanted to come up with something that could be of help. So, the government told everybody to start collecting things: metal, rubber, newspapers, chicken bones, old rags. Personally, I thought that we should have tried to save our methane to use as fuel, and for two years I told everybody I run into that they ought to be burping and farting in a jar and shipping it to the War Department. I thought I made a pretty fair argument, but that never caught on. I did suspect that I was shadowed by Army Intelligence for a couple weeks, but no harm come of it.

Some folks knew it even then, that a whole lot of the collections drives was just to keep morale up and make us little folks feel good about doing something. Even I knew that you couldn't recycle rubber. Still can't to this day, did you know that? And when I saw folks rounding up old tires and garden hoses and galoshes, raincoats and bathing caps, I told them they was wasting their time. They eventually figured out how to make fake rubber, but they durn sure took the winding garden path to get there.

Another thing that Jenny collected was kitchen fat; and that one turned out to be really worthwhile. See you can take old grease and fat and make something called glycerin. Do you know what that is? It goes into medicine and bombs. I didn't find that out until I met a utility infielder at spring training in 1963 who had him a chemistry degree. I don't recall how that came up in conversation, but it did. Made me feel bad on account of I figured that I stole about a hundred sticks of dynamite from the war effort and rubbed it on my rear end. But bacon grease sure does ease a rash better than anything else. And the neighborhood dogs love you.

Well, anyhow, one night in the middle of December of 1943, I had met up with a few of the boys from the team for a spaghetti supper. Beef was scarce, but some of the old ladies at St Bernard's on 14th Street made some pretty good meatballs out of something that I never asked about. This bunch of us had got in the habit of going over there at least one Saturday a month.

Jenny was tired that night, so she said for me to go and have a good time, and that she'd see me when I got back. Wake her up, is what she told me. We were still frisky that way.

Being big overgrown boys ourselves, we decided to stop at a tavern on the way back and swap a few lies. Johnny Allen, who was from Carolina, Dick Bartell, Spunky Weller from the grounds crew. I guess I've put out of my mind who all was there that night, but I'm certain we had us a grand time cause I didn't get back home till after midnight.

You know how you try to sneak into your house after you've been drinking? All quiet. Where you bump into the coat rack and say "Shhhh!" real loud. Well, that was me. I tip toed down the hallway and into our room.

My heart damn near stopped when I saw Jenny laying on the floor about three feet from the bed. Her eyes were open, but she looked so tired, and her skin was hotter than Dante's stove. I could barely hear her, but I made out that she couldn't get up. She just felt weak, she said. Those are words from a loved one that'll sober you up quick. That was three dollars of whiskey down the drain in an instant.

Well, it was the middle of the night, and all I could think of was finding someone to fix her up. Jenny was the strong one, you see. My spark plug. And it wasn't supposed to be like that, with her laying on the floor, all vulnerable.

I bundled her up and carried her three blocks to St. Vincent's Hospital. It seemed the fastest way, you know.

I'll never forget the first face I saw when I got through the door. Sister Joan. Not a handsome woman, except maybe in a Charles Laughton sort of way, but she had a certain grace about her, all reassuring and everything, that made me feel like Jenny was gonna be just fine.

But she never come home.

That was the worst Christmas I ever spent on this planet, 1943, sitting up in the hospital room holding the hand of my beloved.

She lingered for better than two months. There were good days, but when you're close and optimistic, it's easy to lose sight of the bigger picture, as they say. I recollect a drouth year back in Lee County. People think that means that it don't rain at all, but that's not exactly true. There'll be days that it clouds up just to tease you. Sometimes you even get rumbling thunder off in the distance, but the drops of rain that start falling won't be enough to wet the whistle of a parched gnat. The ground is crusted over, and the rain just skitters across the top and never soaks in to do good.

That's how it was with Jenny. There would be a little rally where her blood count improved, and you'd think that a corner was turned. You'd think it because you so badly wanted it to be true. Like that farmer desperately looking for green shoots from the dirt. Fact was that they had no treatment for what was ailing her. It was a cancer of the blood, and she wasted away. Then one day she was gone.

I've been an upbeat soul my whole life, son, but the despair got the best of me that winter. The wolf was in the kitchen. I'd known a handful of fellows who took their own life, old men back in Arkansas, a war veteran who got cut by the Chicks in '21. I always saw it as the ultimate act of selfishness. I wondered how they could do that to their friends and family, the people who cared about them even if they may not have shown it sufficiently.

I don't reckon I've ever admitted this to anyone, but I vowed to share my story with you, and yes, sir, there were nights I was angry at the world just then. Nights when I pondered and weighed whether I could start fresh or whether I had played out my string. I laid awake while I reasoned out how to do the deed. Baseball felt a long way off, and it was the only thing I could imagine soothing my wounds.

Then one night, toward the end of the bottle, I recollected something my old daddy told me.

"Son, when a man gives up trying, he's become no better than a legless mule. No good to himself or anyone else. So, keep giving your best till the good Lord tells you otherwise."

Of course, my daddy was just looking to have mama let him back in the bed, but I reckoned that the lesson still applied. That's what I'd do – just keep walking until life found me again.

Don't miss the conclusion of Rube Wingo's story in Wingo's Redemption coming in Summer of 2024.

Chapter Twenty-Two

Author's Notes

It's a tricky thing to include so many real people in a fictional setting, but my constant goal was to portray them in a manner that made sense given the available historical record. Bottom line, though, is that this is entirely a work of fiction. Many of the choices were made because I wanted a given episode to be funny. End of story. None of this should be taken seriously.

On the other hand, I tried to be precise with all game details. If one of Rube's teams played on a given day or during a described road trip, that should be accurate all the way down to the final outcome and a specific player's line in the box score. If I made a mistake there, it was not my intention, and I apologize. In the midst of so much outrageous fictional behavior, I figured it was the least I could do.

Many of the locations are likewise real, but some are totally invented. Mr. Red's Club on the South Side of Chicago, for example, is named after one of my former dogs. He was a very good boy. On the other hand, Book Row was real, and there really was a Horn & Hardart automat on East 14th Street by Union Square. Whether they had any rhubarb pie that night is anyone's guess. Suffice to say I spent a lot of time entertaining myself by browsing old photos of Manhattan and comparing them to maps. Sadly, old photos of Memphis are much harder to come by via books and the internet.

Since we baseball history folks and SABR types are nothing if not geeky, I need to say that the underlying cover photo is from the Red Sox vs. Senators game on

September 6, 1925. It comes from the Prints and Photographs Division of the Library of Congress, one of our greatest national treasures. What you see is Sox catcher George Bischoff and umpire Dick Nallin watching the Washington center fielder, Earl McNeely, slide safely into home at Griffith Stadium in the bottom of the first. Boston's Ted Wingfield took the 7-6 loss in spite of hitting a homer in his own cause. Win Ballou picked up the W in relief of Dutch Ruether. The photo has zilch to do with anything in the book, but I really liked it as an image!

Books are not a one person operation. Even independent authors have a serious, if limited, team of people helping them out. There are various readers, advisors and editors putting some eyeballs on different aspects of the book. Hopefully, it makes the book better. Think of it like the old maxim that any person who represents himself in court has a fool for a client.

The cover was designed by the super talented Marla Yadira Garcia. She did excellent covers for two of my non-fiction books and has done the same good work for several other book projects I've been involved with through Night Heron Media.

Big thanks go to my beta readers – Carl Faulkenberry, John Farnetti, Jim Kreuz and Jay Trotsky. Those are the folks who first let an author know that they're not delusional and haven't wasted months amusing only themselves.

My beloved script writing partner, Marijane Miller, has supplied terrific support over many years. Chris White, an excellent writer whom I've known even longer, has done the same with a heavy emphasis on the publishing industry. Both Chris and Marijane also read this book in an earlier form.

My wonderful wife, Anne, takes time out of her own busy schedule to trudge upstairs to the Eagle's Nest office, as she calls it, and give me opinions on this or that. She also provides an excellent proof reading eye.

Thank you to all of them and others I've unintentionally omitted.

Coming in the summer of 2024

Wingo's Redemption

A novel by Mike Vance

Rube Wingo finds his way. See how he fares in book two of this duology.

Please sign up for the newsletter at www.mikevancewriter.com to stay up to date on all of Mike's work, and don't forget to follow @mikevancewriter on social media. Above all, if you enjoyed reading Wingo, please spread the word. Thanks!